I Am Mary Dunne

I Am Mary Dunne

Brian Moore

Introduction by Alan Kennedy
General Editor: Malcolm Ross

New Canadian Library No. 128

McClelland and Stewart Limited

The Canadian Publishers
McClelland and Stewart Limited
25 Hollinger Road, Toronto

Printed and bound in Canada

TO JEAN, MY WIFE

O body swayed to music, O brightening glance,
How can we know the dancer from the dance?

—W. B. YEATS, from "Among School Children"

Traditionally, school libraries and librarians teach their young students to differentiate between fiction and non-fiction by some explanation such as: non-fiction contains useful facts and fiction is for entertainment, it is made-up. It often turns out, though, that fiction is far more useful than fact, in personal life as well as in society. It is not useful in any crude pragmatic way, and, in fact, to call the 'use' to which we put fiction in our personal lives a use is almost to overstrain language. The 'use' of fiction is, then, by means of imagination to extend ourselves; or, to put it another way, fiction offers us transcendence. Fiction allows us to live another life as if it were our own, and in this way convinces us – and this is the creative, moral centre of art – of the reality of other lives besides our own. Looked at from a distance, *I Am Mary Dunne* is a book in which the novelist Brian Moore tells a history as if he were the woman Mary Dunne. In this novel the reader should be constantly aware of the fact that this is a man telling a woman's story. This awareness might detract from some stories, but here it is an essential part of the book. Moore deliberately attempts to transcend the limits of his personal view of the world in order to see it through a woman's eyes.

Feminism, or 'women's liberation', is one theme of the novel, but only as a particular example of a larger theme. A passerby on the street says to Mary Dunne: "I'd like to fuck you, baby." and in the theatre of our minds we play at being Mary Dunne (play at being a woman, or another woman) reacting to this street obscenity. At a more distant remove we are aware of Brian Moore's male mind being both Mary Dunne and her accoster, both producing and reacting to this hypothetical obscenity. Now, this playing at being another is an exercise in transcendence, and this transcendence is not only the source of morality, it is the source of human being. Mary Dunne judges that "the real crime of the man I'd just encountered was that to him women were not human like himself, but simply objects he wanted to penetrate and hurt." Mary Dunne briefly fantasizes revenge, but crumbles, like the cartoon cat who has just been handed a bomb, when she thinks of the probable reaction of a male policeman and 'male solidarity'. This theme of male solidarity is, however, presented to us in terms of a more pervasive, more extensive instance of the evil resultant on the failure of imagination. Mary Dunne recalls an article she had read about the obscenities of Auschwitz which argued that the real crime of the camp guards was not sadism but indifference: "The majority of the guards were not sadists; they simply could not conceive of the prisoners (those Jewish and Gypsy bags of skin and bones) as men and women like their German selves." If fiction offers us the opportunity to discover that there are other people in the world like our own selves, it has no trivial function to perform.

So fiction, as one of the realms of the imagination, leads us to see other lives as if they were as real as our own, and one result of this new realization is that we change; we are more than we were, we transcend our previous personal limits. This very capacity, though, gives rise to a problem of personal identity, since whatever it is, personal *identity* must be something which subsists unchanged, identical, through time. How can a thing change and yet be the same? If imagination and transcendence are the spiritual core of our existence, then we are perhaps condemned never to know 'who I am' since we are at our best when we are most transformed. *I Am Mary Dunne* operates on two levels at once then. First, it is a story of a woman growing up, being married, divorced, remarried and discovering things about herself and her past in the course of the narrative. Second, it is a novel of ideas which explores perplexing questions about personal identity, time, memory. We catch a brief glimpse of the way in which the novel deals with such questions by allowing the title once again to put us at a little distance from the inside of the story. At first glance, it is the book itself which speaks to us from the cover; after all, *it* is Mary Dunne. Mary Dunne's personal identity is not really problematical therefore, because it is all there on the pages of the book. She exists only in the book's terminology; or, she is written, therefore she is. This means that, since the book is fiction, Mary Dunne's identity is fictional, it is made-up. If the novel does indeed make some such suggestion, then what it is saying is that personal identity is a product of the creative and sympathetic imagination. One of the ways in which we achieve personal wholeness is by means of imagining what it must be like to be another, and the other way is by imagining oneself. The final ironical magic of the novel is that while we make the effort by means of the words on the page to imagine Mary Dunne's life, we are discovering our own.

The epigraph from Yeats's "Among School Children" is possibly meant to echo the novel's theme; just as one cannot tell the dancer from the dance, so too, perhaps, one cannot differentiate between an individual's personal identity and what he remembers. As Mary Dunne puts it, *Memento ergo sum:* I remember, therefore I am; which is her proffered amendment to Descartes' principle: *Cogito ero sum:* I think, therefore I am. It is equally possible, though, that Yeats's lines are meant to represent an insoluble puzzle; they confuse the mind just as the question of the possible interrelatedness of memory and identity does. It may be that the novel consciously deals with a problem which concerns everyone, one of those problems we cannot help worrying about (or why do we keep photograph albums?) and yet a problem we can never be absolutely sure we understand. It would be too easy simply to accept Mary Dunne as a spokesman for Moore when she says *memento ergo sum*. The novel leads us to consider this idea and then leads us beyond it, tentatively. With a question as complex as the dancer and dance conundrum, one must retain a healthy scepticism without giving up the quest for enlightenment.

Moore is not the first, of course, to worry about the memory-identity question; it is a long-standing problem in the history of philosophy. Moore seems to have had not only Descartes in mind in writing this novel, but also, and more centrally, David Hume. At the end of his consideration of the problem of the existence of the self, Hume sceptically concludes "that all the nice and subtle questions concerning personal identity can never possibly be decided" (*A Treatise of Human Nature*). Hume argues that properly speaking there is no one continuous thing which can be called a *self*; all there is, when we consider the matter, is a bundle of particular perceptions which succeed each other in the mind: "The mind is a kind of theatre, where several perceptions successively make their appearance; pass, re-pass, glide away, and mingle in an infinite variety of postures and situations. There is properly no *simplicity* in it at one time, nor identity in different; whatever natural propension we may have to imagine that simplicity and identity."

As soon as someone says "I don't believe there is such a thing as personal identity," it is open for us to say "Who doesn't?" Hume himself seems at times aware of this irony: to use the pronoun "I" (as in "I am Mary Dunne") is already to assume and assert that there is an identity, or self, to whom the pronoun properly belongs. Mary Dunne echoes Hume's metaphor of the mind as a theatre, and her assertiveness of will at the end of the novel indicates that there is a solution to the philosophical problem of identity:

If Hat killed himself, it was a stupid, selfish thing to do. Hat was always the actor, always making dramas out of his fairly ordinary problems. And, at the end, so caught up in his self-dramatization that he over-played his role. But if I make that harsh judgment on Hat, then what was I doing, play-acting out there on the fire escape? And what are these dooms of mine but a frightening, unreal play going on inside my head, a play I must sit through and suffer, for if I do not fight them, the dooms will not leave me?

The mind is a kind of theatre which has passing in it "an infinite variety of postures", and therefore we all are condemned to be "actors" in life, since we act out in the world the variety of postures that occurs in our minds. Hat was the "complete actor," and even his suicide was a stagey event, intended for effect. Mary too has been an actress, an incomplete one possibly, and we find that she is often posing, as in her attempted suicide, and even in making love to Terence she poses as if she were a stripper, or prostitute, and gives him "an actressy smile." It is important to note, however, that this posing of Mary's is done to keep Terence from realizing the bad state she is in and their love-making leads to an important recovery for Mary. Posing can be positive and selfless, then. In the passage quoted above, Mary has become conscious of her play-acting; she has become conscious of the fact that her mind is a kind of theatre. Further, she has become conscious of the fact that she can choose to exercise her will to fight the "dooms." The existence of that consciousness and will is evidence that she *is* Mary Dunne and that personal identity is more than a bundle of perceptions and memories. Identity, self, somehow transcends merely passive memory; it is active. If identity is active, that means "I" must be an actor and, further, personal existence is established by the same magical logic as is God's: I say "I am," therefore I am.

Since acting is an art and involves the imagination, then personal identity must also be imaginative, or imagined. Hume hints at this when he refers to our "natural propension to imagine" that the bundle of perceptions in the theatre of the mind has an identity. As he continues his analysis, Hume begins to use the word fiction with increasing frequency. For instance:

For when we attribute identity, in an improper sense, to variable or interrupted objects, our mistake is not confin'd to the expression, but is commonly attended with a fiction, either of something invariable and uninterrupted, or of something mysterious and inexplicable, or at least with a propensity to such fictions. . . .

The purpose of this is apparently to convince us that there is no such thing as personal identity; it is a mere fiction, a thing made-up. The passage contains the hint though that personal identity is a fiction that is a creative achievement. Hume does conclude by denying the equation of memory and identity; as, I believe, does Moore. Hume says that memory is merely the *source* of identity: "'Twill be incumbent on those, who affirm that memory produces entirely our personal identity, to give a reason why we can thus extend our identity beyond our memory." Hume suggests that it is imagination that allows us so to extend, or transcend identity. In the course of her narrative, Mary discovers that memory is selective and that the principle of selection is as imaginative and creative as that process of selection from real life that goes into the making of the art of fiction. At the beginning of her story she wonders if the story of her life won't just be "some false, edited little movie." She recalls that children create 'memories' of events they do not in fact remember but have been told about numerous times by their parents. In the scene with Ernest Truelove (who is obviously a travesty of true love) she discovers that she has indeed edited her memories. This editing, though, is to be taken as evidence that there *is* a Mary Dunne who has actively and imaginatively been selecting from her experiences and memories.

The self is imaginative or fictional, at least in part, and forgetting is one of the ways in which the principle of identity reveals itself. It is important to notice that this conception of creative forgetting is directly contradictory to the psychoanalytical one which suggests that forgetting is a neurotic blotting out of facts too unpleasant to be faced. Ernest Truelove says exactly this about Mary, that she cannot face the truth, and by putting the theory in the mouth of this negative character – he does not even like himself – Moore indicates how we are to value it. The scene in Central Park in which Janice and Mary break up in laughter at a peering figure who looks like Sigmund Freud is another clue to the way psychoanalytical ideas of memory are to be viewed. It is simply that imagination, the principle of self-existence, gives life to some events and death to others.

Just as memory can be altered, so too can perceptions. Janice Sloane rushes Mary off to the wrong French restaurant because she had misunderstood, mis-perceived, what Mary had once told her about good places to eat in New York. Similarly, many of the other characters in the novel mis-perceive Mary Dunne. If it is permissible to exercise imagination in the creation of one's own self, it is forbidden to do so in the attempt to create the self of others. It is this exercise of the mind's capacity for fantasy which is most difficult to transcend. Mary's first husband Jimmy Phelan thinks that Mary is sexually frigid while her second husband Hat believes she is highly over-sexed: "I thought of Hat saying, "All you want is to be fucked, fucked, fucked until the come is running out of you." To be sure, Mary does learn to add: "and yes sir, Hat, I recommend it. ..." It is with Terence Lavery though, and not Hat, that Mary ultimately experiences what Blake calls the "lineaments of gratified desire." Mary's other 'lover,' Mackie McIver, tries to transform Mary from the outside to make her fit her private fantasies, going so far as to change her name from Mary to Maria. Mary has to learn to struggle with all the versions of herself, the versions inside herself and the other versions that her acquaintances try to foist on her, including the comic degradation of marriage and sex that Harry and Mother Blodgett stand for. If "I remember, therefore I am" is insufficient philosophy, then so too is "They say it, therefore I am."

Mary, in the face of inadequate patterns of identity, must learn to imagine herself, but it is not only by means of imagination that *self* is assured. The tone of the whole narrative is affected by the fact that Mary Dunne is suffering from pre-menstrual tension. The point of this is that it is the material body that helps establish personal identity. Identity may be partly imaginative, but it is also partly physical. I am a body, therefore I am. In an unusually moving passage at the end of the novel, Mary is waiting to begin to bleed; waiting for the onset of another natural cycle of change in her body that will affect the way in which she responds to the world. As the body rhythm changes, so too the 'identity' we have come to know in this book will be transcended. Her final assertion of identity may be slightly desperate, but it is not despairing nor negative.

If Mary's bleeding is faintly suggestive of the bleeding of Christ, we know that we are faced with no casual reference on Moore's part. The earlier novel, *An Answer From Limbo*, suggests that Art can act as a kind of substitute for religion. Brendan Tierney is scourged and crucified by his need to be a writer. He says, "I have altered beyond all self-recognition. I have lost and sacrificed myself." The virtues of this transcendence are not unequivocal, and Brendan Tierney may just have lost himself, never to find himself again. The theme of art as salvation is taken up again in *I Am Mary Dunne*, through. Mary considers the pictures of Dostoievski, Proust and Yeats that Terence keeps on his wall and says, "They wrote, therefore they are . . . ," a road to identity that Mary herself follows. Terence, a failed artist if a successful revue writer, never thinks of the past. To Mary Dunne, who perhaps thinks too much of it, he holds out the promise of release from time by sexuality. In a beautiful passage, Terence replaces Christ and sex replaces religion: "Terence is my savior, I shall not want, he maketh me to lie down in green pastures, he restoreth my soul. Yes, that's right. He's my new religion. He's my life after death." Towards the end of the story, just before Ernest Truelove arrives, Mary discovers in sexual intercourse that "there is no past." The essence of sexuality, as of art, is "make it new" by means of "that Mass of the senses." Contemporary philosophers are perhaps coming to some agreement that the question of personal identity is solved by regarding identity as bodily. The body changes through time, but it is still the same body. So it may be that Moore is using contemporary philosophers to lead us beyond the conundrum of the sceptical Hume. The truth of the matter, however, is that the resident *genii* of Moore's world are artists, priests of the imagination and the holy body: Blake and D. H. Lawrence, and W. B. Yeats who couldn't separate the idea of the dance from the bodily dancer enacting desire.

Alan Kennedy
Dalhousie University

Cogito ergo sum. I close my eyes and go back seventeen years. Mother Marie-Thérèse writes it on the blackboard. Her arm is bare to the elbow: the sleeve of her habit is rolled up to avoid chalk dust. "I think, therefore I am," she says. Where the Latin was just something to translate, the English jumps and my hand is up (unlike me, that) and when Mother sees me I ask wouldn't it have been more correct for him to have said *"Memento ergo sum"*?

"Memento?"—with that winter frost smile of hers.

"Yes, Mother. I remember, therefore I am."

She sends her smile searching among the other girls in the class. But no one has a comment. As for Reverend Mother's smile, it could mean "A silly girl has misunderstood Descartes," or "See how we have engaged the attention of Mary Dunne."

"And why would you say that?" she asks me.

"Because"—I am fifteen—"we are what we remember."

"Interesting," says Reverend Mother, but did she really think so? Did she remember our conversation an hour after class? I have remembered it seventeen years and now I wonder. If we are what we remember, did that girl I was die because I forgot her? As now, perhaps, I am beginning to die because some future me cannot keep me in mind.

Now why did I think that? I was coming along nicely until I had that thought about dying and now my heart's beating loud again, stop, stop, remember how comforting it was to close my eyes, go back and find them waiting for me, Mother Marie-Thérèse and the class. If I can remember that far back and so clearly, then shut up, heart, calm down, there's nothing to be afraid of.

I tell this to my heart as I would tell it to a very stupid person. I tell it it is a perfectly normal heart: the reason it's acting up is anxiety. I tell it no wonder it's acting up after a day like today, and especially tonight with that story about Hat. But that has nothing to do with me, no matter what people say, it has nothing to do with me, all that is over and done with, I'm in love with Terence, I'm happily married at last, the only thing we haven't got is children, but that will come, the doctor says we're both fine so that will be all right too. In fact, if I were pregnant tonight, my heart wouldn't be thumping like this, because the real reason I'm upset is physical, I'll be starting my period any time now, that's why I was confused all day, that's why this panic about forgetting. It began this morning when the receptionist forgot *my* name, that's what started the whole thing, and I'll bet that, far from losing my memory, I could, if I put my mind to it, remember every single thought, word, and deed that happened to me today. But what would that prove? When people say they remember everything that happened in their lives, they're deceiving themselves. I mean if I were to try to tell anyone the story of my life so far, wouldn't it come out as fragmentary and faded as those old snapshot albums, scrapbooks, and bundles of letters everyone keeps in some bottom drawer or other? What would I remember about my life, wouldn't it be just some false, edited little movie, my version of what my parents were like, the places I lived in, the names of some of the people I've known, and would any of it give you any idea of what I feel about, say, sex, or children, about something trivial like cleaning the oven broiler or something terrible like this thing about Hat?

Down Tilt. I mustn't think about Hat. Far better to do

4

something constructive, like try to figure out why I forgot my name this morning. I should begin there, for the day really did begin there in the Golden Door Beauty Salon about eleven-thirty this morning while I was paying for my shampoo and set. I remember I looked back into the salon and they'd changed the color scheme of the place since the last time I was in. I saw six women wearing scarlet smocks, their heads under the freshly painted pink cones of hair driers, and the cones reminded me of miters; the women became cardinals sitting in their pews at High Mass and that put me in mind of those distorted paintings of cardinals by Francis Bacon and I wondered if I first saw those paintings in the Museum of Modern Art or was it later with Terence at the big Bacon show in the Guggenheim? Anyway, I was miles away when the receptionist asked me about my next appointment. I said Thursday, a week from now, my regular time. The receptionist gave a little cough, then smiled. "Isn't it awful," she said. "I don't know what's the matter with me this morning, but I've forgotten your name."

I remember that I was angry. I thought, damn you, you've seen me often enough, I'm a regular customer, why must you forget my name when you remember the name of every other customer? I've heard you many's the time with your Mrs. This and Mrs. That to anyone who walks in off the street. I know I was unreasonable, but just before my period I *am* unreasonable and there she was, waiting, her pencil at the ready, her book open and my name— Oh God, I couldn't remember it either.

Panic. Standing there smiling idiotically at that idiotically smiling girl, my mind going over and back, over and back, whatsmyname whatsmyname whatsmyname? And, as my mind emptied, a piece of nonsense rushed in to fill the vacuum, a silly English music-hall song I heard years ago and haven't been able to get out of my mind since, so, right there in the middle of my whatsmyname whatsmyname whatsmyname panic, this song started up in my head:

> Big Gertie's daughter I am, I am,
> Yes, Big Gertie's daughter, that's me.
> Big Gertie's daughter,
> Yes, her little daughter.
> No better than I ought to be.

And so there I stood with Big Gertie's daughter, Big Gertie's daughter singing away inside my empty head and what if I told her my name was Big Gertie's daughter and that thought eased the panic so that I found myself saying, "Mrs. Phelan."

"Of course," she said. "Mrs. Phelan." And wrote it in her appointments book. While I opened my purse to put the change away in my little Mark Cross wallet and there, in the wallet, were credit cards. The top card was a Bloomingdale's charge plate, made out to *Mrs. Terence Lavery, 201 East 78th Street, NYC.*

Down Tilt. My name isn't Phelan. Phelan was my name when I was married to Jimmy, and I realized that when Henri who does my hair looks in the appointments book next week and sees Phelan he'll pass me over to one of the juniors, thinking I'm a new customer. But even as all this was going through my mind I was saying to myself what can I do about it except make some joke about my "ex" and I can't bear women who make glib remarks about things like that, so I said nothing, shut my handbag, and went out of the beauty parlor onto Madison, where there was an awful wind coming up the street. I'd forgotten to bring one of those little plastic tie-on things to protect my hair, so eight-fifty, ten with tip, would go down the drain unless I could find a cab at once. I tried to shield my hair with my handbag and ran to the intersection to wait for the light to change so that I could cross over and get a cab.

6

A man came up and waited beside me. I was shielding my hair so I didn't really look at him, but I knew, almost subliminally, that he was an Ivy League type in his thirties or forties, no drunk, no threat. Then the light changed. I went to step off the pavement, but the man put his hand on my wrist, detaining me. I turned to look at him and saw his flushed face, bright eyes, breathy, excited smile.

"I'd like to fuck you, baby."

He was smiling as he said it, the tip of his tongue showing, and I knew it gave him a hard-on to watch the outrage in my face. He let go of my wrist, stepped off the pavement, going across the street quick-quick, disappearing into the crowd on the other side of the street as though he had never been. While I stood there like the cat in the movie cartoon after the sneaky mouse has handed it a ticking bomb. The bomb explodes and when the smoke clears there's the silly cat staring at the remains of the bomb in its paw. Pause. Then (quietly) the cat cracks into a thousand pieces.

Well, in the moment before my crack-up I stood there on the pavement and ran through a revenge scene in my mind. What if I managed to catch up with him? What if I grabbed him and hit him over the head with my handbag? A crowd would collect, a cop would show up, and there I would be, listened to by strangers as I tried to explain to the cop that this man, this well-dressed respectable-looking man had said he'd like to fuck me, and while I'd be telling that to the cop I can imagine the man exchanging meaningful looks with the bystanders, and perhaps saying, "Some people have vivid imaginations, women especially." The cop would digest this, then say, "Tell me, lady, did this gentleman touch you or harm you in any way?" At which point in my fantasy of revenge I splinter like the cartoon cat. You can't fight male solidarity.

All this time I was staring stupidly at the green traffic

7

light, knowing I should cross. But didn't, until the light changed back to red. Then I ran into the traffic, signaling a cab which seemed to be free. The driver saw me and pulled in up ahead (probably breaking some traffic law) while I ran toward him, sure, as are all New Yorkers, that someone else would get to him before me. But he was free. I got in, shut the door, and when I opened my handbag and looked at my hair in the pocket mirror it wasn't the way it had been when they combed it out fifteen minutes before, but it could have been worse. As I gave the driver my address, I remembered an article I read once about the trial of Höss, the commandant of Auschwitz, an article in which the Polish state prosecutor was quoted as saying that the main crime of the Auschwitz camp guards was not sadism; it was indifference. The majority of the guards were not sadists; they simply could not conceive of the prisoners (those Jewish and Gypsy bags of skin and bones) as men and women like their German selves. In the cab, thinking about that, I decided the real crime of the man I'd just encountered was that to him women were not human like himself, but simply objects he wanted to penetrate and hurt. I know that's not well reasoned (as Mother Marie-Thérèse used to say) but it's what I thought then and I went from that pervert in the street to Jimmy who believed he loved me but always said, "You're beautiful. I want you," as though I were a new car he could show off to his friends. And as the cab went uptown I decided that Jimmy didn't want me, he simply wanted a face and body which happened to be mine. Of course I know that's not well reasoned either, but it's what I thought in the cab. I was in a Down Tilt. In a Down Tilt, things are black and white.

And yet. There's no logical explanation, but my Down Tilt balanced out as the cab pulled in at our apartment building and I saw Harold, one of the doormen, coming toward the curb in his bottle-green uniform, white dickey, and clean white gloves, so cheerful and polite with his "Good morning, Mrs. Lavery," opening the cab door for me while I paid off the driver, then moving ahead of me to hold open the glass front door of the building, telling me he had a package for me, moving off to his cubbyhole to get it while I stood there in that pleasant lobby where there's a reproduction of a T'ang horse discreetly floodlit in one alcove and in the other a marble pier table with a white bowl filled with flame-colored gladioli, the whole building so well kept up and pleasant I remember thinking the girls I went to school with would envy me this. I thought of my schooldays because through the glass doors of the lobby I saw a fat little boy who was standing on the curb outside, reining in a poodle on one leash, a beagle on the other and, at the same time, this fat little boy seemed to be waving at me. I smiled at him (who was he?) and as soon as I did he dragged on the dogs' leashes and came across the pavement and in the door. Came right up to me.

"Hi, Mrs. Bell."

"Hi," I said. (Who *was* he?)

"How's Bell? I mean Pete."

While I (whatshisname? whatshisname?) said Pete was fine, just fine.

Wanausek. I remembered I used to have trouble pronouncing it. I was always surprised at the way it slid so neatly out of Pete's childish lips. New York private-school boys have this habit of calling each other by their last names. Pete and Wanausek were classmates when Hat and I lived on East 13th Street.

"Is he still at Lawrence?" Wanausek asked me.

I said I thought he was (although I don't know where he is) and the moment I said "thought" I saw Wanausek give me that changeling look children sometimes assume when, suddenly, their childish bodies seem possessed by the personality of an adult with whom they are in contact. In

9

Wanausek's case the unknown Doppelgänger must be a schoolmaster, for now, miming the gestures of a middle-aged martinet, he dragged the unfortunate dogs to heel and, glaring at me, asked in a censorious bark, "What's the matter, don't you see Bell, I mean, Pete, any more?"

I said no. I said, "Pete's father and I have been divorced."

"Oh." For a moment he stared at the ground, a stiff little schoolmaster pondering a pupil's excuse. Then: "You aren't Bell's real mother, are you?"

"No, I'm not."

"Oh." He nodded again. Excuse accepted. "Well," he said, "if you run into him, say hello for me, will you?"

"I will."

"The name is Wanausek," he said. "Dick W-a-n-a-u-s-e-k."

"Yes. I remember."

He did not believe me. With a name like his, why should he? "Wanausek," he said again. He dragged at the unfortunate dogs. "Come on, Hugo, come on, Rochester. Let's go, you bums." And he and the dogs went out just as Harold came up with my package, which was the Lily Daché bath oil I'd ordered from Bloomingdale's. I thanked Harold and went up alone in the elevator. I only had Pete for a month in the summers and a week at Easter, so I never really got to know him. Except for that two months when his mother was ill and they (the grandparents) sent him to live with Hat. Pete didn't look like Hat. I suppose he looked like his mother.

I remember getting the mail out of our box in the back hall and, going through it as I went up in the elevator, deciding there was nothing interesting there: some advertising junk, a letter for Tee, a *Life* subscription notice, a telephone bill which I put in my handbag to pay; and, when I let myself into our apartment, I saw that Ella Mae, our cleaning woman, had arrived because the paper bag she keeps her street clothes in was plonked down on the hall chair as per usual. I have lots of closets, but do you think I could get her to use one? I called out asking if anyone had phoned, thinking perhaps Janice Sloane might have called, but Ella Mae shouted back, "No ma'am." I put the mail in the Mexican bowl on the captain's chest in the hall and, as I did, a letter slid out from behind the *Life* subscription notice, a familiar white envelope with a blue air-mail sticker and a Canadian stamp. I don't know how I missed it before, but it was my mother's handwriting. I took it up and went into the living room to read it. Even now it jumps up at me, that sentence in among the years of sentences. Sentences like: *Madge Gordon came over and we played a hand of cards, cold all week and snow, the back porch is completely blocked up.* Oh, Mama, I can see you sitting in the little back room because it's warmer, the stove's in there, arthritis in your hands, the trouble you have to hold a pen, but down the years the letters were written, letters to me and Jimmy in Toronto, letters to me alone in Montreal, then to East 13th Street, when I was with Hat. Letters. *It was cold all week and we had some rain, the lawn is flooded, Madge Gordon came over, Dick's eldest boy has the measles, my arthritis is giving me the pip.* Once, long ago, you were the whole world, you were what mattered. I can remember scolding my doll in your voice, standing beside you in the kitchen, learning to bake johnny cakes the way Mama did. And later, away from you, even after the divorce from Jimmy, then Hat, no, it wasn't until Terence that there were no more visits. Still, you wrote: *Madge Gordon came over and we played a hand of cards, it's been hot all week, thank God for the summer, what we get of it, Dick's second has chickenpox, but is mostly over it,* and always, at the end, *must go now, love from Mama.*

Love. I too wrote "love" but I too made tactful excuses,

too busy to come this summer, hoping for Christmas, spring at the latest. And you who once were my whole world, you became—what? A letter from Nova Scotia. A letter once a month, written in that convent hand, the hand the Sacred Heart nuns taught you fifty years ago, that hand which writes *cold all week and snow and Dick's eldest,* a hand which forms sentences I skim over, half reading, until this morning in that same hand, in among those years of sentences, *the doctor says I'm to go in this week and have it out, it's a lump of some sort*—and oh, Mama, darling, darling, darling, oh, my poor old, God spare you now, that God you trust, that God I no longer know.

When I stood up, I was dizzy. I picked up the receiver, direct distance dialed, and your phone rang and rang there at letter's end, off that bleak highway eight miles out of town, down the rutted lane leading to your house, the shingles all crooked, the walls needing paint, rang in the kitchen (I see the wall phone near the scribbled grocery reminder notes under the calendar from Wilson Lumber Company), rang and rang and rang and where were you? Ill in bed, ill on the floor? I thought of Dick but (it's so long since I've written to him or spoken to him) I had to get his number from the long-distance operator and Dick's wife, Meg, answered and when I told her I'd rung you and was worried, she said she believed you'd gone to twelve-o'clock Mass.

"Mass?" I said.

Her voice, very cool: "Yes, Mass. It's a holiday of obligation." Implying I should have known but of course did not. And she was right. A holy day of obligation. Oh, Mama, back there in Butchersville, back where there are holy days of obligation where—rain, hail, snow, or lumps beneath the skin—you are commanded by the Church to rise, dress, back your old green Chevy onto that bleak Canadian highway, and drive eight miles to Immaculate Conception Church.

I said to Meg, "But what about the hospital? I just got a letter from her about a lump she has."

"I'll put Dick on," she said. I heard her call, "Dick? Dick?" And then to me, impersonal as a telephone operator: "Just a moment, please."

While I waited for my brother, the dizziness came back: it was the sort I get when I stoop suddenly, then straighten up again. I go blind for a moment. His voice came into my blindness. "Hello? That you, Mutt?" The dizziness cleared and I felt the small turn of an emotional screw. Mutt was my nickname when we were kids. He is the only person who still remembers it. In a way, that says it all. He knows me as Mutt who tried to chop off her hair when she was eight. I know him as my big brother, Bat, who carried me on his shoulders up a cliff face in the Bay of Fundy, twenty-five years ago. And at the top of the cliff my father waited and my brother was thrashed on the spot. I was Mutt and he was Bat and in the last photograph I saw of him (the one Mama sent last Christmas) he is quite gray.

I told him about Mama's letter and asked about the lump.

"Oh, that," he said. "She's got to go into hospital to have it removed. Just a minor operation, she'll be out in no time."

"Yes, but yes," I said "—but what if it's malignant, aren't you worried at all?"

"I'm not worried," he said. "It's just better to have these things out. No sense taking chances."

"But Bat, I don't even know where it is—where is this lump? She didn't say."

"It's rectal," he said. "A rectal polyp."

"Oh, dear," I said and laughed. He laughed too,

13

for Mama's shyness is a family joke. Although my brother is the only doctor in the Butchersville area, Mama has never allowed him to examine her. She never "felt" right about it and so she drives forty miles to see old Dr. McLarnon in Wolfville. But after the laughing I asked, "Seriously, I mean is it something to worry about?"

"Well, it could be malignant."

"Then what?"

"Then we'll just have to hope they get it all out."

"But supposing they don't get it all out, supposing it's malignant and it grows again?"

"It'll mean another operation."

"But she's over sixty, Bat."

"I know. Let's hope it's nothing."

"I should phone her," I said but he said no, not to, it would only put ideas in her head. He's right. I'd forgotten that, for people of Mama's generation and in towns like Butchersville, long-distance phone calls mean trouble. Then I put my foot in it. "All right," I said. "Let me know, won't you, Bat? As soon as possible?"

"Okay, I'll drop you a line the minute I get the results."

"No. Phone me. Collect, if you like." That was a mistake. It was as though I were saying he's tight. Which he isn't.

There was a pause, and then: "I'll phone," he said. "I think I can afford it. What's your number?"

I gave it to him. I wanted to make some joke, some apology about the collect remark, but he didn't give me time. "Right," he said. "I'll be in touch." And hung up. I remember that he said nothing about Terence. But then I didn't say "Say good-by to Meg for me." Or whatever. Look, he doesn't know Terence. Oh, forget it. No sense making a court case out of something somebody forgot to say.

Mama. I remember thinking I must look up "polyp" in the dictionary and then I thought of my father.

My father died during the war. He died in bed. He died

of a cerebral hemorrhage in the old Park Plaza Hotel in New York. He was on leave from the Canadian Army at the time. Ralph Davis told Dick that Daddy died screwing, that some woman was in bed with him and that the Canadian Embassy in Washington had to do a lot of finagling to avoid an inquest. Died in the saddle. I can still remember Dick as he said it, laughing in a shocked, schoolboy way. I was ten when my father died, fifteen when Dick told me. I wonder has he any idea how that ugly little story has affected my life, how all through my teens, any time a boy made a pass, I froze, afraid that I might become like my father. And sometimes when I'm with people like Janice I see her looking at me and know she's thinking I'm promiscuous, and I have this foolish desire to tell her I'm not, I am promiscuous only in my dreams, those doom dreams where I am naked in hotel rooms with naked men and I know those dreams are mixed up in my mind with the story Dick told me about my father and with my fear that somehow I am like my father.

Am I? I do not know. I was in school when he died. I remember the funeral, the gun carriage, the Scots bagpipes playing a lament, Daddy's service cap on top of the Union Jack that covered the coffin. It rained. Or did it? I was there but do I remember it, wasn't I told about it, time and time again, the gun carriage, the piper, the flag, the cap on the coffin? Adults tell us things that happened when we were small. "You were in Halifax, we brought you from school, don't you remember the funeral? No, I suppose you wouldn't. You were too young." But children are insulted at being thought too young, they want to be grown up, and so they listen to the adults tell whatever it is they're supposed to recall, then memorize it, and in time they come to believe they do remember it. But they don't.

I don't remember my father's funeral. I don't really remember my father. He is, to me, a framed photograph in my mother's bedroom in Butchersville. He wears an army officer's cap. He has a large mustache. His eyes seem amused. He looks young. I hate mustaches. I hate backstairs adulterers who come home to the little woman as though nothing ever happened. I hate officer types. I hate men who like uniforms. I hate charmers. They say he was. A charmer. Daniel Malone Dunne. Dan Dunne, what a charmer. Old and Dunne. That's my secret joke about him, a guilty joke, for he is dead and when I say it I think again of how he died. Malone, according to Grandma Dunne, was the name of an Irish bishop. It seems this bishop led thousands of Irish emigrants to Australia to save them from the famine. My great-grandfather was to have gone to Australia with the bishop's group and had christened his new baby in honor of the bishop. But at the last minute Great-Grandfather Dunne changed his mind, raised his own passage money, and sailed to Quebec instead. If he had gone to Australia I would not have been. Sometimes I think of that.

If I did not know my father, if I can barely remember him, then it is ridiculous to let his manner of death upset me so. Our father who art in hell, cursed be thy name. If I no longer believe in this God I mock, then is it blasphemy to make fun of the Lord's Prayer? And why (since I do not believe) does it comfort me, here in the dark, to say that prayer all wrong, as once, when I was a child, it comforted me in the dark to say it right. Prayers are charms, they are knocking on wood, I know it and yet today, after that phone call from Dick, when I went back into the living room and looked up "polyp" in the dictionary, I tried to pray. *Polyp: a tumor projecting into a natural cavity.* "Tumor" is a word to put the fear of God into a person, and there and then I started, as I have so often before, to blubber out a plea to the Almighty. And then, as always, could not go through with it and stopped, ashamed of my concept of a God who'd place a value on the panicky, God-hating prayers of someone like myself. So, unable to pray, even for you, Mama, I thought of you who can pray, you, lying there in bed in Lord Tweedsmuir Memorial Hospital in Wolfville, saying your prayers before they come with the sodium pentothal to put you to sleep for the operation. I said to myself I would fly to Wolfville to be with you and as I made that vow a trembling started up (I don't know why), a trembling which worsened into the shakes when Ella Mae came into the room behind me, plugged the vacuum in, turned it on, and that noise which is bad enough at the best of times sent me hurrying out of the room and into my bedroom to slam the door and rant in my mind against Ella Mae, a shiftless bitch who gets fifteen dollars for a day's work that she skimps, coming in late, leaving early; it's more like four hours and if she weren't black and I weren't so cravenly liberal, I'd damn well tell her so.

But even as I raged against Ella Mae, I knew it had nothing to do with her, it was my hateful premenstrual tension that put me in a lunatic anger against her, that started the trembling that becomes a shaking, independent of me, as though my heart is an engine which suddenly comes loose inside me and will shake my whole body into pieces. The curse that comes once a month, making me murderous one minute, suicidal the next, weepy, sick, silly, confused, and I sit here appalled, feeling some other self within me begin to go berserk. As I did this morning when I sat in my bedroom raging against the maid, then falling into a mindless panic when the house intercom rang outside in the front hall. Ella Mae shut off the vacuum and went to answer, while I sat there behind my door like a condemned person awaiting the execution party. Ridiculous as it sounds, that is not an exaggeration. And yet I knew, I know (listen to me, Mary Dunne, whoever and

17

wherever you are) that I had no reason to feel that way, I have committed no crime, I am, by all normal standards, a fortunate woman, these fears of mine are without foundation, and it did not make sense for me to sit trembling behind my bedroom door, and how foolish (I know, I know), how foolish my fear would seem to a person who really sat in the condemned cell. And yet I am not exaggerating when I say that this morning I waited for Ella Mae as though whatever news she brought would end me.

"Somebody for you, the doorman say."

I do not remember now what arguments I used on myself to force myself to get up, open the door, go to the hall, and listen in on the intercom earphone. "Hello?" I said, quaking in the dooms as, reassuringly, the doorman's voice floated up, garbled, like something from a spaceship. "Jamanforya. A Misiter Pee-eee-pers." I thought of the television comedian with, I suppose, hysterical relief. "Mr. Peepers?" I shouted back. "What could he want?"

The doorman's voice, whistling in the wires: "Come about eeee-ee—apartment."

And oh, sweet Mother, I'd forgotten all about him, the man who phoned yesterday answering the ad Terence put in the *Times* about subletting our apartment for next summer. A Mr. *Peters.* I'd written his name on the pad by the phone in the bedroom. I told the doorman to send him up, then ran back into my bedroom for a quick self-inspection. I was tidy at least, and Ella Mae was cleaning up the place. The doorbell rang and rang again. Trust Ella Mae not to answer the door when you want her to.

Mr. Peters. From the very first moment there was something about him, a feeling that I should know him. "Mrs. Lavery?" he asked. And then: "My card" (handing it to me). I looked at it: no address, just his name, *Karl Dieter Peters.* I put it in the little silver card tray on top of the captain's chest in the hall, realizing as I did that it's the first real calling card I've ever put there. And, at the same time, the me who'd been in the glooms five minutes before was grinning at the way Mr. Peters doffed his old pearl-gray hat and stepped over the threshold, small and dapper, with rosy old Santa Claus cheeks, little white Vandyke beard, Chesterfield overcoat (beautifully tailored, but so old it was verdigris-green around the black velvet collar), and oh, with his silver-headed Malacca cane, his lemon chamois gloves, his movement into the hall, courtly and formal as though he were tracing the first steps in a gavotte, I tell you he was an old ducky, all right. You'd want to take him in and keep him.

So, there it was, my first impression, me falling for him as he asked if he might take off his overcoat and thank you so much and off with it, laying the hat and gloves on top of it, revealing himself in navy double-breasted blazer, white shirt, and a silk rep tie which, like everything he wore, was almost at the point of being too worn to use but still perfect. And he, like his clothes, very, very old, but at first I wasn't on to that because although he kept his cane he made it seem the action of a dandy, not a dodderer, and it wasn't until he bumped into the captain's chest, his old hand reaching out as though playing piano scales, tra-la-la-ing, searching for the edge of the obstacle, that I realized how blind he was.

Blind? But not so, really, for when he came into the living room he peered around, and, "Haar," he said. "What a lovely armoire." Which I thought was clever of him, for the armoire, although not obvious, is the best thing in the room, it and the Oriental carpet, which he also noticed and said something complimentary about, I forget exactly what. Then asked if he might look at the other rooms, after which the two of us might perhaps have a little talk? I said perfect and so off we went on a conducted tour and as we went through each room he picked just the right

19

things to remark on, my collection of miniatures and those wonderful old copper pots I picked up for nothing on the South Shore. And all the time I was quite calm inside, thinking how nice he was, when suddenly in the kitchen I had this worry: why would a person of his age take an apartment in the city for just three months and why would he consider taking an apartment with two bedrooms and two baths, which was obviously far too big for him? And when no answer came I glided to the edge of a near-panic. Trying to forestall it, I turned to him and pointed out that the kitchen oven has a built-in thermometer "Although," I said, "I suppose that would interest your wife more than it would you?"—looking at him in question marks as I said it. But he didn't pick it up, just nodded and moved on out of the kitchen.

See, said my Mad Twin, he's avoiding you, he's not going to answer you. Now stop that, warned sensible self. You're being silly. Of course he has a wife, she wasn't able to come along. And they probably need the extra bedroom because their grandchildren may come to visit them.

But it was no good. When we went back into the living room and sat down together, I had to tuck my hands under my knees to hide their trembling. His accent, I had noticed, was vaguely British and the conversation between us went something like:

"Haar. I hope I didn't disturb you, not putting you out too much, am I?"

"No, no, not at all."

"I thought the afternoon would, haar, be more convenient so to speak, but you, haar, said this morning, you remember?"

"Yes, I did. Yes, this morning is fine for me. Do you—d'you like the apartment?"

"Charming, yes. Beautiful things you have."

"Well, that's it," I said. "I mean that's what worried us,

20

you see we're going to be in Europe all summer and my husband feels that if we could find a suitable tenant it would be wiser not to leave the apartment empty."

"Haar."

"The rent would be three hundred, which is less than we pay ourselves. And furnished, of course."

Why is it when I get involved in any business transaction I at once feel dishonest, for although every word I was saying is true and the rent is *three-fifty, unfurnished*, somehow, in the business of me being the seller and he the buyer, I felt like a crook, and, Damn Terence, I thought, it was his idea to rent the place, why doesn't he handle it himself?

Suddenly the old boy let a "haar" out of him, so loud I thought he'd begun to choke, but no, he was merely clearing his throat, an action he followed by producing a large white handkerchief, seizing his nose between handkerchiefed thumb and forefinger, tweaking nose hard, then beginning a thorough old trumpeting, sneezing, and reaming out of all nasal passages, an action he concluded with a flourish of the white handkerchief and a sudden smile, cheeks scarlet, eyes watering. "Excuse me," he said. "Haar. Well, Mrs. Lavery, that price is—it's a bargain in this neighborhood. I know. Over on the West Side, all those killings, you know, colored fellas stabbing people in their own elevators, well, Mrs. Lavery, haar, I happen to know in some of those same buildings they're asking more than you're asking here."

I remember thinking, He seems well up on rents, he's well up on everything, because then he started asking all the right questions about watering the plants, defrosting the fridge, very sensible about everything, moving along in the smooth gear of someone who wants to take the apartment, and the moment he implied I was giving him a bargain rate I completely forgot my worries about why he wanted the place. I mean it was one of those situations where he made me feel I was doing *him* a favor and that, of course, made me want to do other favors for him and so my trembling stopped and, although it was after twelve and I was to have lunch with Janice Sloane at one, I remember I got up, went to the butler's tray where we keep the drinks, and asked him if he'd like something.

"Sure I'm not keeping you, Mrs. Lavery?"

"No, no. That's all right."

"Well, then," he said, "a dry sherry, perhaps?" And rose, leaning on his cane, and came over to the drinks tray. He peered at the sherry I poured. "Haar," he said. "Wisdom and Warter. Sherry Wines and Spirits. Very good, very good." And I found myself laughing and saying, "You really do know everything, don't you, Mr. Peters," for to know about Wisdom & Warter—well, I mean. And he laughed too. "No, no, I wouldn't say that, Mrs. Lavery. But Sherry-Lehmann, yes, that's a good wine shop."

And just then, for a moment, it seemed to me I did know him. I remember, as I was about to hand him the sherry glass, I stopped as though I were having my picture taken, for that was the moment at which I knew him and lost him again and was left, angry with myself for having been downed in that fleeting Indian wrestle with my memory. I handed him the sherry and stared at him as he sipped it, an old man in the iron mask of anonymity. Then, I remember, I thought, Look here, if he's to be my tenant I have a right to know who he is, and so asked him if he was a New Yorker and he told me no, he lived at Montauk Point out on the island and he'd heard he could rent his place for a great deal of money in the season, so he'd thought to make some money this summer by renting it and moving to town.

I know Montauk. The year of my "theatrical career" was the one I did summer stock at the John Drew Theatre in

East Hampton. It's quite true, I thought, that an old boy like this could almost make his year's expenses by a summer rental, if he has a nice enough house. But what didn't make sense was his taking our place here. Too expensive.

And with that thought, back came my uneasiness. "But won't it be too big—I mean this apartment?"

He smiled as the deaf smile and twiddled the stem of his sherry glass.

"So," I said, "then you want to—I mean *do* you want to take this place?"

"Haar." Very carefully he placed his sherry glass on the coffee table. "Well," he said, "to be fair, yes, to be fair, there's one other apartment on my list I'd like to have a look at before coming to a final decision. Haar. Is that all right?"

"Of course."

"Good. Well, let me see, I'll look at this other place at once. If you don't hear from me, haar, say within two hours, then that means I'll have decided on the, haar, the other place. Fair?"

"Yes," I said. "I may be out to lunch. But you can leave a message with my cleaning woman."

"Cleaning woman." He nodded, felt his beard, then stood, his hand searching for and finding his Malacca cane. "Very good, Mrs. Lavery. All clear then. Good."

And moved toward the hall, leaning a little on his cane, stopping near the drinks tray to peer at the old Waterford glass pitcher. "Beautiful," he said.

So I told him it was the old Waterford glass. I said the Waterford factories had been closed down for seventy years and only started up again in the forties. I told him this jug predated the modern glass and all the time while I was telling it I was aware how pretentious and vulgar I sounded. The only reason I know about Waterford glass is because Terence's mother's people originally came from there. Old

Mr. Peters listened, his fingers twiddling absent-mindedly with the silver and blue tassel they put on the neck of each Wisdom & Warter sherry bottle, smiling at me all the while as though he expected me to order a drink from him, a sherry or a Bloody Mary perhaps, and in that moment my mulish memory gave up its secret, supplying as background commentary Tom Brooks's Eastern prep-school bray: "Look, look, there's the old bird I told you about. Nancy's find. Over there at the bar."

Surreal as an early Buñuel film, I saw myself, Tom Brooks, and Hat, the three of us walking in bright morning sunlight across a grassy dune, going toward the ocean, while coming at us, bearing trays of scrambled eggs, toast, rolls, and coffee were four waiters, totally incongruous in that seascape, dressed in dark dinner jackets and white cotton gloves. And behind them, snapping pictures of advancing waiters advancing on Beautiful People, were the fashion-magazine photographers, for it was a Sunday brunch at Nancy's place, a pseudo-event ostensibly in aid of some charity, but actually a ruse to promote our season of summer plays, or perhaps, come to think of it, to promote Nancy herself. In any case, it was like most of the social events you read about nowadays. No one can be sure of anything. Were the photographers there because of our elaborate breakfast by the sea, or were we there because of the photographers? Of course poor Hat, avoiding the photographers and trying not to see the waiters with their trays of food, was looking around desperately for a Bloody Mary, and so when Tom Brooks said, "bar," Hat wheeled and said, "Where?" And it was then, following Tom Brooks's pointing finger, that we saw this odd old bearded waiter, standing off to one side behind a trestle table with bottles and set-ups: Mr. Karl Dieter Peters.

And when I remembered, I remembered completely. I even remembered the parties I'd seen him serving at later that summer. It was a summer when it was "in" to employ Mr. Peters, just as the year before it had been "in" to employ a certain New York faggot who cooked Chinese breakfasts. I even remembered Nancy's telling me that Mr. Peters lived on Montauk Beach in a clamdiggers' shack and that he was a retired English butler who had started in service forty years ago, as a footman to some duke. And that Nancy said he was too old to be an efficient bartender. "At least," she said, "not at my parties, not the way some of my guests drink." Which put me on the defensive, making me wonder if she was talking about Hat. And, remembering all this, I remembered that we didn't call him Peters, we called him Dieter—

"But you're Dieter," I said, and as soon as I said it his old face numbed as though I'd struck him. He withdrew his hand from the tasseled neck of the sherry bottle. "Haar?" Now it was a nannygoat bleat of fear.

"I mean, didn't I see you in East Hampton?" I heard my voice trail away, as though I were failing a viva-voce examination.

"Haar?"

I couldn't bear his face. I rushed in and said no, perhaps I'd made a mistake, he reminded me of someone else, yes, a mistake, but all the time I was saying it I avoided looking at him and yet, at last, I had to look, and when I did I caught, as though it were a ball he threw to me, the terrified little smile on his face, caught it and returned it, and for a moment that old man and I were trapped in awful intimacy, each of us knowing that the other knew, that there was no sense in further politicking, that the results were in, Dieter is Dieter, and retired butlers who take summer jobs as bartenders and live in clamdiggers' shacks on Montauk Beach don't have three hundred a month to spend on East Side apartments, now do they?

And then came the Down Tilt, sickening, sure. For of

course this old man, this old Dieter, what was he but a shill, a spy who entered people's apartments under the guise of wanting to rent them, an ex-butler trained in antiques who knew what's worth taking? And months from now, when Terence and I are off on vacation, the smooth customers will move in here, pick the locks, steal the stuff.

Caught in my smile, frightened stiff, the old spy waited for my move. Should I pick up the phone?

"I wonder," I said, "do you know Mrs. Almond? Mrs. Nancy Almond?"

"Who?" He put a trembly old hand up to his beard as though to reassure himself that this part of his disguise, at least, had not slipped. "Mrs. who?"

"Almond. Weren't you—I mean didn't you serve drinks at her parties, oh, about four years ago?"

"Haar," he cried triumphantly. "Almond on Egypt Lane. Mrs. John Bidwell Almond. Yes, I did."

And where did we go from there? He seemed to have trumped me.

He knew where *he* wanted to go. Out. "My coat?" he said, moving toward the hall, picking up his overcoat, wrestling, stiff-armed, with the sleeves so that unwittingly I found myself helping him into it, helping him *escape*, helping this scout for a gang of thieves, this old spy who crept out of his clamdigger's shack at dawn, took the Long Island Railroad all the way from Montauk to Manhattan, took a bus uptown, politely consulted the doorman about my presence, came up in the elevator, was admitted by me, taken on a tour of the place, even given a sherry. And now he'd leave, he'd probably take the crosstown bus to Central Park and sit on a bench near the Metropolitan Museum, writing up an inventory, my fur coat, the armoire, the Oriental rug, the hi-fi, the collection of miniatures, the antique copper pots, Terence's cameras and tape-recorders, the television set, a list which later this afternoon, before taking the four-fifty back to Montauk, he, in some sepulchral Cosa Nostra bar, would pass on to the smooth customers who move in, well dressed (I read all about them in two articles in *The New Yorker*), spring the locks with the thin edge of a plastic DO NOT DISTURB sign, then proceed to gut the apartment with smooth efficiency, smiling at the doorman downstairs as they steal him blind.

"All right then," said the old spy. "I'll, haar, I'll call you within the hour."

"Call?" I said, stupidly, still lost in my Mafiosan dreams.

"Yes, call if I want to take the place. All right?"

I am, always have been, a fool who rushes in, a blurter-out of awkward truths, a speaker-up at parties who the morning after, filled with guilt, vows that never again, no matter what, but who, faced at the very next encounter with someone whose opinions strike me as unfair, rushes in again, blurting out, breaking all vows. And now, enraged by this old spy's obvious lie about calling me back, the fool within me, the blurter-out, put the impossible into my mouth. "But you're not going to call, are you?" I said.

"Haar?"

It was too late to take it back. "I mean," I said, "I happen to know Mrs. Almond, and she told me, I remember she said you live on the beach out there in a clamdigger's shack."

"On the beach?" he said. "Yes, I used to. But not now. Now, I live here. In New York."

Well, that was it, the Perry Mason point, and I became the triumphant prosecuting attorney, swiveling to face the jury, pointing at the true culprit. "So." (My voice almost cracked.) "So you live in New York, do you? Then why do you want this apartment, if you already live in New York? You were lying about living out on the island, weren't you?"

His fingers, touch-typing along the top of the captain's chest, found at last what they sought. His hat. Pulling it toward him, he backed in the direction of the front door. "Yes," he said. "Yes, haar, I'll let you know, Mrs. Lavery."

"No, please, listen to me," I began. "I don't want any trouble, no trouble, but listen to me, if anything is stolen from this apartment in the next few months, the police will question *you* about it. You can be traced, you know."

Even while I was saying this I knew how lunatic it sounded, but that's it, you see, premenstrual tension produces this dichotomy, for while part of me feels lunatic, another me stands by appalled at what the premenstrual self is doing and saying. Or screaming, in this case—anyway, talking in such a loud demented voice that he of course was afraid and, as if to calm me, reached out and patted my arm in such a damn theatrical manner that I struck his hand away, and then he began to say something, make some apology, but, wouldn't you know it, at that very moment Ella Mae threw the switch on the vacuum cleaner in Terence's study, rendering all speech impossible, so, signaling the old man to wait, I turned and ran into the study. Ella Mae switched off the machine. "Yes, Mrs. Lavery?"

"Hold it a moment, do something else, will you?"

Then I ran back into the hall, but of course he was gone. And part of me, the normal, ordinary, shamed me said, Let him go, you warned him, that's plenty, that's enough. But the normal, shamed me can talk all she wants, for in the premenstrual mood her Mad Twin does not listen; it was Mad Twin who ran to the apartment door, ran up the corridor, catching up with old Mr. Peters as he hobbled away toward the elevator, Mad Twin calling out, "Just a moment, just a moment, there."

He stopped. He looked at me. He took off his hat and stood there, holding his hat like a beggar. "Please, Mrs.

Lavery, don't worry. Didn't mean any harm, don't worry, all right?"

"No, it's *not* all right," cried Mad Twin and suddenly, oh God, it wasn't all right, suddenly I was trembling again. He was going to slip away and warn the smooth customers, I was a woman, how could I stop him? "Oh, please," I said. "The things in this apartment, it's not just money, they have a sentimental value, I don't know what I'd do if anything happened to them."

"But I'm not going to steal them," he said. "What a silly thing to say, haar, I'm going to steal, I've no intention, no, no, no, no."

"You mean, you do want, you *are* interested in the apartment? But then why did you lie, I'm sorry, perhaps I misunderstood you, I thought you said—well—never mind." (Mad Twin babbling on, unable to stop.)

"I like to look at other people's apartments. Haar. That's all. I like to meet people. You wouldn't understand."

"No, but I'm trying to understand. Why did you come to look at *this* apartment?"

"Because," he said, his hand reaching up to stroke his little white beard, "because, you see, I haven't much to do. I get the *Times* and read the "Furnished for Rent." Then sometimes, if I feel like it, I, haar, I go and have a look at some of the places."

"But why, what for?"

"Because," he said, "well, I like looking at apartments. And new people, you meet new people." As he said this, his voice carried in it a hint of his anger and humiliation at being forced to explain: implied what he could not say, which was that he was lonely, he probably lived alone in some awful little room and had to find ways to pass the time. His clothes, I'd guess, were the elegant cast-offs of former employers. And now, as he talked, Mad Twin stood in shame, knowing that he was no one to be afraid of, on the contrary, and suddenly (for that's the way in my shaky state) I felt like weeping, hugging him, asking him back in to have another sherry. While he, caught out, waiting to escape me, repeated, at the end of his sad little confession, that he had no intention of stealing, no, no, no, no, and please forgive him for wasting my time.

I said no, it was me should apologize, I was sorry, but I'd been upset today and wasn't feeling well, whereupon, as though afraid I would turn mad again, he hastily fumbled off his glove and shook hands with me, saying, "Well, good-by, then, good-by. God bless. Yes, God bless." And turned from me, gripping his Malacca cane, its steel tip striking loud taps on the terrazzo floor, as, humbled, he went toward the elevator which waited for him, its doors open, went in, its doors shut, went down, an old man I shall never see again, an old man who has already become an anecdote, a story I will tell in years to come. Years ago the Mary Dunne of my schooldays would have written it as a story and sent it out with a stamped, addressed return envelope to one of the magazines she admired. "The Apartment Hunter." That would be a title for it, yes, but where is that me who once wrote stories? That Mary Dunne is dead.

Yet in those days I wanted to become a writer. To become a writer you must want to write. I wanted the condition, not the result. And wasn't that, in some way, true of all my careers, weren't they just roles I acted out? Even acting itself. Who remembers Mary Dunne the actress— who even in the business remembers me? It must be three years since I was in to see them at Ashley-Famous, and they're still waiting for the new photographs and résumé I promised them then. Or are they? Of course not, they've thrown out my file and forgotten all about me long ago. Mary Dunne the actress?

Hamlin's fat, sweating face across from me in Barbetta's. "But that's a character role. You're an ingénue type." It was my acting epitaph, although I did not know it at the time. And in real life it's no different, I play an ingénue role, with special shadings demanded by each suitor. For Jimmy I had to be a tomboy; for Hat I must look like a model: he admired elegance. Terence wants to see me as Irish: sulky, laughing, wild. And me, how do I see me, who is that me I create in mirrors, the dressing-table me, the self I cannot put a name to in the Golden Door Beauty Salon?

When I think of that I hate being a woman, I hate this sickening female role-playing, I mean the silly degradation of playing pander and whore in the presentation of my face and figure in a man's world. I sweat with shame when I think of the uncounted hours of poking about in dress shops, the Narcissus hours in front of mirrors, the bovine hours under hair driers, and for what? So that men will say in the street, "I want to fuck you, baby," so that men will marry me and *keep* me and let's not go into that if I don't want the dooms in spades.

The truth is I did not succeed as an actress, not because I was typed as an ingénue, but because I lacked the drive, the hard-as-nails self-love it takes. Acting is something I did once, did well, I think, but again it was a role. And when success came, the limited success of that season at East Hampton, followed by the offer of an off-Broadway play in the fall, it came too late. I was mixed up with Hat by then. His career took precedence.

The party at Molly Lupowitz's place was last month, the fourteenth, it was, and the *Life* writer (funny, I don't remember his face), and what if I'd never asked him if he knew Hat Bell? But I did. "Hat? Of course," he said. "What a character." And I can see myself standing there, feeling guilty because Terence was only a few feet away, but knowing the man would now tell a Mad Hatter story, and, in some way, still wanting to talk to someone about Hat. "Poor guy," was what the man said next, and I remember I blew up and said, What do you mean, poor guy, who are you, I'll bet drunk or sober he's six times the reporter you are and the man looked at me strangely and said, "I'm sorry, didn't you know? Hat's dead."

"No," I said. "No, he's not, no"—said it so loud that people turned and looked at me and Terence came over at once. "How?" I said. And the man said it was sudden, he died one night in his sleep, and I still didn't believe it, but then the man said, "Yes, it happened about six months ago up in Montreal." And when I heard Montreal, I knew it was true. He had been dead six months and I didn't know it. When I cried, all the times I've cried since, that seemed the worst part: his being dead six months and I not even knowing it.

Hatfield Kent Bell. He used to say he was the perfect English-Canadian stereotype: born of Scots-English parents in Kingston, Ontario, a son of the manse. But, like most of the things he said about himself, it was only a part of the truth. His father *was* an Anglican minister with a living in Kingston. But his mother was a Hatfield, one of the meat-packing Hatfields. How many Canadian sons of the manse go to exclusive private schools, have vacations in England and Nassau, and take over a whole floor of the Royal York Hotel in Toronto for their twenty-first birthday bash?

Hat Bell. He sat in the library room at *Canada's Own Magazine*, looking at microfilm through a viewer. I brought the microfilm rolls, part of the research Mackie and I had prepared for him. I thought he'd be older. I'd read that he was a war correspondent with the First Canadian Division in Italy. I was five when the war started. It was my father's war. Besides, in the one-column cut on the standing head over his column, HATFIELD BELL IN OTTAWA, he looked like a British barrister, grayish, an eminence. He was not gray, he was blond, no eminence, but one of those long-legged untidy men who remain boyish all their lives. Yet, like everything about Hat, that wasn't the whole truth. He *did* look distinguished in a careless way, he *had* been a law student at the University of Toronto before shipping overseas to become Canada's youngest war correspondent. And drunk, broke, no matter, one thing you guessed about Hat: his people had been rich.

When I put the second roll of microfilm into the machine, I stood behind him, waiting to show him which part was relevant. He said in a cold voice, "Don't lean over me." I could have killed him, who did he think he was, rude bastard, the big writer lording it over humble library slave. But then he laughed his Mad Hatter laugh and said, "You're too distracting." Was it that night he took me to dinner or was it the night after? I don't remember. What I remember happened about three months later. I shut my eyes now and see myself coming out of the bathroom of a suite in the La Salle Hotel in Montreal, my face made up, my hair down around my hips, and me naked, having at the last moment decided to make my entrance without my slip. I was feeling high from the Bloody Marys and the wine at lunch, feeling terribly excited, yet guilty about doing this to Jimmy. I remember there was a moment as I entered the bedroom when I began to hope, foolishly, that by some miracle Hat and I would just lie together on the bed and kiss and feel each other up and perhaps it wouldn't count as adultery. And at the same time a little part of me was worrying that I hadn't taken off my lipstick, would it smear all over the pillow? Then I thought of my bra and girdle, which I'd hidden under a towel on the towel rack in the bathroom, and what if, afterward, he went in first and pulled that towel out and my bra and girdle fell on the floor? The girdle was cheap and old.

So there I was, going naked into adultery, and as I went into the room Hat stood waiting, looking at me. He was naked too and I couldn't help staring at it. He had no hard-on, which frightened me. I thought, He admires me in my clothes, he always says I look like a model, maybe my body is a disappointment to him?

But in that uneasy first moment he did the right thing, coming toward me, kissing me, leading me toward the bed, lying down beside me. At once I felt his penis stiffen and throb against my thigh and oh, then we had lots of kissing and hugging and feeling each other up and, at last, loving, but the thing was I didn't come and neither did he, although, not knowing him then, I thought he had. Afterward, I remember, there was a tenderness between us, there were I love you's and do you love me's and yes I do's, the first prayers for our earthly kingdom, the first of those litanies I would come to know as the prayers of failure and then I hid in the bathroom while Room Service came in with the ice, and it grew dark, and I remember us sitting naked on a little love seat, arms around each other's waists, glasses of whisky near us, looking down at the snow as it silted slowly into the back courtyard of the La Salle Hotel. We had a feeling as though we'd both run away from home and everything was a joke with us, a guilty joke, a world turned on its side. And later, very late that night, I lay awake beside Hat in the dark and I remember a tiny feeling that it hadn't been all it might have been, a feeling so small, so unwelcome to my mood that night that I dismissed it. I never should have dismissed it. Never. For the central thing was no better than it had been with Jimmy. I was still as I was, still as I had been that first time in the motel room in Calais, Maine. The tenderness, the I love you's: that was fear. The jokes and giggles were mild hysterics. I knew it, yet I did not want to know it and that was my fault, my fault, my most grievous fault.

Did Hat know it too? What did Hat really think, what thoughts drove down the back roads of Hat's mind when he stopped pretending and became himself? I was supposed to be the actress, yet for me acting was an enthusiasm, something I did, yet never mistook for what it is not. But Hat acted his whole life, every day, every hour, devising all sorts of business, character touches, lines, for the role he created as Hatfield Bell. The total actor, the Hat type, has no need to appear on a stage, no time to learn another man's lines, pretend another man's play. An actor like Hat is his own play. Yet does he understand it? Underneath all the Hats, who was really there? Will the real Hatfield Bell please stand up? But oh, Hat, old Hat, you can't stand up any more, you're six feet under. Show's over.

Hat in Kingston under a stone. My father's grave in the snow in the military cemetery in Halifax, the little stone cross so packed around with soft wet snow that it no longer was a cross but a phallus. Old Dan Dunne. "We will all die soon enough without us dwelling on it," my Aunt Maggie used to say. She was my father's older sister and like old Dan Dunne she too is dead. I remember that she had a mustache. And that she was very tall, nearly as tall as old Mrs. Dowson, Janice's mother. It's funny, I haven't thought about Janice since we said good-by today. She phoned this morning at the very moment I went out into the hall, chasing after poor old Mr. Peters. When I got back into the apartment the receiver lay waiting on my bed. "Mrs. Sloane, she say her name was," Ella Mae informed me. I picked the receiver up. Janice on the phone is like no one else. She talks into it as though she were sinking on the *Titanic* or taking the last plane out of Saigon.

"Mary, I'm not late?"

"No, no. Where are you?"

"I said I'd call at one. It's not after one, is it?"

"No, no, that's fine."

"Oh, thank God. I was at the Gotham Book Mart and I decided to wait until I came uptown before calling you. I made a reservation at that place you told me about, Le Plat du Jour. It's not far from you, is it?"

"The where?"

"Le Plat du Jour. The one you told me about in Montreal. All right?"

I had never heard of Le Plat du Jour but, knowing Janice, I thought it better not to argue. "Fine," I said.

"So I'm—let's see, I'm at Seventy-second and Third now. I'll get a cab and pick you up in, say, ten minutes? Okay?"

"Fine."

I put down the phone, looked again at my face, put on some lipstick, went into the hall, and left fifteen dollars in the Mexican bowl for Ella Mae. We're shy about money, she and I. I did not tell her when I'd be back. If I say I'm coming back late, she leaves early.

So, eight minutes after Janice's phone call, I went out with no farewells. When Janice says ten minutes, she means it, and no sooner did I step out of our building than I saw a cab pull in across the street and in the rear window, waving like a drowning woman, Janice, signaling me.

When I think of Janice Sloane I see her eyes, those enormous ice-blue eyes which are her distinguishing mark, like De Gaulle's height, or Churchill's cigar. But after her eyes I think, Janice and Charles, for there is that about the Sloanes, they are a couple, indivisible, so when I saw Janice there in the cab it occurred to me she'd said she was here on her own and, as I crossed the street, I wondered why Charles wasn't with her.

She opened the cab door. "Darling Mary. Oh, you look

gorgeous. God, I feel so dowdy. I should have worn my Dior. I mean my lousy Dior copy, oh, God, is it terribly chichi, this place? Reassure me?"

"I don't know," I said. "Are you sure it was I who recommended it?"

"It *was* you, of course it was you, you told me about it last year in Montreal. I wrote it down, never mind, God, I look like Methuselah, Dior copy or no, so forget it, how *are* you, are you happy, you *look* happy. You look wonderful."

"Lady?" said the driver. (He was one of those surly morons whose boorish sentence-inversion New Yorkers mistake for wit.) "So, are we going someplace?"

"Oh, I'm sorry." Janice pulled open her handbag, took out a little English leatherbound pocket diary and hunted among its scribbles. "It's Le Plat du Jour, at one-ten East Sixty-fifth Street."

"That supposed to be a restaurant?"

"Let's go," I said to him very crossly. "You have the address, okay?" (Why is it people like him are always putting down people like Janice?) I turned to her, determined to freeze the cabby out. "So," I said, "you're here till Monday?"

"Yes, Monday." Impulsively, she leaned over and kissed my cheek. "Mary, it's so good to see you."

And I—I'm sentimental or easily moved or empathetic or whatever, but I felt like weeping and I gave her a squeeze and kissed her cheek and I thought, I *do* miss her, there's something about people from home, about Canadians—we were all so involved with each other once, perhaps that's it. Oh, this feeling of love, it's false, I know it, but I did feel it and, as I say, I almost wept. In reunions, first moments are the best moments. For during them we have not realized they are all there is.

"Oh, Mary," Janice said, "it's so good for me to get

to New York. Not that, as you know, I don't love Montreal, and things are happening there, it's getting better all the time and the house, we've really done a lot since you saw it, but anyway, oh, well, there's something so liberating about being here, even just sitting here in this cab going down Park Avenue and being with you and going to lunch —oh, listen, let's have Bloody Marys, okay?"

I said yes, of course we would, said it as an adult might say it to reassure a child, smiling at her, but at the same time a cold little thought started up in me, a "there but for the grace of God go I," for if I had stayed with Hat I would be back in Canada, trying to convince myself Montreal was something it isn't, still coming down to New York, like Janice, a kid to a party. Except that I knew it would be worse for me: if I had stayed with Hat, New York would have been a reminder of Terence, a reminder of what might have been.

"Gosh," Janice said, sweeping all of Park Avenue into her gesture. "How I envy you this. Yes, I do. But not the way you think. I envy you because you can live here and not miss Canada. You don't miss it, do you?"

"No," I said. "Although sometimes I miss people from home. My mother, for instance." But if I thought I was going to get a word in about my mother, I had another think coming. "There you are," Janice said. "You see? We're different, I mean I'd miss Montreal. Of course you weren't born there, you don't feel that way, only people who were born there do, I suppose. But you know, when I think of all those years I used to dream of living in Paris or New York, I know now that was daydreaming because, no matter where I was, I'd miss Montreal. I used to be ashamed to admit that even to myself, but Dr. Raditsky says it's part of finding out, you know, finding out what it is I really want behind what I think I want. And guess what? I think I want beautiful hardwood floors. Isn't it disgusting, but the thing that really pleases me now when I feel a bit down is to go into the living room and look at my new hardwood floor. The *floor,* for Godsakes. But it's so beautiful. Isn't that silly?"

She laughed, and I laughed with her, for it *was* silly, but I was thinking, Yes, she's right, perhaps Dr. Raditsky's doing her some good after all. This is probably the truth, and now she can admit it.

"Hardwood floors!" She exploded it again. "Oh, listen, have you seen the *Marat-Sade*?"

I said no.

"But why not?" She looked upset. "Is it awful?"

I said no, I'd hardly been to any plays this season. I said, "You know, when you live in New York you get lazy, and besides, Terence prefers movies."

"Oh, does he?" Her wonderful eyes went blank, turning off Terence in a way which at once angered me. "Anyway," she said, "everybody thinks it's stunning theater. The *Marat-Sade*, I mean. But a bad play."

Who is everybody? I wondered. Which magazine? And how could bad plays be stunning theater? I suppose I was irritated at her cold look when I mentioned Terence and so I wanted to get back at her. I said, "I hear the most stunning thing about it is that one of the actors shows the audience his bare bum."

She laughed. "Of course," she said, "it's a fag play, they all are nowadays. By the way, Davy Powell sends you his love."

I thought of Davy, I saw his gray hair, his gray suit, his air of "sincerity." He's a druggist, a dull man who grows faintly bitchy in drink, his voice slurring into queer talk. The boy who used to live with him committed suicide by jumping off Jacques Cartier bridge. Janice and Charles whisper this fact to other guests, usually while Davy's holding forth in their living room. Oh, God, oh, Montreal, where it's still "chic" to know a queer. How great to have left it forever, to have said good-by to Davy Powers, Blair and Peggy O'Connell, the Leducs, and all of them, so smug and small, so sick for horrors and gossip.

"And Blair," Janice said, as though I'd spoken out loud, "sends you *his* love. Of course he's still your slave. And oh yes, I meant to tell you that other fan of yours, Ernie Truelove, he's broken up with that girl, Sally something, Sally . . . ? But oh, I'm *here,* I'm in New York, what am I doing talking about poor old Montreal, my God, this place, I love it. Wait, is that the Pan Am Building?"

"That's it, all right," I said.

"And do helicopters really land on it?"

"Yes, I think so."

"They don't land there no more," the cab driver said. (Oh, he was determined to get in on things.) "The service don't pay," he told us. "Yeah, it's too expensive. Besides, people was complaining about the noise."

"How interesting," Janice said, and of course that was enough, he was off, talk, talk, talk, all the way over to a restaurant I was sure I'd never recommended, but which looked fairly promising, the sort of place the guidebooks list as Moderate to Expensive. I paid the cab, although Janice tried. I remember thinking, Not a Bloody Mary but a martini. For suddenly I felt trembly and tense. I knew she was going to mention Hat.

We went in, down two steps into a little entrance foyer with a cloakroom on the left and on the right a reservations desk, a sort of podium with an electric-light fixture over it, the kind used to light expensive oil paintings. And at this podium, in a black suit, a fat butter-complexioned Frenchman. Owner? Headwaiter? Who knows?

"*Madame Sloane,*" Janice announced. "*J'ai réservé pour deux.*"

40

Owner-Headwaiter listened, staring at Janice as though she were a remarkable talking myna bird. He gave a little sigh, then, without consulting his reservations chart, picked up two menus from a pile, waved them in our faces to show we should follow him, and follow him we did, two women going by the stares of the martini men at the little bar, down into the long narrow room, all the way down to (wouldn't you know it?) a place right next to the kitchen door, where Owner-Headwaiter pulled out a table and indicated two places on the banquette by the wall. I prefer to sit opposite my fellow guest, not side by side, but if I did that I would be in the direct line of waiters backing out of the kitchen with plates of food. So I accepted my fate and sat beside Janice while Owner-Headwaiter locked us in by pushing the table back into place. *"Je vous remercie bien,"* Janice announced loudly, although why she should thank him for the worst table in the room is beyond me. Owner-Headwaiter put down two menus. *"Bon appétit,"* he said, finger-snapping for a waiter, turning away, leaving us. The waiter came, a stout, bald man in his late forties, wearing a waiter's short red jacket and black evening trousers. I don't think Janice looked at him; she was too busy seeing who, if anyone, had noticed that she speaks French. "Would you like a cocktail, madame?" the waiter asked and at that point Janice turned and said loudly, *"Oui. Deux Bloody Mary, s'il vous plaît,"* nodding in a dismissing way, causing the waiter to back off at once, and so much for my thought that I'd like a martini. Then turned to me, her face anxious. "Seriously, Mary. I look like hell, don't I?"

"Nonsense, you look wonderful."

She sighed. "How could I?"

"What do you mean? What's wrong?"

I waited, but got no answer. Instead, she lifted her head,

a movie heroine facing the firing squad, picked up the menu, and asked, "Have you seen the Turner show at the Museum of Modern Art?"

I said no, not yet, I'd heard it was very crowded, and she said she must go, it was one of the things on her list, and by that time the waiter was back with the Bloody Marys.

"Oh, I need this," she said, gulping hers.

"What is it, Janice? Could I help?"

"It's nothing," she said. "What do you hear from Montreal these days? You still keep in touch with the O'Connells, don't you?"

I said no, not really, Christmas cards was about it, I'm a bad correspondent. I said I supposed she, Janice, was my closest contact there nowadays.

"You mean you don't write *anybody*, none of the old crowd?"

I said no. I said my mother was the only person I wrote to regularly and then I was going to tell her about today's letter from Mama, about the polyp and my worry about it and how I'd phoned home and spoken to Dick. But before I started, she asked what time it was. I looked at my watch and told her one-fifteen, and as I did she drank down the rest of her Bloody Mary and held up her empty glass. "Listen, would it be awful if we had another?"

I remember that I'd drunk only a little bit of mine and I felt less trembly, less worried about her mentioning Hat, and so I said I'd still got some, but why didn't she go ahead? After all, she was the one who was on holiday.

"*Eh bien.*" She moved her voice up a register so that the other diners would hear. "*Garçon? Garçon?*" The waiter, who was coming along the aisle of diners, three plates of roast beef on his right arm, a bottle of red wine and two glasses in his left hand, nodded, harassed, as though to say he'd be there in a moment, and there was Janice, her left hand raised, looking around at the other

42

diners, then calling loudly to the waiter as soon as he had deposited his roast beef and wine. *"Quand vous avez un moment, un autre Bloody Mary, s'il vous plaît."* The waiter, coming back past us, said, "Just one?" and Janice nodded, and then at last the waiter spoke his first words of French. *"Bien, madame."* And Janice called back, *"Merci,"* as though she were delivering lines from a stage, then turned to stare quite shamelessly at a man who was lunching with two other men on the banquette across the way from ours. The man looked up, looked at her. He was just a man, in his thirties, with a tab-collared shirt and a freckly face, but I went stiff in embarrassment because Janice pointed straight at where he was sitting.

What was she going to say? I stared at her. The man stared too, his fork in mid-air.

"Is that the Sainte Chapelle?"

Above the banquette where the poor man was lunching was a French government poster of the Sainte Chapelle, and so I said yes, it was. The man, chewing inelegantly, swiveled around and looked at the poster on the wall behind him while I sat there, my face hot, wanting to pinch Janice, thinking, My God, we Canadians are always going on about Americans, how loud and show-offy they are, but what about this? And so, ashamed of Janice, anxious to dissociate myself from her, I picked up the menu and pretended to study it.

"Ah," she said. "Now I'm going to prove to you that it was you who told me about this place."

She opened her purse, produced her little notebook, and hunted in it. "Here we are," she said and pushed a scribbled page under my eyes, and there was my name, MARY, and after it: *Le Plat du Jour: speciality. Endives flamandes.* I read it and then realized what it was I'd told her, to try *endives flamandes,* which was one of the *plats du jour* at Chez Napoleon at Fiftieth and Ninth. She had misunderstood, written down Le Plat du Jour as the name of the restaurant, and by coincidence found one by that name. If it were anyone else but Janice I'd have laughed and told her about her mistake, but instead I picked up the menu, hoping that by some crazy luck I'd find *endives flamandes* on it. For I remembered Janice's moods, knew that somewhere close to the surface of her seemingly large self-esteem there is another, terrified Janice, a Janice who could break down and weep over this trivial error, a Janice capable of turning a small misunderstanding into an hour-long session of recrimination in an effort to prove that somehow she had not been wrong, could not be wrong, never was, never would be, world without end, amen, wrong.

"Oh dear," I said falsely. *"Endives* doesn't seem to be on today."

"Isn't it? Too bad. Never mind, perhaps there's something else you recommend?"

"Rognons," I said. "Do you like kidneys?"

"Are they good here?"

"Yes," I said. And then, going on with my lie: "At least, they were the last time I was here."

Good, she said, *rognons* it was, and she ordered *moules ravigotes* to start with and a small carafe of white and a half-bottle of Brouilly, making it all very much a *commande* in loud French, the waiter nodding, saying, *"Très bien,"* and Janice looked around her, smiling as though for an audience, and then, I forget, what did we talk about before Hat? I don't remember. How did he come up? Yes. Janice said, "I bumped into MacKinnon the other night at a party. Do you remember him? He remembers you."

I remembered him. I thought of him coming out of his private office at *Canada's Own Magazine* one winter afternoon. The Warm Brown Turd, Hat called him, and it was dead on, he even looked like a turd in his perennial fawn shirt, brown tie, brown suit, and shiny brown shoes. That

44

terrible time, with me trying to get Hat to slip away quietly, everybody on the magazine working against deadline, everyone suddenly aware of the trouble, as Hat, obviously drunk, came in very late and sat down to write his column. And MacKinnon's voice: "Get your coat on, Bell, do you hear me, Bell, or are you too rotten stinking drunk? Go on, get out." And Hat so very drunk I don't think he *did* hear MacKinnon. Then MacKinnon looked at me and asked, "Who let him get this way? Were you with him?" And I, Simon Peter to Hat's drunken Christ, yes, I denied him.

"Of course," I said to Janice, "I remember MacKinnon. He hired me on *Canada's Own*."

"Gosh, yes. Silly of me," she said. "I always think of your acting, I forget your magazine days. Anyway, he asked after you. He knew you were divorced from Hat, but he didn't know you were living in New York. He told me they're putting out an anthology of Hat's wartime stuff: McClelland and Stewart, I think. And they've asked MacKinnon to write a preface."

"But why MacKinnon? That turd. Hat used to call him the Warm Brown Turd. God, Hat would be furious, why couldn't they get somebody else, anybody'd be better than that bastard, what's he got to do with Hat, that shit, all he ever did for Hat was try to fire him."

And, oh, my voice, talk about Janice being close to the surface of panic, there I was, far too loud, saying filthy words, turd and shit, shaking like a madwoman in simple bloody anger at the injustice of MacKinnon writing a preface to Hat's one and only book, Hat, poor Hat who'd wanted all his life to write a book, first a novel, then a biography of Louis Riel, and then something else—I forget, it came to nothing. And now, at long last, someone decides to put those wartime pieces of his between hard covers, and Sweet Jesus our Saviour they ask R. M. Mac-

Kinnon, the Warm Brown Turd, to write the official foreword to the words of Hatfield Kent Bell. Dear old Canada, wouldn't you know it, the people who shat on Hat while he was alive will be the first to rise up and claim they knew him when. And what can *he* say? He's dead.

And I, what right have I to act holy about all this? I left him. They say that killed him.

But there, in the restaurant, I blamed MacKinnon. I remember saying in a loud voice, "It's just not fair." Then I tried to drink some of my Bloody Mary and spilled it, and Janice gave me Kleenex from her purse and said she knew Jack McClelland, the publisher, he was a very nice guy and if I liked she would write Jack and suggest somebody else, someone Hat would approve of. And who would be the right person to do it, who did I think?

Which was the very best thing she could have said, for it made me forget my shaking in an effort to think who *would* be the right person to do a foreword, who would Hat have chosen? Meanwhile, Janice signaled the waiter and there was a second Bloody Mary beside me, I remember thinking she did that efficiently, just as Hat would have done it. Who could write the foreword? Names: A. J. Liebling, Scotty Reston, Edmund Wilson—impossible, of course, none of those people ever heard of Hat. But they were who he would have liked. Liebling especially. Then I remembered that Liebling is dead. And Hat is dead. And that there just isn't anybody in Canada.

"What about Reid Stanfield?"

"Oh God," I said. "That ass. Why do they need a foreword, anyway?"

"I suppose to tell who he was?" Janice said.

When she said that, tears came into my eyes. Oh, Hat, who *were* you? Did anybody know, did you know? Will this little book of your writings bring you to life, will it prove that you thought, therefore you were? I doubt it, and there, in the restaurant, the sadness of it would not leave me and so, holding Kleenex to my mouth and nose, pretending I'd had a fit of the sneezes, I rose and went down among the crowded tables to the ladies' washroom, where (alone, thank God) I stood in a one-minute silence by the washbasin and wept for Hat. Remembering that sad epitaph:

"Why do they need a foreword?"

"I suppose to tell who he was?"

I wonder: Why, why do I still feel our lives must have some purpose? I don't know. But there in the bathroom, thinking of the sadness of this meaningless posthumous book, a book which would have so delighted Hat if Hat were alive, I wept. I stood at the washroom mirror, great black coal-miner smudges of mascara around my eyes, my lipstick all washed off, and there in the midst of my tears I thought of the man at the traffic light and laughed, for I thought, If that sick bastard walked into the ladies' room and saw my face now, he wouldn't say, "I want to fuck you, baby." No, he wouldn't. But my laughter, which began by liberating me, refused to leave me and became hysterical. Which frightened me, so, still laughing, I wet a paper towel and wiped my forehead, then washed my face in cold water, another me taking charge, the sensible me who talks to Mad Twin in a condescending grown-up way, saying come on, girl, get a hold of yourself, stop this nonsense. A hateful person, this Girl Guide mistress, an amalgam, I suspect, of all the grown-ups who lectured me when I was a child. Anyway, that sensible person talked that other person I fear out of her hysterical laughter; it was sensible self who stretched out an arm very straight, inspected the tips of fingers for tremor, and announced that make-up could again be applied.

Then, as I began to put on my eyeliner, a third self took over, an indulgent My Buddy persona who suggested

47

I go back and have that second Bloody Mary Janice had ordered for me. Enjoy your lunch, My Buddy advised me.
Get a little bun on. Just keep Janice off the subject of Hat
and the old days. She said she didn't want to talk about
Montreal. Remind her of that. Make a joke of it.

Sensible self and My Buddy having done their work, the
make-up job satisfactory if not great, I went back into the
restaurant, which now seemed very crowded, waiters everywhere, not an empty table or chair, and everywhere that
noise, noise, noise which is the heart of the New York lunch
hour. I remember consulting my dress watch as I went toward our table, and it was one-forty-five. I remember Janice looking up, worried, then smiling, reassured at the
sight of me. By now the table was cluttered with the remains of my first drink, the fresh drink Janice had ordered
for me, her own drink, then a carafe of white wine with
two glasses, two portions of *moules ravigotes,* a blue Gitanes
ashtray, Janice's handbag and gloves. And as I sat down
she said, "Don't you look marvelous, sometimes I hate
you, what am I talking about, I *always* hate you, that marvelous hair of yours, you never have to do a thing to it,
do you? My damn hair's so fine, every hairdresser I've ever
gone to has thrown up his hands in disgust."

I said, "I just spent an hour at the hairdresser's before
coming to lunch."

"Did you? Well, it was worth it, I must say." She put
the fresh Bloody Mary in front of me. "Come on, now,"
she said. "You're behind. Oh, Mary, what *fun* to see you
again."

But it wasn't the same as when she'd said it in the taxi.
Now she was a reminder of days I do not want to remember and so, anxious to hurry through lunch and get away
from her, I picked up the fresh Bloody Mary, poured half
of it into her glass, and said, "Please? Help me with this,
will you?"

48

She smiled and nodded. She clinked glasses with me. We sipped, then put the glasses down, looking at each other, she fondly, I pretending. "Did I tell you about Woody and Kate?"

"No," I said.

"They've separated."

I nodded. The wrong thing to do, for she said at once, "Aren't you surprised?"

"It's not that," I said. "It's—" But I couldn't say it's Hat, Woody knew Hat, it all reminds me of Hat, and so I said, "It's—ah—it's the past. I don't like to remember those times, that's all."

I could see her turn this over before she accepted it. "Well," she said, "of course you're not a real Montrealer, you were only there for a few years, it was just an episode in your life. It's not like me." She stared at her drink, jiggled her glass. The green slice of lime rotated slowly in the tomato-red slime of her Bloody Mary. "It's my whole life," she said. "That's the sad part."

"Why sad?" I asked but she wasn't looking at me, she was looking across the room again and I looked to see what she saw and there, under the Sainte-Chapelle poster, was the freckly-faced, tab-collared man, grinning at her. The other men at the table were also looking in our direction, and one of them, catching my eye, winked at me. Furious, trapped in this flirtatious exchange of glances, I turned to Janice. It couldn't be, it just couldn't, she couldn't be trying to pick those men up, could she?

"My mother is ill," I said. I don't know why it came out like that. Yes I do, I said it because it was the one thing I could think of which might get her attention. She turned to me, looking serious, and said, "Ill?" And so I began to tell her about Mama's letter and my phone call to Dick. But as I started to tell it I watched her the way I'd watch a thief. Sure enough, by the time I got to Dick and the polyp,

49

her glance began to slide past me to the men and, seeing this, I felt ashamed to be discussing something as important as my mother's illness, with Janice staring across the room like a silly high-school girl trying to pick up boys at a soda fountain. And so, cutting my story short, I said, "That reminds me. How is *your* mother?"

"Mother?" said Janice. "Well, at least it's harder for her to descend on me these days."

"She's still living in Montreal, isn't she?"

"Well, yes," Janice said. "But didn't I tell you? She's in Briarwood now. Charles and I arranged to get her in. We had hell's own trouble, too."

"Briarwood?"

"The convalescent home for old people. It's very good. You know she fell last winter, and she just couldn't look after herself in her own flat any more. So we got her into Briarwood. We were lucky, there's a huge waiting list."

"And does she like it?"

"Are you kidding? It's out in Senneville, it's more than an hour by bus. So of course she can't just pop in on us any more."

She shook her head and I saw her eyes seek out the man across the way. "Gratitude is something mother just doesn't know exists. You should hear her, you'd think Charles and I were her worst enemies. She's so selfish, it never occurs to her I have a life of my own and that she just doesn't fit into it."

"How old is she?"

"Oh, early seventies. Of course, she had me very late. These *moules* are delicious, don't you think?"

I didn't think so but I said they were. It struck me that, after two Bloody Marys and half of mine, anything would taste good to her.

"The phone is still the trouble," Janice said. "She still phones me every morning. It's her umbilical cord."

She looked back at the men. Old Mrs. Dowson, Janice's mother, is a handsome, frail old lady who reminds me of the late Queen Mary, Princess of Teck. What I remember about her is one day I went to see Janice and Janice was out and there was her mother, also arrived to pay her a visit, waiting in the little back garden of Janice's house in Montreal West. It was a hot summer's day and Mrs. Dowson, who is very tall, sat hunched up uncomfortably in a garden chair, leafing through a copy of some French magazine. I had met her once or twice before but had never really spoken to her. We exchanged some vapid remarks about the weather and Janice's whereabouts and then, out of things to say, sat in silence. Her eye went to her magazine, so I picked up *The New Yorker*.

Then, as we turned magazine pages, suddenly she said, "Nonsense, he did *not* smell."

I looked at her. She was shaking her head over the magazine. "Who?" I asked.

"Rasputin. They say here he smelled badly. Not true. Not when I met him."

I remember wondering if she was going a bit senile, but no, I asked where she'd met Rasputin and she told me that before her marriage she was a governess, she had spent five years working for the Duc de Mirepont: in 1913, it seems, the Mireponts went on a grand tour, taking their *miss anglaise* with them, and in Moscow, at a tea given by the Czarina for the Duchess, Rasputin walked in, sat down, ate three cakes very greedily, drank a cup of tea, showed the children a conjuring trick with a coin, behaving all the time as if the Czarina's private apartments were his own. "I knew no Russian, of course," Mrs. Dowson said, "so I have no way of judging him. But he seemed very pleasant, and certainly he was fond of children. I sat next to him. He did *not* smell."

Dowdy, old, hunched uncomfortably in that garden

chair. I remember staring at her, at this woman who had traveled in Imperial Russia, who had taken tea with Rasputin and the Czarina. Is there anything in Janice's life, in my life, as strange as that? I remember when Janice came back I said how extraordinary, her mother's life. Janice said, "Oh, she met Proust too, didn't you, Mother? And the pity was, of course, Mother didn't know who he was, she thought he was someone mixed up in the Dreyfus case." I looked again at her mother, who smiled a timid smile. "Proust?" I said. "What was he like?" But Janice gave me a warning look and at once called me into the kitchen on some pretext. "Look," she told me, "I don't want to sound mean, but mother will stay here all afternoon if you encourage her." And that was that. I never really heard about Proust and when once or twice, in front of other people, I mentioned Mrs. Dowson and Rasputin, Janice said, "Oh, yes, that," as if that was far less interesting than the sex life of Davy Powell or what Dr. Raditsky thought of Graham Greene's new novel or the colors and design of the North African rug Janice and Charles were having made up to go with the new hardwood floor in their living room.

And so today, listening to her complain that her mother is selfish and phones too often, I thought of *memento ergo sum.* Does that unwanted old widow who sits staring into the sad, colored glooms of a television set in the lounge at Briarwood really remember the young governess who took tea with Rasputin in the Czarina's apartments long, long ago? Perhaps Rasputin did smell but the old woman does not remember? Perhaps she recalls that afternoon only as I do my father's funeral, as a story whose details she has mastered by repetition, a story she tells to strangers, hoping it will hold their attention? And, when I thought that, I became frightened, frightened not only for poor Mrs. Dowson, but frightened for me, for the me who cannot remember that young Mary Dunne I was. And so, frightened, I foolishly burst out, "But Janice, I feel sorry for your mother. I'd phone too, if I were all alone. Wouldn't you?"

Janice. Her eyes turned on me, eyes cold as the tiger's eyes as he watches you watching him, watches you as he walks his measured beat in the zoo's cage, waiting for his keeper and the day's meat. Those eyes which saw me but did not see me, which inspected me as the tiger inspects the frieze of visitors' faces, faces of no interest to the tiger, who waits only for the slap of the bloodied hunk of horsemeat in the concrete gutter under the iron bars, the tiger to whom my interruption was just that, an interruption; who must now dispose of it with an angry flick of the strong tail, the ice-blue eyes remote, withdrawn in reverie. "But she's been alone for years," the tiger said. "You don't understand. She *likes* to be alone. Why do you think she divorced my father, why do you think she sent me to a boarding school when I was twelve? She's always liked to be alone. If she wants company it's only for a few hours and on *her* terms. Oh, yes."

The tiger, having swatted down the fly of my objection, looked steadily across the room to where the men were sitting, at first ignoring the waiter, who brought our *rognons*, set them down in a great hurry, and began opening the half bottle of Brouilly with his waiter's pocket corkscrew, having trouble with the cork, saying a tiny "crotte" under his breath as the cork came out broken, using the edge of his napkin to get the bits out, listening to Janice, who, suddenly noticing him, informed him loudly for the benefit of her audience across the way, "*Dommage, dommage, ces tire-bouchons, je me demande comme vous pouvez vous débrouiller avec ce machin-là.*" The waiter nodding, saying meaninglessly, "*Oui, madame. Ça chauffe, vous savez,*" while I sat thinking, What *is* it that heats, what does he mean, does it heat the bottle, the bottle-opener, or what?

53

Why do waiters and workmen say these meaningless, menacing things about their tools when the tools fail them? But while I thought this I thought it in an automatous trance, the way people recite multiplication tables to keep their minds off something else. The something else was Janice smiling at those men across the way, her smile becoming a caricature, and I remember thinking that when women start worrying about their age or sex appeal they fall into self-parody, for now the coquettish smiles and becks are sincere at last; the man, any man, is wanted. But even as this thought went through my mind I said to myself, It's not age in Janice's case, she's only thirty-three, she's a good-looking woman, so it must be something else. (Is she sex-starved?) Oh, eat your *rognons*, I told myself. Drink your Brouilly. I drank it and it was sour. I asked Janice about Blair and Peg O'Connell (anything to distract her from coming on with those men) and it seemed to work, for at once she started in on what was supposed to be a very funny story about Blair and some mad patient of his who developed a crush on Peg. (I *think* that was the story.) In the old days when I lived in Montreal it might have interested me. Now it bored me. Blair and Peg are no longer part of my cast of characters; they are the past as Montreal is the past. When one rejects a city, one seems by implication to reject the friends who have remained in that city, and so, afraid that Janice would detect my inattention, I overacted my interest until suddenly, shocked out of all pretense, I saw her, still talking, openly wink at the men across the way. Absolutely no sense pretending, Mad Twin screamed inside me, it *is* happening, it *has happened*, and slap! like my hand coming down on the table, I heard my voice: "Are you trying—" (That's what I started to say, but when I am near my time of month my rages alternate with an equally unreasonable terror that other people will injure me physically and so, faced by Janice's

54

cold tiger eyes, I felt myself flinch in mid-sentence, felt a grin of fear form on my face as desperately I tried to turn my accusation into a joke.) "To—ah—to pick those men up?"

Her tiger eyes studied my grin. Did she sense Mad Twin's anger underneath? Then she laughed, a great gushy, gee-shucks laugh, which by its spontaneity managed to chase Mad Twin up a tree, leaving me up there wondering if after all I'd imagined the whole thing because, damn it, Janice is good-looking and of course men ogle her and, as for her peering around, remember she's a visitor to New York, it's all exciting to her, and when I used to come down here from Montreal I was always peering myself, trying to suck all the juicy excitement out of every minute of my visit.

"I'm kidding," I said, and she laughed even more and then I said, "Pay no attention to me. After this morning I'm a nut on the subject of men."

At once she stopped laughing. "What do you mean?" she asked, looking upset. I had no idea why, so I said hastily that something unpleasant happened outside the hair-dresser's and told her about it and at once she was all sympathy and told me about a similar nasty thing that had happened to her and suddenly, what with this and that, we had finished our *rognons* and the wine and it was time for dessert and it seemed unfair of me to have worried about getting through a lunch with her for, if it wasn't quite like old times, we at least had enough of a savings account of shared experience to last a few hours in each other's company. We picked on chocolate mousse for dessert and ordered *café filtre*. Then there was a pause. She looked at me significantly.

"Well," she said, "if you *do* know, you've been very discreet. I'll say that."

"Know what?"

"About Charles. Are you sure you haven't heard anything from some of our dear friends in Montreal?"

"No, what?" I asked (in my trembly mood, people beating about the bush, mysteries, I can't stand them). "What?" I said. "Please tell me, what is it?"

"Charles is having an affair. I suppose it's self-centered of me but I thought, his being in and out of New York and all that, that you might have heard about it."

"I never see him," I said. "We just assume he's busy when he's here. After all, those news shows are pretty hectic, I guess."

"Not hectic enough," Janice said. "He brings his poppet with him. Or so I'm told."

I looked at her.

(I remember I was trying to think what I would say to her.)

"Don't feel sorry for me," she said. "He's not going to have it all his own way. I came down here for revenge."

"Revenge?"

"Perry's here now, remember? Two can play at that game."

Perry Grandmaison works at the UN. He's something in the Canadian delegation. He was Janice's first love; they lived together for a while. Perry's wife wouldn't give him a divorce, so he and Janice split up on Janice's twenty-fifth birthday. I remember her telling me about it, long ago, and oh, I didn't want to hear any more of this, revenge, who is revenged by revenge of this sort, what did she mean, revenge?

"Well," she said. "Surprised?"

"About you and Perry?"

"No, about Charles. Charles of all people. It's as though he's suddenly taken leave of his senses. I mean he never looks at another woman, never has."

Charles. If surprise was the reaction she'd wanted, she

had it now. Was it possible she could remain blind all these years to the dog eyes of foolish lust Charles turns on every presentable female in sight? I remember the meaningful grins which met me when I went to do my first show at the CBC and said Charles Sloane had hired me. The Casanova of casting was their nickname for him then. Surely Janice knew, surely some gossip had come back to her over the years? Surely she couldn't be so innocent, so self-deluding?

But as I looked into her tiger's eyes, those eyes fixed always on a world which, for Janice, spins endlessly around the axis of herself, I thought, Yes, she *could* ignore the truth about Charles if that truth doesn't suit her fantasy. There is a madness, autopsychosis, a disorder in which all ideas are centered around oneself, and (I don't know why) it jumped into my mind at that moment in a joke headline: LECHER SAVED BY SPOUSE'S AUTOPSYCHOSIS, and there I was, beginning to smile, the smile becoming a giggle while Janice, shocked, sat beside me, her mouth forming an O of outrage.

"What are you laughing at?"

"Nothing, I'm sorry."

"I suppose it's funny to you that my husband's planning to leave me?"

"Oh, Janice, are you sure? I can't believe it."

"It's true, he is. He never comes home any more. I suppose that's funny to you too."

"Janice, I'm sorry. Really I am."

"No, you're not. For some reason you're glad, for some reason my bad luck gives you a big laugh. I suppose you hate me. I suppose that's the truth of it."

"Nonsense."

"Well, then, why are you laughing? I hardly think it's a laughing matter."

I sat there, not knowing what to say, autopsychosis wasn't one bit funny, of course, how could I explain it? And then, because I could not, I wound up, idiotically, saying something worse.

I leaned toward her and put my hand on her wrist, trying to calm her. "Janice, listen. Charles has always had an eye for the girls. That's not new. It's well known."

"Well known to who? To you? Was there something between you and Charles?"

"Now, that's a silly thing to say."

"Is it?" she asked. "I know he's always saying how pretty you are. Come to think of it, he got you started on your career as an actress, didn't he?"

I felt Mad Twin jump in my skin, felt new shakes, adrenalin shakes, anger shakes. "Leave me out of it," I said.

"Why should I? You're the one who brought it up."

"All right," Mad Twin said, "if you won't take my word for it, forget it. Your husband's a lech, everybody knows that. Everybody except you."

"A lech?" she said. "You mean he sleeps around, is that it?"

"Look, I don't *know*. Now can we drop it?"

"Fine. Yes, fine. You perform a complete character assassination on my husband and we're supposed to drop it? Good. You—well, according to you, you don't know one single person he's slept with. Yet you call him a lech, that's a lovely word by the way, how would you like it if I said your friend Terence is a lech? Which he is. Of course, come to think of it, I'm not as experienced as you are about whether men are leches or not. I haven't been married three times."

"Exactly," I said. (After that remark she could go to hell.) "Now," I said, "shall we drop it?"

"No, we will not drop it." And of course she wasn't going to drop it, she wanted to talk about it, it was her great drama, she was here in New York to sleep with a man in order to get revenge. Her husband had taken up with another woman. This was drama. Her life wasn't boring at the moment. In fact, in all its horrid fascination, being deceived was the biggest thing that had ever happened to her, and I, like a fool, had opened up a new lead for her to explore, and explore it she would, she'd discuss it, analyze it into the ground. "All right, now," she said. "You can tell me, in fact I think you owe it to me to tell me anything you know at this point. I had no idea Charles was the sort of person you say he is, but then perhaps there are none so blind as those who will not see. I mean—did anything happen between you and Charles? I won't be angry. Just tell me."

"There's nothing to tell," I said. "Word of honor."

"Mary, I think you're trying to spare my feelings. When was it? Was it the time you worked with him at the CBC?"

"Do you mean casting couch?" Mad Twin blurted out. "Is that what you mean?"

She dropped her glance to her plate. "Well, wherever," she said mulishly.

"Do you want to know the truth?" Mad Twin asked.

"Yes, I do."

"The truth is I couldn't bear to have him touch me."

She glared. "Then why do you say what you do about him? If he didn't make a pass at you, how do you know?"

"Janice, there was a joke at the CBC when I worked there. Charles's office was called the free feel department."

"Charles?"

"Yes."

"Then why didn't some of those girls complain? Brewster or Conrad would have fired him."

"Oh, Janice, grow up. Nobody took him seriously. Besides, if men were fired for making passes at girls, most of the men we know would be out of a job."

"I suppose you'd know more about that than me," she said. "I've always felt most passes are made because the man suspects he'll have some measure of success."

"Thank you."

And after that we sat looking at each other, saying nothing. Her face seemed rouged, for her anger showed in little slaps of red between her cheekbones and her ears. Silence at such times is more dangerous than spoken insult: silence builds hatred as invective never can. In those moments, as Janice and I sat side by side, the voices of the other people in the restaurant, the crash of crockery in the kitchen, the noise of a bus going past in the street outside, each sound was amplified as though to draw attention to the silence it replaced. We sat like that for perhaps thirty seconds.

Then Janice opened her purse, removed her billfold, and laid a ten-dollar bill beside her plate. "I have an appointment," she said. "Would you mind paying? This should take care of my share."

I nodded. She put on her white gloves and stood up, clumsily using her thigh to push the table away from the banquette, the table making a harsh scraping noise as it moved. She eased herself past me into the aisle, then looked down at me, as in afterthought. "Do you know what people say about *you*?" she asked.

I did not answer. I did not look at her. "You know what someone called you?" she said. "The Un-Virgin Mary. You have sex on the brain, don't you? That's why you left Hat. Poor Hat. Talk about being a lech. You, God! Look what you did to him when he was down."

Standing over me, her big hat shielding one side of her face, one tiger eye glaring down at me.

"You were late," I said.

"Yes."

She walked away. I saw the three businessmen looking at her as she went toward the door, looking at her bottom and at her legs. One turned to his companion and smiled. The smile could have meant anything; approbation, dismissal. Janice did not see it.

Look what you did to him. That's what she said. Had she gone? I looked down toward the restaurant foyer, where Owner-Headwaiter stood at his little podium. Yes, she had gone, and now, four years later, I knew it was she who had told Hat.

Ranald MacMurtry swiveled around in his office chair behind his desk on Redpath Crescent in Montreal, while I, in the armchair opposite him, looked over at the analyst's couch, with the tidy detail of a fresh paper towel laid on the headrest, ready for the next patient, that couch on which Hat was spending so many hours, and now my friend Ranald swiveled back and forth, his large hands destroying wire paper clips, picking them up from a little cardboard box, straightening them out, laying them on his desk; then looking at me almost surreptitiously over his glasses, quick look, then back to straightening out another clip, his voice slow with a hint of Scots in it, although Ranald was from New Brunswick and had never been to Scotland. And then, in that slow voice, the bad news: "Well, Hat seems to feel there's someone else. Y'know, Mary, people are awful gossips."

Quick look over his specs, pause, then pick up another clip. I said nothing.

"Anyway," he said, "whoever it was told him is no friend

of his. They have no notion how serious a worry like that could be for Hat. In my judgment he's very near the edge just now."

At the time Ranald said this, Hat and I had been back in Montreal for two months. Nobody in Montreal (nobody anywhere) knew about Terence and me. The only person who had ever seen Tee and me together was Janice Sloane and that had been an accident, her meeting us in Central Park that day when I went down to New York on a morning plane and was home the same afternoon so that Hat never knew I had gone. Janice, who happened to be in New York, met Terence and me as we came out of the park exit at 72nd Street. Janice knew nothing. As far as she was concerned, Terence was merely someone I introduced her to, very briefly. There was no reason for her to jump to any such conclusion.

So I told Ranald, that day, I thought it was merely Hat's way of dramatizing his fears, and I said we both knew what a self-dramatizer Hat was. Ranald nodded, broke a paper clip in two, then looked directly at me for the first time in our interview. "Aye, but *is* there somebody else, Mary?"

I said, "Yes, there is."

"Well," said Ranald, "in that case you'll just have to take my word for it that somebody *has* spilled the beans to him."

"But that's impossible," I said. "Nobody knows about it. You're the first person I've told."

Ranald shook his head. "Not so. You must have told somebody else. A thing like this is very hard to keep under the rug, you know. So, if you don't mind a word of advice, try not to upset Hat with it, at least for a month or two. He's very near the edge, as I said."

Afterward, when I phoned Terence in New York, he suggested that maybe Hat had engaged a private detective to follow me. We didn't even *think* about Janice Sloane, but the point is, it *was* Janice. I cannot prove it but I know it. I know it because I read it in her eyes that moment in the restaurant when she said, "Poor Hat. Talk about being a lech. You, God! Look what you did to him when he was down."

And, of course, in those days Hat *was* down. Nobody knew about it, though. We had come back to Montreal from New York for Hat's one last good chance at a job. He stopped drinking and worked hard but he got depressed, very depressed, and went quietly to Ranald for psychotherapy and pills. He hoped and I prayed that Ranald would pull him out of it. "You, God! Look what you did to him when he was down."

Yes, it was Janice, all right. But, as I said, even though Ranald warned me that someone had blabbed to Hat, I didn't believe it. And that was why, a week later, I risked telling Hat that I was going back down to New York for a few days. Which ended it.

There, in the restaurant, I remember, I did not feel anger or a wish for revenge. What I felt was a heaviness, a feeling much like the one I have when I leave an airport and drive back to town after seeing someone off on a plane. It's a Down Tilt, it's the knowledge that someone has gone off on a journey and that you have stayed behind. They have gone; you have stayed behind. It's hard to describe. I am thirty-two; I do not forgive easily. I do not make friends as once I did. I sat there and in the slight muzziness from the Bloody Marys and the wine I felt dull and misunderstood. I thought, If someone called me the Un-Virgin Mary, then it does not matter if I am promiscuous or not. They say it, therefore I am. It was the same at school. If I refused to neck with boys, sometimes they revenged themselves by telling other boys I had gone all the way with them. As later, I guess, men who never

63

touched me have boasted to other men that they slept with me. As those three men, sitting across from me in the restaurant, were probably saying something filthy about me. Janice had flirted with them, but she had left and I was the one they were talking about and when one of them looked over and caught my eye I knew what he was thinking, he was thinking, I could fuck you, baby, yes he was. Oh, I was sad, I sat there in an old brown study, my sadness, almost without my knowing it, settling into that dull, mindless gloom which is depression. Depression is when things are not the world's fault, they are your fault. Maybe I am not promiscuous, but I have been married three times and I am only thirty-two. Maybe, without my knowing it, I am old Dan Dunne's daughter after all.

My father the lecher. My father who art in hell. In my dream about men, the men differ, they are nameless strangers, tall, small, blond, dark. But I am always the same. I come out of the bathroom in a hotel suite and walk naked into the bedroom where the man waits. My hair is down (it falls to my hips) and my make-up is on straight and I smile but am nervous. The man is sometimes naked and sometimes has a shirt on, but always he wears no trousers and his prick stands up. Naked means lying down, it means feeling each other up, it means I feel his prick throbbing in me as my mind miraculously erases all other times I ever made love, making it new like art is supposed to make it new, making it as it is with Terence, every time a first time. And so I lie down with the nameless man but, as I do, he is no longer nameless, nor is he Terence. He is Hat. And now the dream is truth, I live again that first evening Hat and I went to bed together, in the La Salle Hotel in Montreal. I walked out of the bathroom, my hair down, my make-up on straight, and I was nervous, I was naked for the first time with Hat, old Hat, and he was naked too, but his prick wasn't stiff and the panic started, the panic I lied myself out of, a lie paid for over and over, for in the years that followed, no matter in what city, in what season, no matter what the window-dressing of each sexual encounter, nakedness between Hat and me was the overture to panic, a panic no longer of not knowing, but a panic of certainty, a certainty, no matter what we did, no matter how well and fondly we lied to each other, asking was it all right, oh yes, it was for me, was it for you, yes, for me it was fine, honestly, fine, was it for you, was it really? Yes, really. Lies, lies to let your partner sleep in peace that night, lies to make possible the fiction that Hat and I were lovers. We had five years of it. It seems impossible now, but we had five whole years, the five years from the La Salle Hotel that winter afternoon, through my divorce from Jimmy, Hat's trip to Europe, Hat's divorce, our marriage, the big job at *Life* which brought us to New York, then, after *Life* fired him, his year as a free-lance. Until the summer I met Terence. And then Hat came back from Washington.

I seem condemned to relive those few days, to go over and over them in my mind so that now, with time and repetition, those events are a play of which I remember every line, stage direction, entrance, and exit. The first act was the Algonquin, August 3, 1962. I even remember that the thermometer registered ninety degrees as I got off the Hartsdale train that night and walked across the main concourse at Grand Central Station. The clock in the concourse said six-twenty-one and I was wearing a green and lilac Swiss silk dress, expensive, but I did not like it. Hat and I were living out in Dobbs Ferry, and for the past three weeks Hat had been in Washington doing a story for *Canada's Own* on ex-Harvard professors in government. Three weeks was too long for research on a story like that for a magazine like *Canada's Own*, so there had to be some lost time, a bender in there someplace. But for once I had not been angry or worried. A few days after Hat left for Washington I took Hat's boy, Pete, into New York to catch the plane for Toronto. Pete had been visiting us for six weeks, and after I put him on the plane I went up to Jody Terrel's for a drink and that was how I met Terence. That was something, I can't explain it, but we met again the next day, and then every day I took the train to town to be with him, sometimes even staying overnight in his apartment on the Lower East Side. Which was foolish and dangerous, of course, but how can I explain it, I was living in a state of elation, waking up in excitement every morning, finding myself smiling in the street when I thought of Terence and me, hating to go to sleep, feeling there never was, never would be a time like this, that New York was the greatest city, that, oh, that I had no nerves any more. For the first time in my life, I was happy.

Actually, as I crossed Grand Central concourse, it was my third time there that day. I had come up that morning to have lunch with Terence. I had taken an afternoon train back to Dobbs Ferry and was hardly into our house (it was, I remember, five to five when I got back, and Hat phoned at five) when, as I say, Hat phoned from La Guardia saying he'd just come home on the shuttle flight from Washington with McGeorge Bundy (who was to be the leading figure in Hat's magazine piece on professors in government), and would I put on my best bib and tucker and come into town and join him for dinner on the expense account? And I said, "Join who? McGeorge Bundy?" And Hat laughed and said, "No, McHat Bell." And he sounded fine, not smashed and very up and he said he had something important to tell me but it would keep until we met and could I make the five-forty train, which would get me into Grand Central about six-twenty, so we'd meet in the Algonquin at, say, six-thirty. Best bib and tucker, though. Right?

I remember when I put the phone down my only thought was relief that I'd been home in time to get his call. I opened my closet and looked at my dresses and there was no doubt which dress would be prettiest for dinner, but then I thought, What if there's a chance for me to have dinner with Terence, say tomorrow night? And so I did not pick out my best bib and tucker, or even my second best. I picked out the green and lilac silk, which was expensive and okay for a good restaurant but not something I'd ever liked. After all, I was going out with Hat, only Hat. I was not in love with Hat, I was in love with Terence. I had never loved, will never love anyone the way I love Terence. Yet when I remember picking that green and lilac dress I did not like, it makes me want to cry for Hat.

But that evening, sitting in the cab going toward the Algonquin, I had no sorrow about what I had done to Hat. I know it was selfish of me but I was so happy I wasn't even nervous about meeting him. I remember, as we drew up at the Algonquin (how strange that I remember this and so clearly), I looked up at the sun visor above the cabby's head. He had it half pulled down, and wrapped around it were notes to himself, business cards, and a watch on a cheap steel bracelet. I can see that watch now: I was early, it was only six-twenty-five, and I remember wondering for a moment, What if Hat notices how changed I am? Will he see that I am a way I never was before, will he know I am in love?

I doubted it. Hat's radar was for bad news, for hidden irritations, for tension beneath the surface. He lived with such things; they were his emotional language. Happiness (other than the spurious, momentary happiness of a booze euphoria) was something he did not know, had never known. I had no guilt for him to sniff. I had no nerves. I remember how calm I was as I walked into the Algonquin lobby and saw Hat sitting there with another man.

Terence and I had not planned this, but it had happened, and my one thought as I approached Hat was this: My God, if I had not met Terence, that person there, Hat Bell, poor, damned, arrogant Hat—he would be my life.

The man sitting with Hat was introduced as Jack Freed. He had been in Washington too, doing a piece for *Harper's* or was it *The Nation*? I don't remember. Anyway, I wondered if he'd be having dinner with us. Hat hated to see people go in those days, and so, I suppose, did I. We needed other people, we were nice to them, we tried to amuse them. They were our buffer against being bored with each other. And people liked us, we were considered good company in a way in which Terence and I are not. So when this man, Jack Freed, finished his martini and stood up, I expected Hat to try to keep him. Freed said his train was due in fifteen minutes. He said he'd better try to make this one.

"We know," Hat said, standing up and offering his hand. "We're commuters ourselves, God help us. Or were."

When the man had gone and Hat sat down, smiling and happy-looking, I asked him, "What does that mean? Or were?"

"Damn," he said. "I meant to spring it on you when I had you properly primed with wine and food. But probably I couldn't have kept it to myself that long. Waiter?" He rang the little brass bell they have on the tables there and hitched his armchair close to mine, his long boyish leg jiggling as he talked. That nervous trick of his. And it came out. Unknown to me he had been flown from Washington to Montreal for a one-day chat with De Belleville, the magazine's publisher. Parsons, the articles editor of *Canada's Own*, had had a sudden heart attack and they were considering Hat as his replacement. So Hat met De Belleville, but nothing had been said directly. De Belleville simply talked to him, then sent him back to Washington to complete his story assignment. Hat didn't phone me. Superstitious, I suppose. He sweated it out alone down in Washington and two days later De Belleville phoned from Montreal and offered him Parsons' job. If Hat accepted, we were to move to Montreal within the month.

"It could be permanent," Hat said. "We could buy a house. Something in Westmount, madame? Or would you prefer Outremont? And what about a kiss?"

I kissed him on the cheek and the woman across the way smiled at us. Hat took my hand and held it between his own. I noticed he had not touched his drink. "Now, look, Mary," he said, "I know you love this town and I know you were glad to leave Montreal. So, remember. It's your life too. I'm not going to twist your arm. If you say no, we won't go."

"What do you think?" I asked.

"Well," he said, "this last week, finishing up my assignment in Washington, I've thought a lot about it. I wanted to dope it all out before I put it up to you."

"And?"

"And I think it's my chance." He picked up his glass and looked at it. "This is my first drink since I went up to Montreal to talk to De Belleville. I knew they were worried about that. I lied to De Belleville. I told him I'd quit drinking. Then, when I got back to Washington, I decided that if I got the job I really would quit. And you know? Since I heard I had the job, I haven't needed a drink."

He put the drink down, Scotch and water, still untouched. His right hand, fingers browned by nicotine, combed through his hair, which was streaked with gray. "Dammit, Mary," he said, "let's face it, I know now I'm not going to set the world on fire. Since I got the boot from *Life* I've been going downhill. I'm forty-three. Jesus, I'm

69

too old. I hate free-lancing, I hate doing junk assignments just to pay the rent. I need this job. It's the last good offer I'm likely to get."

His drink untouched, the ice melting, his handsome face worried now, skin a little puffy, fingers combing through his graying hair, yes, he was getting old. He had said it. He needed this job, he needed me to say yes to this, the last good offer he was likely to get. And I (how can I describe what I thought when I still don't understand it myself?), I remember saying to myself with false calm, Well, Hat has leveled with me at last, he's right, this *is* his chance. If I say yes to him it means not seeing Terence again, not ever, and I had better get with it right now and say yes and go to Montreal and hope this last good chance will work.

Hat sat waiting for my answer. His wild black eyes, which used to frighten me, had become dog eyes, dark brown, not at all sure of me. And then I noticed the left hand, the one which was not combing nervously through his gray-streaked hair, the left hand had reached for the glass of Scotch and held it like a gun, a gun with which, if refused, he would again blow up his whole life. I guessed that a no from me meant a yes to that, but it was not the threat of that which made me act. It seemed to me I had no choice.

"Hat," I said, "that really is good news. When would we leave?"

"As soon as you're ready. How long would it take us to pack and get out?"

"A week," I said. I did not care if it was too short a time. I would have said a day if it were possible, for if I was not going to see Terence again I wanted to be far, far away from the temptation of ringing his doorbell. Oh, it hadn't sunk in, it hadn't sunk in at all; I remember that I drank two martinis while Hat virtuously nursed his Scotch, and of course he was full of plans, he wanted to take me to

Café Nicholson but I vetoed that because I felt sick at the thought of facing a big table d'hôte dinner and so, as Hat didn't really care much for food, we wound up having a bowl of chowder at Grand Central and taking the nine-thirty back to Dobbs Ferry. And it was there, driving out of Dobbs Ferry station in our car, sitting beside Hat, going down a dark country road, that I thought, I am alone with him. I will spend the rest of my life locked up with him. I turned and looked at his face in profile as he drove the car, and I thought of those horror films where ordinary people turn into vampires, and for a moment Hat seemed a vampire and I wanted to scream, as though a scream would release me, end the panic, let it all out.

But I did not scream. And as I turned the key in the front door the phone began to ring in the living room. I went for it, but Hat came through the garage and got there first. It was a quarter to eleven. I knew it was Terence, calling to say good night. Hat picked up the receiver. "Hello?" he said. "Hello?" He listened, then put the receiver back on the hook. "Another silence heard from," he said and went into the bathroom, loosening his tie, saying something about our taking up skiing in the Laurentians once we got back.

I remember listening to him going on about skiing as I stood there by the phone, thinking, Terence, you are there, all I have to do is pick up the phone and call. Terence, I am here and I can't do without you, no, I can't.

I thought Hat would want to stay up and talk half the night but from the bathroom he called, "What about going to bed?" and I said, "All right," and went and sat at my dressing table, which was in an alcove between the bedroom and the bathroom. I began to take off my make-up. He knew I liked to be alone while I did that. I heard him washing his teeth in the bathroom and then, as I sat at the mirror wiping off eyeliner, I saw the bathroom door open

71

and he came out, naked. His penis was erect. He came toward me, bent over me, and unzipped the back of my dress. He began to undo my bra, and as he did his hands shook. (It was three weeks since he'd been home: he was nervous and not drinking.) He slipped the bra down and cupped my breasts in his hands. In the mirror I saw his face, the slightly reddened skin ending in a white line at his neck, his wild eyes, now brown and pleading, his hairless chest, his slightly sloping shoulders. I felt faint. I leaned forward, shut my eyes, and put my head down. My forehead was damp and as I bent over I felt something brush against the small of my back. It was the tip of his erect penis touching, very lightly, moving along my skin. I stood up, deathly sick. I ran to the bathroom, got there just in time, clutched the basin, threw up.

He was worried, of course. I lied and said I'd had trouble with my period. But Hat had radar for bad news. He lay awake beside me, saying nothing. I wonder which of us slept more than two hours between the time we went to bed and the time we got up next morning? Anyway, when I did get up I had coffee and began to pack. I packed all day and when the phone rang I let Hat answer it and when he went out for a while in the afternoon it rang twice. I let it ring.

The next day I went on packing and throwing stuff out, and by eight in the evening I had finished. We went down to Hartsdale and ate some pizza, then came back and fell into bed. He did no more than kiss my cheek, and as I turned over to go to sleep I told him I wanted to leave the next day, if possible.

"Why?"

"Just—if we're going I want to go and be done with it."

"You don't really want to go, do you?"

"I do."

"All right," he said. "Maybe, if I'm lucky, we can make

72

it the day after tomorrow. Tomorrow I'll drive into New York first thing in the morning. I have to do something about the bank and the car and see about subletting this place, and—well, anyway, it will take all day. Do you want to come in with me?"

"No. I have things to do here."

He was up at eight and gone by eight-thirty. At ten I broke the promise I'd made to myself. I phoned Terence, told him Hat was back, and asked if I could meet him for lunch.

"Of course," he said. "I've been worried about you. How about Chez Napoleon at one?"

Some time before all this, when Hat's back seized up, a doctor gave him some double-strength reserpine pills to ease the tension. Hat had said they calmed him. I remembered that and hunted in the medicine cabinet for the bottle. There were two of the pills left and I took one just before I phoned for a taxi to drive me to the Dobbs Ferry station. I caught the eleven-ten to New York and it was as I sat jiggling on the wicker-covered seat going in to Grand Central that the pill began to work. It was stronger than I could have believed. I remember leaving Grand Central and going in the direction of the restaurant, and then, as though waking from sleep, found myself standing on the steps of the Public Library at Fifth Avenue and Forty-second Street, tears in my eyes, staring up into the muzzle of a stone lion. And in that moment of sad clarity, knew how wrong it had been to take the pill. There are pains a person must face without prescription: there are times when attempting to avoid the consequences of a misdeed is more wicked than the misdeed itself. This was such a time. I felt stupefied; I could not seem to comprehend or care about what was going to happen. Even my tears were not real: they were therapeutic, not grieving.

But my moment of clarity was just that (false girl star-

73

ing at false lion, both equally stone-stupid), for I remain hazy about most of what followed. Our luncheon and what was said are as unclear now as those long-ago details of my father's funeral. And unclear in the same way, in that I am not sure what part I remember and what part I remember only because Terence retold it to me. Yet a few things do come back; they float isolated on a wave of memory and are washed up again and again for my examination. I pick them over, but they are detritus, I cannot put them together to form the shape of those events. The first is a moment before lunch. I had arrived early at the restaurant and, not wanting to wait alone at the bar, remained outside, standing in the doorway of one of those little news-agent-grocery corner stores at Fiftieth and Ninth, two doors down from Chez Napoleon. I remember I was looking dully at the sex headlines on copies of *The New York Examiner* and *Midnight* which were stacked alongside the *Daily News* outside the place when someone called "Mary?" and I turned and saw Terence wave to me from across the street; crazy Terence with his long British hair and bright clothes, isolated as in a color snapshot. I even remember what he wore, his black and white houndstooth jacket, tan corduroy trousers, blue workshirt, red kerchief, suede boots. I remember it because for the first time the sight of Tee did not produce the usual Pavlovian leap of my heart; instead, staring dully at him as he paid off his cab across the street, I remember thinking, He's too young for me, he looks like a schoolboy. (Which is nonsense, he's only a year younger than I am, and even then he'd done much more than I had, he'd written and illustrated three children's books, sailed the Atlantic in a ten-foot dinghy, he'd been a singing waiter in Greenwich Village, he was writing lyrics for an Off Broadway show.) But if I feel compelled to rehearse all the things he'd done up to

74

then, then, methinks, I do protest too much. The truth is he does look young; then, he looked like a schoolboy.

And that lunch. It frightens me still to think that, drugged as I was, I might have blown the whole thing sky-high. Even now I remember only isolated moments from that awful afternoon. There is one moment in particular: Terence sits opposite me in the booth, his head to one side, a tall Liverpool-Irish stranger who is doodling elaborate dodo birds on the tablecloth. The birds' heads form a circle around the base of his untouched Dubonnet cocktail. And as he draws these neat, fantastic birds he is listening to my reserpine babble about how much Hat needs me, how it's Hat's last chance for a decent job, how I can't walk out on Hat now, no matter how much I want to and on and on, and none of it do I remember any more, but I do remember that moment, watching Tee as he listened to me, watching him doodle the dodo birds, hearing his voice say, "Quite. . . . Yes, quite," not knowing then as I do now that for Terence "Quite" is "Shut up, damn you, why did I ever get mixed up in this?"

But that awful day, even if I had known what he was thinking, I would have been incapable of changing my behavior. I went on, boringly sleep-talking my way through lunch, and, fool that I was, never even mentioned that I'd taken a pill.

But I'm getting ahead of myself. I did most of my explaining *before* we ate lunch. Then, Terence tells me, there was a silence until the waiter brought the food, a silence in which Terence suddenly decided he could not bear to sit there much longer, so he made a pretense of eating, swallowing a few mouthfuls, then called for the check and said if I didn't mind he had an appointment and would I mind having my coffee alone as he had to go? And then, without waiting for my answer, put some money on the table, stood up, and said, "Good luck, Mary. It will be all right, you know," and before I in my drugged dullness could think to protest, he had gone. And it was then, thank God, that I had my third brief moment of clarity that afternoon, for it came to me that unless I did something, and at once, I would never see Terence again.

I rose up and ran, fuddled, out into the street, and there on the corner of Ninth Avenue was Terence, having just flagged down a cab. "Terence? Terence?" I shouted, so loud that people turned to look at me and the taxi driver, stopping near Terence leaned out of his cab window and pointed me out to Tee, and I remember Tee turned and came toward me, looking worried, as though I were going to make a scene.

Like a drunk, I put my arms out, and when he came up to me and did not embrace me, I reached out and caught hold of his wrist. "Listen," I said in a stumbling voice. "Hat's going to be in Ottawa next month, the twenty-fifth to the twenty-eighth. I could come down here and we could see each other."

When I said that, the way I said it, something happened. Tee held me off and looked at me, his face puzzled. "Are you all right?" he asked. "What's the matter with you?" And I said, stammering it out, "Listen, I'm sorry. I shouldn't have, but I took some pill, I think, I mean I can't think straight."

"What sort of pill?"

"Reserpine, a doctor gave them to my husband once. Please, I'll come down to New York on September twenty-fifth. Will you see me if I call you then?"

"Reserpine," he said. "My God."

The cab he had flagged down had made a U-turn and now came up alongside us on the pavement. "So, you want a cab?" The driver shouted and Terence turned, nodded, then turned back to look at me.

"Please?" I said.

He bent down and kissed my brow as you would a child's. "The twenty-fifth," he said. "All right. If you still feel like it, I'll be here."

He let go of me, jumped into the cab, and pulled the door shut. The cab moved away from the curb, and I tried to see him through the window but the sun shone at an angle, making the glass just a gleam. And the cab went off down the street. He had gone, I could no longer see him, but in that moment it was decided. I would go to Montreal with Hat, but only until Hat was settled in the new job. I would not stay with him. I left Hat at that moment, although, to be honest about it, I did not know it then. I walked off down 50th Street, going toward Times Square, and all I knew was that I had a small chance of being with Terence for a day or so, six weeks in the future when Hat would go to Ottawa. I was still woozy from the pill. I don't remember what I did for the next hour or so. What I do remember is suddenly coming to in the commuter train going home to Dobbs Ferry, knowing that the pill had worn off, sitting staring out at the long rainy film strip of sub-urb going past the train window, and quietly beginning to cry, the cry of my life, the tears that for the next weeks recurred and recurred, often even in front of other people. Tears that came on when I heard music (for music made me think of Terence), tears that were mixed with a sad-ness in those six weeks of waiting, a sad, foolish certainty that Tee had only agreed to see me that day to prevent me from making a scene, poor Tee, trapped in the street by a drugged woman who didn't know what she was saying when she made her foolish proposal.

"More coffee, madame?"

I came up from the dooms as from a dive into deep water, finding my bearings in the poster of the Sainte-Chapelle on the wall opposite me. At my right hand the waiter, middle-aged and familiar in his short red jacket, a brass coffeepot in his hand, his face a question which asked for my answer.

"Yes, thank you."

He bent over me, took my cup, turned away from the table as he poured the coffee. The back of his red jacket rode up, revealing the suspenders which held up his black trousers, their leather stays forming a V as they gripped the trouser buttons, straining against the bulge of his thickening middle-aged back.

In Montreal, years ago, Hat and I out walking on a Sunday morning, turning the corner of Metcalfe Street, found there in pale winter sunlight a parade. As it came close, the band struck up: it was a Shriners' convention, old and middle-aged men from towns in the eastern United States and Canada, red fezzes incongruous on their aging Protestant faces as, still hung over from last night's whoopee, they marched six abreast behind the bright uniforms and the buck strut of a teen-age high school band. Failed men, as Shriners seem to be, druggists, salesmen, shoeclerks, stepping out in the cold winter sunlight, all together now, hup-two-three-four, dispatchers, drapers, deliverymen, dentists, brothers all in the Ancient Arabic Order of Nobles of the Mystic Shrine, and as I stood on the corner of Metcalfe Street, watching them march past in their red fezzes and cheap suits, seeing some of them smile

78

shakily and wave like good sports to the good sports among the watchers in this Canadian Gay Paree where they'd convened to have some fun and good fellowship and help Little Crippled Kids, I wept, I wept, I could not explain it to Hat, how could I explain why those failures in foolish hats, those old joiners, looking so damned silly as they marched behind the blue and gold shakos of the boys in hussar uniforms from Rosewood Central High—why did they make me weep?

I do not know. But I remembered the Shriners as I looked at the waiter's suspenders showing beneath his fancy-dress red jacket, straining against his middle-aged spread, and, remembering, looked away, afraid that again, inexplicably, tears might come.

"And the other lady, does she wish coffee?"

I realized he did not know Janice had left. I looked up to tell him but as I did he turned and faced down the aisle of diners, holding up his coffeepot questioningly, smiling at someone who (my God, why?) was Janice coming back to our table. Who nodded to him, yes, she wanted coffee. He poured some and took himself off, just as she reached our table.

"May I sit down?"

Avoiding my eye as she said it, staring instead at the wall above me.

"Of course." Clumsy, I must struggle up, pull out the table from the banquette, while she, equally awkward, must wait, then edge past me, almost upsetting the cups, glasses, napkins. I pulled the table close, locking us together again.

Wondering, Is she mad? I heard all she said, I didn't imagine it, did I, she *did* say those things?

I side-glanced at her, saw her touch the coffee cup's handle with the tip of her thumb and forefinger, lift the cup, then, her mind changed, set it back on its saucer.

Surely she wasn't going to ignore what she'd just said to me?

Her hand, rejecting the coffee cup, moved along the table. Her fingers gripped my wrist. "I'm sorry. Very, very sorry, Mary, will you forgive me?"

"Yes, of course."

But I did not mean it. I do not forgive her.

"Thank you," she said. She hesitated. And then: "Mary, do you think we could go somewhere else? I can't talk to you with those men sitting over there. You were right. I *was* flirting with them. Did you get our check yet?"

"I will." I signaled the waiter, who nodded that he would come but he was waiting on an old, old man and a girl who might be the old man's granddaughter. The old, old man was having trouble reading the menu. The waiter, helpful, bent to point out something on the printed card while I willed him to hurry, to come to us, get us out of there. Not looking at Janice, yet looking, seeing, yet pretending not to see, the flush of shame which reddened the line of her jaw as she sat there, humble, staring at the tablecloth.

The waiter came, but oh, so slowly, flipping through the bills on his pad to find the right one, checking with me about the bottle of Brouilly—"Was it a half-bottle, madame?"—slow to add it all up, and, when he had finished, I left too much as tip because I couldn't stand to wait for my change. Janice, humble, saying nothing, picked up the ten-dollar bill she had left on the table and pushed it into the open jaw of my purse.

Then the pair of us, awkward, deliberately blind and deaf to our surroundings as though the other patrons were shouting abuse at us, blundered down through the room, fleeing the place, hurrying past Owner-Headwaiter in the little foyer, up the steps, and out into the street, where Janice took hold of my arm, turned me in the direction of

Lexington Avenue, and, looking into my face for the first time since her return, began in a monotone, like a child reciting a memorized speech, saying something apologetic about her wanting to get back at me because what I said about Charles hurt her, although, mind you, she knew I had said what I did say without malice and for her own good.

And then she stopped and waited for me to say something, but what could I say? Anything I said might insult her all over again, so I compromised by nodding my head and saying, "Yes, I understand," and by now we were at the corner of Lexington and she had decided to say something else, something very important to her, for she stopped walking and stood facing me for an awkward, silent moment, her eyes open in great O's of near hysterics until she got it out. "Yes," she said, "it's true, that saying. There are none so blind as those who will not see. Oh, Mary, I know I deny the truth, I always did and now I know why. I do it because I'm afraid and I'm selfish and— Oh, *look!*"

And I staring at her, my heart going out to her as she made this confession, startled when she suddenly said "Oh, *look!*" for, as she said it her voice dropped to a whisper and she grabbed my wrist so dramatically that I was sure some horrible accident had happened just behind me, something she'd seen and I had not, so, afraid to look, I turned and saw—nothing abnormal, a girl coming out of Delight Dry Cleaners, a girl carrying a dress on a hanger, a girl whose hair and costume might cause stares some places but not here, anyway she was no reason for Janice's sudden spastic pause, until I looked again and the girl was Julie Harris, the actress, very slight and childish in a short-skirted dress of yellow wool, long white jacquard stockings, and white Courrèges boots, her long red hair streaming free down her back, her eyes nunnishly on the pavement as she passed us by, acting out her unawareness of Janice's vulgar nods and becks and wreathed smiles, Janice suddenly so hateful, so hicky, as she shook my wrist, whispering, "It *is*, isn't it? Julie Harris?"

I nodded yes, frowning at her to shut her up, but, oh God, she let go of my wrist at once and ran after Julie Harris, who had stopped at the intersection, waiting for the light to change, and then I heard, "Excuse me, I know this is rude, but you *are* Julie Harris, aren't you?"

And Julie Harris smiled and muttered something, allowing, I suppose, as how she was Julie Harris.

"But I just had to speak to you, I just want to say how much I admire your acting. I saw you in *The Lark* and, yes, in Montreal I saw you in *Member of the Wedding*. Anyway, I think you're one of the finest actresses alive."

Julie Harris scuffed her Courrèges boot and stared at it and smiled, mumbling something that, again, I did not hear. And stepped off the pavement (thank God the light went green for her), escaping to the other side of the street. Leaving Janice in an orgasm of hero-worship, and me, the third visitor on this scene, my face scrooged up in contempt.

Janice, returning, all smiles: "Wasn't that *something*?"

"Oh, for God's sake, Janice."

"What do you mean?" (And, believe it or not, I don't think she knew what I did mean.)

"What do you think I mean? Running after that poor woman. 'Oh, I just think you're one of the finest actresses alive.' How could you say such a thing?"

"I know," Janice said. She laughed, then covered her mouth with her hand, pretending embarrassment. "Wasn't it terrible of me? I know she's not great. But she is good, don't you think? Did you see her in *Member of the Wedding*?"

"God, Janice, I'm not talking about that."

But Janice pretended not to hear me. Grinning, she drew me to her, holding my wrist in false collusion. "Oh," she said, "come on, now. Famous people just live for praise. You *know* that."

"No, I don't," I told her, wondering as I said it how on earth we got sidetracked like this.

"Well, they do. Especially actors. They're so dumb."

She stopped and said, "Oops. Present company excepted. Anyway, you weren't just an actress, you did so many other things. I'm sorry."

Smiling with the pretty woman's confidence that she will be forgiven. But I stood there thinking, You silly bitch, if you have such a low opinion of actresses, then explain to me why you run after them in the street? I despised her, I despised myself for being a friend of a person who would interrupt herself to run after a celebrity. Anyone who would do a thing like that was not worth my attention, I decided, and so, unable even to look at her, I turned away from her and looked instead into the window of Delight Dry Cleaners, which was a mistake, for the Negro delivery man inside stopped his job of covering cleaned garments in cellophane bags and began making sucking motions with his lips, pretending to kiss me through the windowpane, an action which, stupid as I was with premenstrual tension, frightened me, making me start and turn back toward Janice and so run full tilt into her next question.

"All right, Mary. Look, let me begin over again, do you have a date or could you spend, say, another hour with me?"

I, flustered by the delivery man's gestures, not expecting Janice to ask this, couldn't think of an excuse so, weakly, I said, "No, I'm not busy," and of course she looked delighted and said, "Wonderful. Let's go somewhere quiet."

My apartment was quiet, but by then I realized what a mistake I'd made. Better someplace neutral. "What about Central Park?" I asked her. "It's a nice day, we could get some air?"

"Good. Let me get us a cab." And with that she stepped off the pavement, waving, into the traffic coming down Lexington. A cab, empty, slewed in ahead of her with a great flounce of its body and squeal of brakes. As I went toward it, Delight Dry blew me a mocking kiss good-by. Appropriate, for now I really *was* stuck with Janice. "Central Park, please," I said to the driver. "Whichever's the nearest entrance."

"You want to go to the zoo?"

"No, just the nearest entrance."

"I mean, it depends on what you want to do. I mean, maybe you want a cup of coffee, something to eat, maybe you just want to see some kids play ball. I mean there's all kindsa things to do, you know what I mean?"

"Just the nearest *entrance,* please."

"*Okay.* Only trying to help, you know."

"We'd like a quiet place," Janice said cravenly.

"Thank you, lady." He turned to me. "*You* should of told me that, I mean, you want a quiet place, I take you to the Ramble, you know, that's paths to walk, rustic, like they say. Real nice, you'll like it."

Two gabby cab drivers in one day. I have all the luck. The *nearest goddamn entrance, you fat, stupid bastard,* Mad Twin yelled inside me. But I bottled her up and slumped on the seat, letting him get away with it.

"The Ramble, imagine," Janice said. "It sounds so British. The Ramble."

"It's one of the most dangerous parts of the park," I said, which was a mistake, for of course *he* picked that up and said, "That's right, lady, there was a murder in the Ramble a couple of years ago, yes, it was a college professor, you know, he was killed, nobody knows who done it, they found a woman's shoe near there, at first they thought some woman done it, you know." And on and on. I suspect his plan was to talk us all the way up to the Ram-

84

ble, which was probably on his way home. And then, almost equally infuriating, Janice started to talk back to him; she's one of those people, if she's out with you she'll ignore you completely the minute a waitress or a cab driver starts talking to her. She feels guilty about asking them to do things for her so she pretends an interest in them which is completely phony. Anyway, she and the driver nattered away to each other all the way up to the Ramble, which is a maze within the park, trees, little winding paths, wooden fences, rustic bridges, glades, all of which make excellent cover for the queers who use it as a place of assignation, loitering palely along its paths, looking over the field, so to speak. It's a part of the park I hate. When Terence and I first discovered the park as a place to be together in, we walked over every section. There were some we only did once. The Ramble was one of them.

But Janice isn't sensitive about where she is, and as soon as we'd paid off the cab she took my arm and started marching me down toward a rustic bridge. I remember thinking she might as well be walking into a subway tunnel, for all she notices. I looked at her: she was the tiger again, pacing the cage of her thoughts.

"Mary, I need your advice. What am I going to do? Should I call Perry, or shouldn't I?"

A sudden spring wind blew hard on the path, blowing my hair into my face, my skirt tight against my legs. A dry, muddy scrap of newspaper plastered itself to my knee. I read: "Delta Viet Cong." I moved my leg, and the paper swirled up grandly toward the sky. Janice waited for my answer.

"What has calling Perry Grandmaison got to do with this business of Charles? There's no guarantee that your sleeping with Perry will annoy Charles. In fact, it might be just what he wants."

"How could that be?" She stared at me.

"Well, it might lessen the guilt he feels toward you. I mean his guilt about his own behavior."

I could see this thought was new to her. "Do you think so? Yes, well, of course you'd know better than me."

"Now look," I said. "Keep a civil tongue in your head."

She laughed at that. "I've called Perry," she said. "I'm having dinner with him tonight."

Her eyes searched my face to see my reaction. "Well? Should I?"

"Should you what?"

"Have dinner with him?"

"Look, Janice," I said. "It's none of my business, but it strikes me that taking up with Perry just to make Charles jealous is a cheap thing to do. I mean to yourself and to Perry."

The tiger looked at me, looked through me. "Oh," said the tiger.

Silence. We walked down the path. A pretty uniformed nursemaid overtook us, wheeling one of those huge English prams. As the nurse passed by I looked in the pram, and there was nothing inside, no blanket, no pillow, no child. The pram was new, the nursemaid's clothes were new, and there was no child in sight. And, I know it sounds silly, but suddenly, irrationally, the nursemaid was sinister, part of some plot. What awful thing has happened or is just about to happen? I said to myself as I watched the sinister nursemaid draw ahead of us.

"Well, what's the alternative?" Janice asked. "I mean to my having an affair?"

"I suppose, a divorce."

"Divorce?" You'd think I'd suggested murder. "No, that's out of the question," she said. "Although I could, couldn't I? But let's face it, I don't want a divorce."

"Does Charles want one?"

"Why should he? He's having his fun, with no responsibilities."

"Well, then," I said, "why not ignore it?"

Ahead of us, the nurse had come to a fork in the path. She adjusted her headdress, then wheeled the pram down the left fork. I decided that we would take the left fork when we came to it.

"But supposing he won't stop? Supposing he goes on with it, what'll I do then?"

"Oh, Janice," I said. "How could anyone advise you on something like this? Nobody can. You'll just have to make up your own mind."

"Maybe. But I know what you *can* advise me on. You know a lot about furs."

I thought, "Furs" is what I heard, it must be the curse, there *is* something wrong with my ears today.

"You see," she said, "there are two things I can do to get back at him. I can go off and sleep with Perry, but, as you say, that might be a mistake, it might work against me by absolving Charles. So that's out. I won't even call Perry."

"I thought you said you *did* call him?"

"Did I?" Her stare: the brass mask of the habitual liar. "I meant I was going to. But anyway, that's out now, you're quite right, the thing I really had in mind when I decided to come to New York, the thing I had in mind when I phoned you about having lunch with me is quite different. I think it's more subtle. It's going to hit him where he lives. I'm going to buy a fur coat."

She looked at me to see what I was thinking. "A fur coat?" I said, sounding like the straight man in vaudeville.

She smiled. "Not an ordinary one. I mean a sable. I mean ten thousand dollars. I mean one I love, one I really love. One that, when I go back to Montreal with it on

87

my back, it will make him wonder if his slap-and-tickle is worth it; I mean ten thousand bucks' worth. When I think how I've denied myself all these years, saving up his money for him, well, he can afford it, don't you worry, he has lots of pennies socked away. Anyway, that's what I want to do. And you *know* furs and you have marvelous taste. I want to get one styled by someone really good, someone from New York. For ten thousand I should be able to find something pretty nice, shouldn't I?"

Ahead of us the nursemaid had halted and was signaling to someone further up the path, someone I could not see. An accomplice?

"I mean," Janice said, "when I think I've given that man the best years of my life, I'm entitled to something, don't you agree?"

(And he, didn't he give you his best years?) But the nurse had signaled again and now she began to walk forward very slowly, pushing the pram ahead of her. (I guessed it then: Ahead, in some little glade, a child is playing. The false nurse will pretend the child is her charge, pick it up, hurry it to a waiting car. Oh, why, I thought, why is there never a policeman around when you want one?)

"I know it sounds selfish," Janice was saying, "but why should I divorce him? I mean what would I *do*? I've spent the past seven years of my life fixing our house up, slaving over every detail, giving dinner parties to help *his* career, ignoring my own career, anyway, what am *I* apologizing for, he's the one's been running around behind my back all these years. The office lech, God. When I think that people have been laughing at me behind my back all these years, I could spit."

"Oh, that's not true," I said, but I was no longer really listening, for ahead of us a tall young gangster stepped out of the bushes, waved the fake nursemaid on, then came up to us, his palm up to stop us, policeman fashion. He was just a kid: black vinyl cap over his greasy blond locks, black leather windbreaker, black riding boots. But he frightened me.

"Hold it a minute," he said—this with a grin at me. Then turned to Janice. "We're filming down there," the liar said.

"No kidding?" Janice was all interest.

"Yeah, TV commercial," the liar said, but I stared past him, saw no camera, nobody. Mad Twin trembled inside me, but as she did two men pushed a little dolly out from behind some bushes, and there was a man sitting on the dolly, and the man was peering into a movie camera, and from the bushes opposite came another man, in a yellow sweater, carrying a big silver reflector. The nursemaid walked toward the camera, pushing her empty pram. I felt weak, as though wakened from a nightmare.

"How long will you be?" Janice asked the young gangster, and he said about ten minutes, then suggested we cut across the grass and take the other path. "Shall we?" Janice asked me and, not waiting for an answer, started off across the grass, and there was I following, feeling my feet sink into the grass, which was dry on top but spongy wet earth underneath. I felt my shoes getting wet, asked myself why I was following her, why I was going now to Reveillon Frères or Bergdorf's to help her spend ten thousand dollars on a fur coat to revenge herself on her husband. And I said to myself, Janice isn't rich, none of us are rich people who do things like this. Why, I bet my father never earned more than—what? Ten thousand dollars a year. Before the war? Oh, more like seven thousand, more likely. And there, following Janice across the grass, I thought of you, Mama, I wondered what you would say if we were sitting at home now in Butchersville and I was telling this story to you and maybe to Madge Gordon, who'd dropped in. And you and Madge, you'd smile afterward and say,

"Oh, that Mary, she'll not let a story spoil in the telling of it," but Mama, Mama, if only you knew, most of the things I've told you, I didn't hype them up, I toned them down, for my life, this life I live, isn't believable, not even to me. Who would believe that this afternoon Janice Sloane wanted me to help her spend ten thousand dollars on a fur coat because Charles is sleeping with some girl?

And there, plodding after her across the grass, thinking of this, I found myself suddenly calling out, "Janice? Janice?"

She turned and looked at me.

And it happened again, panic, panic, I did not know why I had called her or what I had meant to say to her. I stared across the park at the skyline, while Janice stood waiting, looking at me, her blond hair blowing into her ice-blue eyes.

I knew her name. She was Janice, Janice Sloane, but I, who was I? I was Big Gertie's daughter, Big Gertie's daughter, that's me, I did not know why I had called her or what it was I had meant to say to her.

"What is it, are you all right?" she asked, and I nodded and smiled, afraid she would find out that whoever I am had gone away and left me in a panic with nothing in my head but a silly music-hall song, and now, worse, like the ticking crocodile in Peter Pan, the clock inside me started up, the metronome tick-tock-tick-tock between each word-that-came-in-to-my-mind-I-was-in-the-tick-tock-tick-tock-the-tick-tock-

"Are you sure?" she asked. "You look all trembly. Are you ill?"

Her-hands-took-my-hands.   Her-face-came-close-my-mind-went-ve-ry-sl-ow-

"Mary?"

Ma-ry-she-said-Ma-ry—

(I remembered then.) Mary Dunne. Old-and-Dunne.

"I want to go home," I said.

"Home? Well, yes, of course, if you're not well," she said reluctantly. "What is it, do you feel dizzy? Perhaps you'd like to sit down for a while?"

The tick-tock had gone. My name was once Mary Dunne, and now I was Mary Lavery. I was General MacArthur stepping ashore, returned to memory, wading back up the beach through the shallow water. So damn relieved that I said out loud, "Do you ever have moments when your mind—I mean when just for a second everything goes blank, you can't remember who you are, it's like fainting without blacking out?"

"Is that what it was?" she asked. "Oh, I know, I used to have those spells. It's funny, isn't it, how women never faint any more, yet in our grandmothers' day they were always doing it. Of course, they used it as an excuse to get out of things."

I looked at her, silently thanking her. I would be her grandmother. "It's my period," I said. "Often I have a bad time just before it, and this seems to be one of those times."

"Maybe we could go and have a cup of tea someplace? Would that help?" Smiling a charmer's smile, but I said no, I really did think I'd better go home.

"Damn," she said. "Oh, dear. I'm sorry. I was hoping to spend most of my day with you. Well, never mind, it's New York, after all, there must be things I can do." Looking helpless, a lost charmer, but I took lessons in this from Hat, who was a master at making you feel selfish, so Janice's effort, good performance though it was, was amateur. I hardened my smile and said yes, it was a shame, but I did feel rotten, I thought I'd better take a cab home right away.

Ahead of us, above the treetops, was the roof of the Museum of Natural History; the whole building, big as a Roman basilica, came into view as we went down the path toward the West Side. A yellow rush of cabs moved downtown on Central Park West, passing the museum entrance. I thought of the statue of Teddy Roosevelt in front of it; the place was built for him, it's his sort of museum, stuffed animals, Boy Scout enthusiasms, dinosaur bones and scale models. I hated it when we used to go there, Hat's kid, Pete, and I, and Pete's little school friend Skip. At the other end of the block was the Hayden Planetarium; we used to go there too and I remembered there was a bus stop on the corner. I could get a bus there which would take me crosstown, right to the corner of Seventy-ninth and Third, all the way home in maybe ten minutes. Perfect, I thought, then asked Janice what she wanted to do, saying, "I could get a bus over there by the Planetarium if it's all right with you?"—pointing out the Planetarium, trying to ignore her sudden effluvium of hurtness, damn her, I wasn't going to let her make me feel guilty any more.

And then: "You want to get rid of me, don't you?" she asked, and the worst was happening. I looked at her and saw wild, staring eyes, the beginnings of tears, the thread of her self-control unraveling by the second, and I was not up to another emotional scene with her. I just wanted us to leave each other be.

"No," I began. "It's just I'm not feeling—I mean I'm very nervous today, I can't concentrate on anything, honestly, I wouldn't be any use to you."

A man and his wife, out for a walk, were coming up the path toward us. It was crazy, but the man looked like Sigmund Freud. He was tall with a shovel beard and a gray tweed suit, his watch on a waistcoat chain; arm-linked with his wife, a small dumpy woman in green velveteen with a fox boa around her neck, the little vulpine jaws biting a bushy tail under the fold of her chin. Both she and Siggy had big ears for Janice as, melodramatically, Janice paced upstage, going away from me, then, turning on her mark, threw out her hand, pointing at me, her voice going into high register. "Oh no, Mary. No, no, you're just trying to get rid of me."

I saw Sigmund Freud look at his wife, significantly. (*Paranoia, liebchen, ja, ja!*)

"Janice, that's not true."

"Oh, but it is true. And, look, I don't blame you, I know I behaved badly back there in the restaurant, walking out on you, insulting you. Yes, it *is* true, why can't I learn it, nobody wants to hear anyone else's troubles, least of all mine."

Sigmund and Frau slowed to an almost-stop, not wanting to miss any of this.

"It was the fur coat," Janice said. "I knew the minute I said it that it put you off. Yes. But isn't it better to go out and buy a fur coat than do the other thing?"

At which moment she became aware that Sigmund and his wife were part of her audience and turned, magnificently, I admit, to glare at them. Sigmund tightened his grip on his wife's arm and, watched by both of us, the Freuds passed by.

"Yes, the other thing," Janice said again. She pointed at the underpass beneath us. Cars rushed under a little bridge, coming up into the park. "Which is to go to that bridge and jump off it."

I looked at Sigmund's back. Had he heard? But he and the missus were hurrying toward the Ramble.

"Or," said Janice, "going into these bushes and calling out to the first man who comes along and pulling down my pants and letting him screw me and screw me, when I think that for the past seven years I never as much as looked at a man, when I think of the propositions I've had, damn, I'm not ugly, if you knew some of the things men have suggested to me, I suppose I don't have to tell you, but anyway all that time I never even looked at another man, while according to you Charles has been the office lech, he's probably had a dozen affairs, this one's different, I suppose, only because he's decided to come out into the open with it at last. From now on probably he'll get his kicks by humiliating me in public. Oh damn, damn, why am I telling you all this, you don't care, you *don't*, do you?"

Weeping now, covering her face with her hands, and there were other people coming up the path, I had to calm her down, get her away somewhere. I put my arms around her. "There, there, come on, it's not as bad as you think, let's find a bench and sit a moment." And so off we went down the path, she still weeping but letting me lead her, and I saw Sigmund Freud and his Frau peeping back at us and felt like shouting out at them, "Mind your own damn business." Yes, yes. Madness is catching; it seemed so silly, it was funny.

"Why are you laughing?" Janice asked, shocked out of her weeps.

"I don't know. I think we're both lunatics, I do, I do."

I know it makes no sense, we must have been mad, both of us, for at once we switched from tears to giggles, hysterical, I guess, but such a relief and what fun to look back and see the cheated faces of Freud and Frau, who glared at us, then at each other, then stamped off, affronted, giving us their backs in what was the cold shoulder if ever I saw it.

"He looks like Freud, did you notice?" I said, choking with giggles.

"You're the end. Freud, oh, Mary, you *are* mad."

Holding on to each other, staggering along the path, two women, people would have thought us drunk. "Did you see the face on old Sigmund?"

"And you—ohh—going on about taking your pants down, I wonder if he heard that," I said, and it was so liberating to laugh again, laugh as we once laughed long ago when we were young and silly, when simple things were funny, when life was ordinary and often dull. When I was Mary Dunne.

But no, I wasn't Mary Dunne when I met Janice, I was still Mary Phelan. I met Janice the time I came to Montreal with Hat to do that first story for *Canada's Own*. When I think of Montreal at that time, for some reason I remember one winter evening, snow on the ground and very cold, we were all bundled up in winter overcoats, scarves, fur-lined gloves, and overshoes, coming out of a bar called the Blue Chip near the Stock Exchange, walking arm in arm, five of us, coming up a steep, slippery, icy little street toward St. James Street. It was a Friday night and Hat and Charles (they'd been to school together at Upper Canada College) had run into each other after work. Janice and I had come down to the Blue Chip to join them, and Eddie Downes, the photographer, was there too, and as we came out of this side street into St. James Street there was a line of six or seven limousines, black Cadillacs and Chrysler Imperials, waiting outside the Transportation building, the chauffeurs walking about, stamping their feet, flailing their arms to keep warm, and, as I say, just as we turned into St. James Street, the revolving doors of the Transportation building started turning and the chauffeurs stopped their foot-stamping and went rushing to their limousines, opened the doors, revealing pearl-gray interiors and neatly folded lap robes, while out of the building came ten, or maybe fifteen, old financiers, most of them in old-fashioned long raccoon coats and black Homburg hats, and one, I recall, in a black overcoat with gray mouton collar and a long cigar. They were so perfectly the capitalists of fancy that we stopped and grinned and Hat suddenly shouted out at them, *"Mange la merde, mange la merde,"* which means "Eat shit" and was the insulting punch line of an old French-Canadian joke, and we five guffawed as the old tycoon faces turned, worried, staring at Hat, hoping a policeman would happen along to protect them. Then, bending, folded themselves into their limousines; the chauffeurs slamming doors, running to get behind their steering wheels, the tycoons peering out at us through back-seat windows as, laughing, reeling about in the snow, we five linked up again and went past the limousines, silly, happy, and young. Yes, young. When I remember that now, I feel empty.

"Janice," I said, "do you remember *mange la merde* one night on St. James Street, long, long ago?"

"No. What was that?" And I told her and she laughed and nodded and held me and for a moment we were old friends, arms linked, remembering.

"Those awful winters," I said. "Just think. Those were the days of Duplessis." I saw Duplessis' face as I said his name, the face of a cheap dictator, a tinpot provincial tyrant. In my time, he ran Quebec. I hated him, his graft, his crooked government, his arrogance, but, more than that, I hated the fact that most people, and particularly those English-Canadian industrialists, paid graft to him, encouraged him, and feared him.

"And that slogan of his," Janice said. *"Notre maître, le passé."*

"And everybody went along with him. Even *Canada's Own.*"

She nodded. "It's all so different now," she said. "Those days are gone forever, thank goodness."

"I know. I'm glad he's dead. I'm glad to see his name

wiped out," I said. "But that Montreal, Duplessis' Montreal, is the only one I know. And it doesn't exist any more. When I go back now I don't know the place. It makes me feel old."

"I know. Me too," she said, but she was just saying it to agree with me, it cannot be like that for her, for she has never left Montreal, the city has aged for her as a husband's face ages, she sees it every day, she is not aware that it's completely different from the Montreal of my day. But for me it is gone, my old Montreal. That is true of all my old towns. I move away and they change and, in their changing, they die and so live only in my memory. *Memento ergo sunt.* Remembering Montreal, there in the park, I felt I had become the Wandering Jew, the Flying Dutchman. Down Tilt. "Janice," I said, "I really must go and lie down. Let's make a date to meet tomorrow, all right?"

She looked at me, at last believing me. "Poor you, you're shaking."

She noticed my hand. Bad tremor. "Doesn't mean anything," I lied to her. "Call me tomorrow; I'll probably be feeling better then. And why don't you go and have a look at the Turner show this afternoon? It might take your mind off this other stuff."

She nodded. "Yes," she said, "it might. And you're right, it's better not to get involved again with Perry."

My turn to nod agreement.

"As for the fur coat," she said, "Maybe I should think about that, too. No sense doing something silly."

I nodded again. Emphatically.

"I don't know," she said. "Perhaps, after all, a divorce is the only solution."

"Please, Janice. Try to forget it for today. Call me tomorrow. I'm sorry to poop out on you like this."

"Do you want a lift?" she asked. "I'm going to take a

97

cab and go back to my hotel and freshen up." I told her no, we'd be going in opposite directions. Then I walked her down to Central Park West, where she went into her now familiar kamikaze act to get a cab. And as she turned to get into it she held me and kissed my cheek. "Oh, Mary," she said. "You're still my best friend, do you know that?"

What could I say to this lie? I nodded and smiled, but I was trembling as she held me. Hat. *Look what you did to him.* I stood with a forced smile on my lips, those words of hers in my head as she waved from her cab and the cab moved off and I crossed the street, going toward the bus stop. In a Down Tilt; the dooms again. *Look what you did to him.*

"New York?" Hat said. "Again? I didn't realize you'd be commuting back *there* every month. What is it this time?" I told him an audition for an acting job; it was an explanation that had always satisfied him in the past but now that Ranald MacMurtry had warned me that someone had been talking to Hat, I was awkward in my lie. Anyway, Hat's nose began to twitch in a way I'd learned to hate. (He had become a cross, edgy person since he gave up the booze.) And there, in that half-furnished living room in Montreal, in a house he'd just made a down payment on, he glared at me like an old-fashioned Victorian husband and said, "Well, you're not going, that's all." It was so unlike him, I laughed and said, "For goodness' sake, don't be ridiculous. Since when did you order me around?" Risked saying it because even then I couldn't quite believe Ranald's warning that someone had talked to Hat. How could they? Nobody knew. It all happened (when it did happen) five hundred miles away in New York, and nobody I knew knew Terence, which was why I risked laughing in Hat's face. And when I asked since when did he order me around, Hat said, "Since now." I asked him who did he think he was, talking to me like that, and he looked at me with those sad dog eyes and answered, "I'm your husband and it seems I'm too old for your taste. You want kids now, don't you?"

I misunderstood. I thought he was talking about having children. Hat had never wanted children with me: he already had his son, Pete. We had talked about it and I'd said that was all right with me. So I was angry at his bringing it up like this and I said, "Look, you're the one who brought this up. We've agreed. You don't want kids. Fine. I'm perfectly happy. I'm not going to New York out of spite or anything like that."

"I'm not talking about babies," he said. "I'm talking about Beatles. You know the one I mean. Lavery, isn't that his name?"

"What?" I said. When I said that my face must have told him the thing he wanted to know, confirmed the thing Janice had told him, for he nodded as if I'd said yes.

"Right," he said. "If you go to New York, don't bother to come back."

"Right," I said. "I won't."

And today I remembered that, as I stood at the bus stop after saying good-by to Janice, who had just told me I was still her best friend. Janice, who does not know that I now know she was the one who told Hat. And thinking of it, waiting for the bus, I began to tremble very badly. I was standing behind a mother with a small child, and behind me, shuffling his clipboard, arranging his textbooks, all the time inspecting my legs, was a pimply student type in a Columbia University windbreaker. I remember as I waited for the bus I was thinking how Hat followed me into the room that night when I began to pack and how that was my mistake—packing, I mean—for it gave Hat a chance to talk to me some more. And gave me a chance to say the things that, I suppose, killed Hat.

Look what you did to him, Janice said, and I was still thinking about that, thinking about that night, when the bus came and interrupted my thought. The mother got on with her child, then fumbled, finding her change, while I stood on the second step of the bus, holding my quarter, waiting for her to move on inside. Behind me, the student type moved onto the bottom step and accidentally on purpose rested the back of his hand against my thigh. I moved, but there was no room for maneuver, and was it worthwhile to start something? Besides, I felt too trembly to deal with him. Ahead of me the money receptacle, spun by the bus driver, revolved its little treadmill, chasing down the mother's change, clearing the box to receive my fare. The mother moved on down the aisle, pushing her little boy ahead of her, as I, released from the student's surreptitious touch, stepped up and offered my quarter. The driver took the quarter, made change on his machine, spilled two dimes and a nickel into my palm. I put the money into the fare box and as the driver spun the treadmill, chasing my money down, I turned to look at Hail Columbia, he of the nudging knuckles, who now, holy as an altar boy, ignored me to stare up at a transit advertisement which asked him if he would like a career in the Coast Guard. I moved down the bus, which was half empty, picked a seat on the right-hand side, and sat down, seeing my reflection in the windowpane as the doors whirred shut. The bus moved out into traffic, and my face's reflection in the bus window floated glassily over the shapes of passing buildings and passing cars, floated past trees and buds of spring foliage as the bus entered Central Park. *Your face, my thane, is as a book where men may read strange matters.*

My face in the glass was Macbeth's, the face of the murderer, and no matter how I tried not to think of that night I could not exorcise it. I cannot make it go away once it has entered my mind; my purgatory is that I am compelled to relive it from the time Hat came into the bedroom that night as I was packing and said, "Look, are you sick or something? I've been thinking. Maybe you're the one needs a few skull sessions with old Ranald, not me?"

"Why am I sick?" I asked, and he replied, "Don't you think it's sick to be running down to New York to go to bed with a kid who's only half your age?"

"Who told you that?"

"Never mind," he said. "It's true, isn't it?"

"No, it's not true. And even if it were, why would that be sick?"

"If you have to ask why—" he said. "I mean, there's the answer. Good God, Mary, weren't two husbands enough for you, do you have to go robbing cradles as well?"

"Stop it, Hat," I said. (I felt Mad Twin inside me but I kept her down.) "Go away, Hat," I told him. "There are things I don't want to say."

"What things?" His eyes, dog-brown and beaten, changed as he asked it, became, as in those first days I knew him, fine, angry eyes, luminous as the eyes in a Rembrandt portrait. He sat down on the edge of the bed and knitted his fingers around one kneecap, swinging his long leg. "What things?" he asked again, eager to hear, self-destructive as always.

Gentlemen of the Jury, I remember distinctly that on that very night as I packed for New York I was, as now, on the point of having the curse, Mad Twin was in charge, I know it, I was not myself. But that excuse will not satisfy me. I am my own judge, it is still *mea culpa, mea culpa, mea maxima culpa,* for the next thing I did was tell him in one long tirade, throwing clothes into my suitcase at the beginning of it, then, forgetting the clothes, simply standing facing him in that almost bare bedroom as he sat gripping his kneecap, his long leg swinging at first, then dangling limp, quiet, quiet, as he listened to the truth, the whole truth at last, so help me. I started by recalling our very first time in the La Salle Hotel, me coming out of the bathroom, both of us naked, and the panic that it wasn't quite right, that we were faking it, that it was not what we had hoped, yet how we lied to each other that it was, and I told him how that lie had come back to plague us, year in, year out, every time we made love to each other, for, no matter what the time or place, it was never right between us. And how, after a while, it had become for me, at least, a sort of death, a foreknowledge that each time we approached each other naked something would be faked, something would be sad and false. For (I said to him) when sex cannot be made new, it cannot be made, and all attempts to fake it are a cancer. I said I had become resigned to that cancer; I told him I had no hopes of there ever being anything different in my life. I had not expected Terence, and even with Terence I had not ever hoped it would be as perfect as it was, and, I remember, Hat stopped me at that point, his face frightening in sudden, flushed anger, his eyes black as murder, and he shouting, "Fuck Terence, fucking Terence, what's his name? Terence Lavatory." And laughed like a lunatic, repeating, "Lavatory, yes, Lavatory, yes, that's the name." Then raised his hand as though he would slap my face, but did not. And shouted, "You know what you are, you're a bitch, a bitch, you don't give a damn about affection or love or marriage or any normal, decent emotion, all you want is to be fucked, fucked, fucked, until the come is running out of you, that's why you left poor Phelan, because he couldn't satisfy you, and now you're running out on me for the same reason and after this poor Beatle bugger has fucked you blind, you'll ditch him too, but I'll tell you something, you'll have your day of reckoning, even you can't go on forever, you know. You'll wind up like every other sick bitch—paying for it. Say, six Beatles from now."

"Have you finished?" I asked.

"No, I haven't. Jesus Christ, you're obscene. I'll bet you don't know a goddam thing about this poor Beatle kid, he could be anybody at all, what's it matter to you? All you want is a stud, right?"

"Right," I said. "I don't know much about Terence, come to think of it. He's not like you, he hasn't informed me about every girl he's ever slept with. In fact, I know very little about him. Outside of bed. Whereas you—I know you out of bed, but the you I meet in bed is somebody I never know and won't ever know. Now if that makes me a bitch and bed the most important thing in my life, all right, that's the way it is. I've changed, Hat. I've grown up. I want something more than a dirty little sex fantasy when I lie down to make love. I suppose that's what I'm trying to tell you. It's late. I'm twenty-eight. But better late than never."

"With the Boy Wonder," he said, his face pricked by rage. "With Terence Lavatory."

"Yes, with Terence," I said.

"Terence, your savior."

"That's right," I said. "Terence is my savior, I shall not want, he maketh me to lie down in green pastures, he restoreth my soul. Yes, that's right. He's my new religion. He's life after death."

"And to complete the analogy," Hat said, "I am death, right?"

"Right," I said. I was shaking. I had thrown my bomb, I had blown everything up. But Hat was very quiet now. He sat on the edge of the bed, stretched his long legs out straight, and examined the toes of his shoes. Then stood up, not looking at me, and went back into the living room. I went to the closet and got my coat and handbag. I walked into the front hall, and as I did Hat came out of the living room and crossed the hall in front of me, going into the kitchen. He had an unopened bottle of Scotch in his hand and was tearing off the tinfoil. He did not look at me. I opened the front door, then hesitated and looked back into the kitchen. The last time I ever saw Hat Bell he was standing in the bare kitchen of that house he had hoped to buy. He'd taken down a glass from the cupboard above him and was pouring Scotch into the glass. He must have heard me open the front door, but he did not look up. He raised the glass. He drank. I left.

Through the glass panel of the bus window, my face slid past the façade of the Metropolitan Museum. My bus had crossed the park from West Side to East and now I was reminded that the Met, for me, is Terence. The Met where we met. Even today, sitting on the bus in the Hat dooms, the sight of the Met raised me in joy, remembering thee, O Terence, remembering how I would begin to run as I drew near the main entrance, for I was always early for our secret meetings, I'd know it was too soon for you to be there, so I would walk into the main hall, past the guards who check to see what you're carrying in, and up to the bronze statue of the naked man. He is, perhaps, the Emperor Trebonaius Gallus, but no one knows for sure. There used to be a bench beneath him. I used to sit on that bench. When Tee arrived he would always know where to find me. Under the naked man.

People who get on the bus at the 79th Street stop are usually people who have been to the museum—art students, tourists, Europeans, Japanese. But the woman who sat beside me today with her little daughter on her knee—I doubt if she had ever been inside the Met. She seemed Puerto Rican, with a tired yellow face. Perched on her mother's knee, the little girl stared at me with chocolate-drop eyes, examining me as I examined her. She looked at my mustard suit. I looked at her dress, which was white with a lace collar, probably her First Communion dress let out. They had pierced her little ears and fitted them out with ugly tiny gold earrings. How old was she? Nine? Hers was the Juarez face: it could be Mexican. No matter which country they came from down there, they are Indians, with that Indian face, the face of the three little girls of my Juarez dooms, the three little girls who sat on the public bench in the Plaza San Jacinto on that dry, dusty afternoon in El Paso. They had the same stare this child had, the stare that judges without judging. Two years ago (my God, is it two years already?) in the Plaza San Jacinto in El Paso, Texas, three little Indian girls stared me into the dooms. Remember those dooms? Please, God, let me forget them. Dry hot winds blow down through Texas, down to the Mexican border, rushing into El Paso del Norte, filling the streets and squares with dust. A border town; it made me think of a cheap army-surplus store. At noon lawyer Guzman's jitney brought half a dozen of us back to it from Ciudad Juarez and our quick divorces, the jitney crossing Cordova Bridge over the muddy ditch that is the Rio Grande, going past the United States customs building and along a long dusty road to a bus terminal where the bus from Mexico was unloading people with Indian faces, poor people who crossed the street from the bus terminal like pilgrims going to a shrine, the shrine a long block of cheap clothing, furniture, and appliance stores filled with shoddy goods "Made in the U.S.A."

But El Paso is what I remember best. After the divorce in Juarez I went back to El Paso, ate lunch, and then, depressed by the drummers' atmosphere of the Hotel Cortez lobby, went out into the main plaza of El Paso, across from the hotel, to wander and wait for the plane that would take me back to New York and Terence. The plaza had trees, concrete paths, small formal plots of grass, dusty shrubs, benches with many people sitting on them; and in the hour I had to wait I dawdled and stood, read the bitter pro-Southern Civil War inscription on the small monument on the northwestern side of the square, then came to a more interesting monument on the northeastern side, a monument that was a little horse-drawn streetcar, its driver a store dummy in a Zapata hat, his reins connected to a fairly lifelike dummy mule. A plaque near the mule's hoofs explained that this was the original streetcar which linked El Paso and Ciudad Juarez, that it had been donated by its last owner to the city of El Paso. And there was the very car, lettered: TRANVIAS DE CIUDAD JUAREZ, 1882. I looked at its iron guardrails and wooden panels, looked through its dusty windows, and inside, more imaginative than the dummy driver, were large cardboard cutouts of the old streetcar's passengers, crayon-colored, as by a child. Two of the cutouts were of Mexican men in Zapata hats; there was a cutout of a woman with a baby in her arms; and, at the rear of the car, a one-dimensional gringo gent with Vandyke beard, and, by him, a boy in knickerbockers. Imaginary passengers in a real streetcar, cutout ghosts from those days when El Paso and Juarez were just sleepy border towns and not, as now, a one-day happening for hordes of nervous strangers.

And while I stood there staring at the Tranvias de Ciudad Juarez as once it was, someone began to yell in Spanish. I turned to look, and there, marching up and down along the lines of Mexicans who were waiting for the bus back to Juarez, was a stout young man, blond and sweating, wearing a black and white checked shirt, green chinos, orange work boots. In his left hand was a large open Bible, and from the Spanish he shouted, I distinguished only the words: "Jesus Jesus Cristo." I stared at this poor Fun-

damentalist shouter, bringing (he thought) God to the
heathen. The Mexicans never looked at him: they stood on
the pavement or sat on the public benches like cows in a
field at noon. He was flies. They ignored flies. They
twitched their heads and gazed about them. The bus would
come, yes, the bus would come and carry them back to
Juarez, and when that happened this noise would be left
behind. I remember that at first their silent unity reminded
me of a similar silence that morning when we, the divorce-
seekers, sat waiting in the lobby of the Hotel Cortez, each
of us knowing we were on the same quest, yet each of us
alone, like people on a religious retreat in which a vow of
silence and contemplation has been taken, travelers on a
shameful journey who had abjured our normal American
garrulity, preserving in our silence the privacy of defeat.
Yet how false that silent unity seemed when, two hours
later, the deed done, the papers signed, my companions returned to normal in the jitney coming back across the Rio
Grande, normal being nervous jokes, normal being too
informative, too eager to be at once restored to that gabby,
indiscreet, phony friendship which is the posture of Americans as travelers.

And so, there in the Plaza San Jacinto, I admired these
silent Mexicans who felt no need to joke or grin at each
other as they endured the God shouts of the mad gringo.
The bus would come. The Mexicans waited in patience,
and I, taking my cue from them, sat down on one of the
public benches, knowing that my plane would also come.
And, as I sat there, three little girls sat down on the bench
opposite and turned their collective gaze on me. The middle one whispered something to the one on her right, who
giggled and set them all three to giggling, and then the
giggles stopped and they sat staring at me with unblink-
ing chocolate-drop eyes in carved Indian faces. I looked at
them and thought they must often see women of my sort,

young, well-dressed, alone, nervous: strangers they glimpse once in the plaza but never again. And in that moment I wondered what sort of woman they must think me to be and then began to wonder myself.

I was a woman who had come from New York, flown thousands of miles to a city I had never seen, slept alone in a strange bed in a strange hotel, risen that morning to eat in silence and wait in silence with nine other nervous strangers until a jitney came to take us into a foreign country, to meet a lawyer who hurried us to a foreign courthouse, where I was declared a resident of a state (Chihuahua) whose very name I had not known until that day, then was led before a judge who hurriedly unmarried me, changing my name from Bell to—what? What was my name that afternoon in the Plaza San Jacinto? I asked myself but did not know. Was I now Phelan? No, couldn't be that, I was divorced from Jimmy, I had to be Mary Dunne, but would I be called that or would I still be called Bell until I remarried and became Mary Lavery?

The three little Mexican girls stared at me. They had always had their names. Soon they would take the Tranvias de Ciudad Juarez across Cordova Bridge and the Rio Grande, and then they would be home in Juarez City beneath the Sierra Madre Mountains in the State of Chihuahua in the Republic of Mexico, and so it was natural and right for them to be here in this dry, dusty Plaza San Jacinto, but it was not natural for me, although I too could remember when I was a little girl, not so different from them, I was Mary Dunne in Butchersville, in the Province of Nova Scotia in the Dominion of Canada, and how strange it would have been for me to sit under the War Memorial Cenotaph in Confederation Square and stare at some odd Mexican lady and wonder who she was. And when I thought of that I smiled at the little girls, but the little girls did not smile back. They stared. My smile failed, and it was then that I had the very first of these moments, the first because I could not blame it on a pill, I could not blame it on anything that I knew about; it simply happened and there I was: I could not remember who I was or where I was. I sat in a hot dusty square, stared at by those childish Indian faces, a blond man shouting "Jesus Cristo" in back of me, and it was panic, I couldn't remember my name, and I got up from the bench and ran past a line of Mexicans who sat and ignored me. (I was flies.) I ran and then stopped when I saw the front entrance of the Hotel Cortez and it came back into my mind, *I am Mary Dunne.* I said it over and over, I am Mary Dunne, it's all right, I am Mary Dunne. But somehow it was not true any more and in the bus that afternoon going back to the airport, to the plane which would take me to New York and to Terence, I remember thinking for the first time what I have thought many times since. I am no longer Mary Dunne, or Mary Phelan or Mary Bell, or even Mary Lavery. I am a changeling who has changed too often, and there are moments when I cannot find my way back.

The bus had left the Met, crossed Fifth, Madison, Park, Lexington, Third. My stop came up. I smiled at the mother of the little Indian-faced girl, and the mother smiled back at me and moved her knees to let me pass. (VAYA CON DIOS said the Chamber of Commerce sign that day, long ago, as I left picturesque El Paso.)

There was a cold spring wind as I got off the bus, cold on my thighs between my stocking tops and girdle, a cold puff of wind up my spine as I hurried to the corner and crossed on the changing light.

Harold, our doorman, came to hold the door open for me and, as I went in, signaled that he wanted to speak to me. I thought it was probably another parcel. Harold is tall and stout; he makes me feel small. He has a trick of teetering on his heels as he talks. He teetered, looking down at me confidentially, taking a notebook from the hip pocket of his uniform. "Mrs. Lavery, do you know a"—flips pages—"a, wait now, let's see, this gentleman?"

A penciled name on the lined page: L. O. MacDuff.

"Do you know him?" Harold asked again.

"No."

"Well, he says he knows you. He was here asking me questions. Said he was a friend of yours."

Harold, looking down at me. Harold's head is quite small, too small for the six-foot body and his football-tackle fat. The uniform cap makes him seem older than he is. Actually he's just a kid, not much more than twenty. "No," I told him, "I don't know anyone by that name."

"Well—uh—uh—I phoned up on the house phone, you weren't there, I told him that, then he start ask me all kindsa questions, said he was here on a vacation, he wanted to catch you, then he wrote his name down, told me, 'Be sure you show it to her and tell her I stopped by.'"

Robbers, more robbers, came into my mind. "What sort of questions?" I asked in a shaky voice.

"Well—uh—uh—" Harold seemed embarrassed. "He asked if you had a job now, I mean what hours and what time your husband—I mean he ask if your husband worked at home."

His eyes caught mine, then avoided my frightened stare. "I mean, I thought he was a friend of yours, y'know."

I told Mad Twin to be quiet, it wasn't a robber, it must be something else, but she wouldn't—

"What did he look like?" I asked. And Harold pondered, screwing up his little face in a visible act of intellection.

"Well—uh—uh—he was—uh—uh—kind of a tall gentleman, didn't look like nobody from a collection agency, you know. I can tell those guys, they often come around and ask about the tenants."

"And he wrote his name down. And asked you to tell me he was here?"

"Yes, ma'am. Oh, and—uh—uh—he said he'd call you. Phone, y'know."

"When?" (I was trying to get hold of myself: I was shaking and Harold had noticed.)

"Didn't say any special time, Mrs. Lavery."

"Well, if he comes around again, you just be careful. There was another man here this morning, pretending he wanted to look at our apartment. I wouldn't be at all surprised if they were collaborators; there are these gangs of apartment robbers I read about. Now, you were on this morning, do you remember sending a man up to our apartment, an old man with a little white beard?"

Harold thinks. "A beard? Uh—uh—yeah, yeah, I remember. Ah, don't worry, Mrs. Lavery, we don't let nobody go up unless the tenant is at home. I mean that's our job, y'know."

"I know. But still, well, there are these—these crooks nowadays are very smooth. This article I was reading— well, you'd be surprised at what they get away with."

By now I had offended him. He reached up his hand, tilted his cap down over his nose, scratched the back of his head, and eyed me under the peak of his cap in a way which said I had gone too far.

"Knock wood, Mrs. Lavery, we haven't had no robberies here. Not the kind you're talking about. No, ma'am."

"All right. Thank you, Harold." (Thinking: I must get upstairs, take an aspirin or something.)

"That's all right, Mrs. Lavery."

He watched my progress toward the elevator and I knew

that it would never be the same again between Harold and me. Doormen divide tenants into mad and sane, and now, with my babble about crooks and magazine articles, I had crossed the line and joined the complainers, the dotty old dames, the suspicious tenants he must jolly along. From now on, he will wink behind my back as I have seen him do when old Mrs. Spritzmayer goes into her plaint.

At the elevator a wan-looking woman in a plaid pants suit waited, tugging at a big brown poodle on a chain. As we went into the elevator together, she smiled at me. The poodle's wet nose touched the back of my hand. I jumped.

"It's all right, he's friendly," she informed me in a twangy voice. (I don't give a damn if he's friendly, take his great wet snout off me.)

But, craven as we all are in face of Man's Best Friend, I smiled and nodded to his owner and pretended to smile at the animal, which reciprocated by shoving his nose up under my skirt. At last she tugged on the leash. The dog yelped. She ruffled his ears affectionately as I watched for the reprieve of my floor. I got off without looking back.

There was no paper bag on the chair in the hall. So Ella Mae had gone. I heard voices, Terence's and some other man's, but not what they said, for Terence's study door was closed. I closed the front door with a bit of a slam, hoping Tee would hear. And he did. His door opened and he smiled at me. I thought, I love him.

"Somebody called MacDuff rang you up," he told me. "I left the number in the living room. He said it's important and wants you to call. How are you?"

"Fine," I said. Two men looked out at me from Terence's room. Beau Sales, a composer, and Sam Schactman, a choreographer. I gave them dinner here about two months ago when Terence and they started talks about a revue Tee is writing with them. I hadn't seen them since. "Hi there," said Beau, who is smart and showbiz, and didn't even try to put a name on me. The other, Sam, more *gemütlich,* knew he should know me, my name was on the tip of his tongue. But not quite. "Hi there," he said. "Ah . . ."

"You remember Sam and Beau, don't you, Martha?" Terence said.

"Of course," I said. "Hello there."

Sam took the bait. "That's a nice hairdo you got there, Martha. Cool."

"Thank you," I said. I looked, straight-faced, at Terence and he gave the smallest wink. Only yesterday I bet him none of his show-business friends even knew my first name. Terence remembered. *Martha.* I love him.

Yet yesterday when I made that bet with Terence it was not funny; it sounded like a complaint. Perhaps part of my uncertainty about who I am these days is because, living with Terence, I am introduced to everybody as Mrs. Terence Lavery. "You mean *the* Terence Lavery, the British playwright, that one?" Yes, that one. When Terence and I meet new people, eyes go to him. If I start talking to a stranger at a party and Terence comes up, I find I may as well forget whatever it was I was saying. Oh, I suppose men still look at me, but with this difference: When they hear who I am they at once ask if Terence is with me and what he's doing these days. Then we talk about Terence.

"We won't be much longer, will we, fellows?" Terence asked Sam and Beau. They, eager to please him, said no, not long. I went into the living room, where, on the writing desk I found a pad with Terence's handwriting on it.

MARY

Call L. O. MacDuff, Room 2020, Barbizon Plaza. Says it's urgent.

The Barbizon Plaza's where Janice Sloane is staying. A lot of Canadians stay there. I decided it was better to find out who L. O. MacDuff was than to stand about worrying. I got the phone book and dialed the number.

"Barbizon Plaza, good afternoon."

"Room Twenty-twenty, please."

It rang and rang and rang until the operator came back on. "Room Twenty-twenty does not answer. Would you care to leave a message?"

"Yes, please." I thought I would leave my name, so that whoever it was would know I'd called.

"One moment, please."

Click-click-click. Then a new voice, male: "Front desk, good afternoon."

"I'd like to leave a message for a Mr. MacDuff in Room Twenty-twenty."

"One moment, please."

I waited.

"Did you say MacDuff, madam?"

"Yes."

"I'm sorry, we don't have a MacDuff registered."

"But I got a message from a Mr. MacDuff in Room Twenty-twenty."

"I'm sorry."

"Well, who do you have in Room Twenty-twenty? Perhaps my husband got the name wrong."

"I'm sorry, madam, we're not allowed to give out guests' room numbers."

"I see. Well, would you leave a message for whoever is in Room Twenty-twenty that Mrs. Lavery called?"

"Yes, madam. Mrs. Lavery. Thank you."

I hung up and, I don't know why, suddenly became convinced that this L. O. MacDuff person was from Butchersville, was someone my mother had instructed to look me up in New York. Then I remembered Mama and her polyp and decided, Never mind what Dick says, it won't hurt to call her. Besides, I can use this MacDuff person as an excuse for calling. So I looked up her number and direct distance dialed.

It rang, it rang.

An operator's voice: "What number are you calling, please?"

"Area code nine-oh-two and the number is six-seven-eight-two-seven-six-two."

"Thank you, and thank you for giving me the area code. That circuit is overloaded; let me try to get your number for you."

She dialed. I heard a number of clicks and then a crackly small-town voice. "Butchersville."

"Operator, this is New York calling. We are trying to reach six-seven-eight-two-seven-six-two. Will you try that for us, please?"

"Six-seven-eight-two-seven-six-two," said the voice back home. A dialing sound. Then the phone rang in my mother's kitchen, rang and rang and rang, while we three women, none of whom had ever seen the others, sat listening across the wires. It rang, it rang.

"That would be Mrs. Dunne, wouldn't it?" said the voice from home. I could imagine her, some Mrs. Tiggy Winkle in a knitted gray cardigan, having a cup of tea as she answered the calls.

"Yes, that's right," I said.

"Guess, she's not home," said Mrs. Tiggy Winkle. "Want to leave a message?"

Big Time Operator relayed the question. "Ma'am? Care to leave your number, the party could call you back?"

"No thanks, it doesn't matter."

"I could try for you in, say, half an hour?" Big Time offered.

"No, it's all right."

"Thank you, then," said Big Time. "And thank you, Operator."

115

"You're welcome," said Mrs. Tiggy Winkle. We all hung up, and I decided I would try Mama later, maybe after dinner. I tried to remember if Terence had said something about going out to a movie. I wasn't sure. I love movies, but when I'm nervous they sometimes don't work, I can't get with them, I simply sit in the dark, my mind dithering, waiting for them to end.

Movies. Jimmy was the one who started me going: he and I would go five nights a week in Toronto when and if we had the money. Hat disliked movies, although he pretended to like them. The only films he ever really wanted to go to were big colored excitements, which bore me. Terence likes movies and we go a lot. But Tee is professional in his interest, so most of the time we go to foreign films. And that's all right. I go where I'm took, as the girl said. The only time I had rows with anybody about movies was during the period Hat and I lived in New York. There were so many good ones on then, but we hardly saw one of them. Sometimes I'd ask if we could go to one and Hat would say sure, and even pick a night, but when that night came suddenly he'd have an article to finish or some phone calls to make and he'd go into his study and stay there until minutes before the last show, then rush out and we'd take a taxi to the theater, almost always arriving after the last show had started. Then Hat would say he wasn't going to see only part of the film and why didn't we pop around to Downey's for a nightcap instead? Hat always did what he wanted, not what you wanted. Always.

But Jimmy, I was thinking of Jimmy, he was the moviegoer. James Patrick Phelan, the Jimmy of twelve years ago when he was twenty-one and I was twenty. When I am an old woman, Jimmy will remain unchanged for me, a twenty-one-year-old boy with a big Adam's apple, laughing with a nervous bark, inhaling his cigarettes the wrong way and coughing as though he will choke. Always the young boy, as Hat will always be the man I knew in those last months, irritable, touchy, skin slightly red and puffy, fingers combing nervously through his gray-streaked hair. Yes, Hat is cast as growing old, Jimmy as the boy I ran away from home with. Jimmy and I and the idiot, driving all together to Toronto, that's how we started our married life. If you could call ours a married life.

The idiot's name was Tom Dawkins; his family was very rich. Poor Tom had a mental age of five or six and was afraid of planes and trains, so every year when he spent Christmas with his mother in Toronto (his parents were separated), he had to be driven there. The old father, who lived in Halifax, offered Jimmy two hundred dollars and expenses to drive poor Tom to Ontario in a rented car, and Jimmy (who knew I was daydreaming about joining Catherine Mosca's acting school in Toronto) came to me and said that he had this big car and two hundred dollars and why didn't we get married and go live in Toronto? Jimmy was on the outs with his family at the time: his mother had hoped he'd become a priest, but instead he had flunked out of Dalhousie and was refusing to go to Mass on Sundays. I had just finished university, but all my B.A. had gotten me so far was an offer of a filing clerk's job at the government forestry lab in Fredericton. At twenty, my life stretched ahead of me like an empty horizon. I wanted to act, I wanted to do something which would take me away forever from Butchersville, from the Maritimes, from the lives and jobs and ambitions of the other boys and girls around me. I know. It sounds mad to the me I am today. I liked Jimmy but I didn't love him. Nor did he love me (he thought I was beautiful and wanted to go to bed with me), and I suppose you could say we used each other. But we didn't know that; all we knew was the hopeless feeling of that empty ordinariness stretching down the years ahead of us. And suddenly here was something mad, a ride to

117

Toronto, a two-hundred-dollar grubstake (it seemed a lot to us; neither of us had ever lived away from home), and so, without a word to Mama or to Dick, I got up one morning, smuggled a suitcase out of the house, and took the bus over to Dartmouth, where Jimmy and Jimmy's friend O'Keefe were walking about in the snow on the street corner in front of an old white frame house belonging to a Unitarian minister, and a few minutes later we were in the minister's parlor getting married, with O'Keefe and the minister's sister as witnesses, and afterward we got on the bus and came back to Halifax and had our wedding breakfast in a greasy spoon. (I remember O'Keefe had bought a bottle of Irish whisky in honor of Jimmy and Jimmy put some in my coffee. It was the first time I had ever had any liquor and I thought people must be crazy to drink it.) Then, after breakfast, we all got on another bus and went out to the rich part of town and got off at the very grand avenue where the Dawkinses lived, and Jimmy set off all alone, going up the driveway beside a huge old gray mansion while O'Keefe and I waited, farther down the street, stamping our feet to keep warm behind the snowbanks shoveled up on the pavements, me with the remains of a ten-cent bag of confetti in my hair and bits of rice in the collar of my good coat and down my neck, O'Keefe holding my suitcase and cursing because Jimmy was gone for ages, until finally along the street came this huge black Chrysler Imperial limousine with Jimmy driving it, and beside Jimmy was the idiot, only he didn't look like an idiot, he was a tall stout man with blond hair and a black Homburg on his knees and he wore a suit with a vest and a beautiful black overcoat with an astrakhan collar, and O'Keefe and I both had the same idea, this was the idiot's father, so even when Jimmy stopped the limousine right by us we pretended we weren't with him, we didn't even look at him until he got out of the car and came up and said, "What's up, aren't you coming?" And O'Keefe said, "That's not him, is it?" And Jimmy said, "Sure it is, it's old Tom." And he went over and opened the front door of the limousine and old Tom smiled at us and Jimmy said, "All right, Tom, you get in the back, I want Mary to sit up front with me." Right away old Tom stopped smiling and then a six-year-old in a forty-year-old body said, "No, I won't. It's my car and I always sit up front." So Jimmy thought about this for a moment and then he said, "No, it's not your car, Tom, it's just a rented car. Now, you get in the back." But old Tom shook his head. "It's my daddy's car," he said, and that was that, there was no budging him, so I got in the back with O'Keefe and took a back seat to the idiot on my wedding day, and we drove to O'Keefe's house, where O'Keefe kissed me and gave Jimmy the rest of the Irish whisky, and then we started off like escaping convicts, driving down those winter roads to freedom. I had told my family I was spending the weekend in Halifax with Shirley Davis. My plan was to announce my marriage as soon as we reached Toronto, which we thought would be in three days, and so for that reason we drove late into the night until we reached the United States border at Calais, Maine. Which was our first mistake, because old Tom was hungry and kept wanting us to stop for dinner, and when Jimmy said he wanted to get on to the border old Tom asked for a drink instead and Jimmy let him have it, which was mistake number two, because it seems old Tom wasn't allowed to drink and this was written down with a lot of other instructions which the old father had given Jimmy but which Jimmy had put in his pocket and hadn't yet bothered to read. Anyway, by the time we reached the motel at Calais old Tom had had a couple of big belts and was high and fell asleep over dinner so that we had hell's own job getting him back to the motel. Jimmy, of course, had been instructed to share a double room with old Tom, but naturally, it being our wedding night, Jimmy had other ideas, so we registered at the motel as Mr. and Mrs. Phelan in the double and put old Tom in a single cabin next door.

That was the first night I ever slept with a boy. It was a disaster. Jimmy knew even less than I did. I remember we went to bed in our underwear and after he had taken off my bra he clutched me to him suddenly, pulled down his shorts, and ejaculated on my leg. And then we got all hotted up again, kissing and feeling each other, and after an awful lot of fumbling he ejaculated again, and again it was too soon. I felt like crying but didn't and pretended it was all right and asked for a drink, and Jimmy got out the bottle and I had the second drink of my life and we talked for a little while and then I felt sick and was sick and we talked some more and he kissed me and kissed my breasts and rubbed himself against me, then suddenly fell asleep. I lay holding him for a while, then got up and was sick again. I have a vague memory of myself in that motel bathroom at four in the morning, sitting on the throne and telling myself, Well, you've done it now, this is the first real mortal sin in your life. And I didn't mean the sins priests say are sins, such as sex and drinking. I meant Jimmy. I said to myself, You *are* a rotten person, Mary Dunne, you've married him, yet you don't even want to kiss him, let alone live with him the rest of your life. Talk about my rotten father, I felt I was twenty times as rotten as he ever was, I deserved to be sick, I deserved not to sleep, but I did sleep; I got back into bed beside Jimmy and we both slept a dead sleep until almost ten in the morning. When we woke up and saw the time we panicked, because what about old Tom, he had to be taken out for his breakfast. I dressed the way I used to dress when I was late for school and ran out into the snow, Jimmy just ahead of me, but old Tom's cabin was empty, the door ajar.

We turned and looked at each other. I remember we didn't say a word but ran together to the cabin marked OFFICE, where was a nice old lady behind a desk. "Good morning, dear," she said to me. "Your father's gone up the road a piece, for breakfast. He'll pick you up later."

Jimmy was standing behind me in the doorway. He turned and ran out, then came back in. "The car's gone," he said. "But how could it be? I had the keys."

And the old lady smiled. "You're on your honeymoon, right?" she said.

We nodded. "Well," she said, "your dad came and explained that, so I made an exception and let him into your cabin, oh, about eight o'clock, I reckon. You were sound asleep, the pair of you." She smiled and winked. "He just took the car keys off your dresser and went out again like Santy Claus. We reckoned you both needed your beauty sleep."

Jimmy and I went outside. I remember to this day that I felt then the way I'd felt when I was a little girl and my ball hit and broke the window in McArdle's Store and I ran away and an hour later they said a policeman was asking questions. I felt the same way that morning: I mean, too young to deal with this adult world we'd got mixed up in. We went back to our cabin and sat on the bed. Jimmy said old Tom would be back soon because his father had told Jimmy old Tom didn't know how to handle money, therefore how would he be able to pay for his breakfast, so he'd realize he needed us and come back for us. But I didn't believe Jimmy. I sat there thinking, Look at us, we're only married twenty-four hours and here we are sitting in this bedroom like two people married twenty years, worrying and worrying, and he never even thought of kissing me this morning, I don't think he even likes me, he just lusted after me, that was all. So we sat and talked and worried and then we walked up the road and got coffee, and the people in the coffee shop didn't remember seeing old Tom, so what else could we do, we were stranded, we went back to the motel and waited. It was awful, that wait, the morning was like weeks. At noon we made up our minds old Tom had ditched us, so we checked out and took a taxi into the town of Calais, where Jimmy got his courage up and phoned the old father in Halifax. A servant answered and told Jimmy Mr. Dawkins was on his way to Maine to pick up his son, and Jimmy asked where old Tom had been found but the servant said he wasn't allowed to answer any further questions. And that was that. We still had the expense money, we didn't know what to do, we had some vague fear that my mother might have sent the Mounties after me, and so, confused, like children, we decided to go back across the Canadian-American border and take a bus and go on to Toronto.

I remember the moment, as we walked toward the border point, that we saw the Chrysler Imperial. I wanted to run away, but Jimmy had hopes he might be able to square things with old Tom and the old father, so we went into the customs, and there, sure enough, was old Tom. What had happened was he had no car papers, or even a driver's license, and at first they had booked him on suspicion of drunken driving, but after talking a bit to him they'd twigged what he was and searched him and found a card sewn into his jacket with the old father's address and phone number. And it seemed they had phoned the old father and he was on his way in a private plane he had chartered. So, although Jimmy kept trying to get the immigration men to release old Tom into our custody, it was no soap and we were still there an hour later when the old father phoned to say he'd landed at the local airport, and when the cops mentioned Jimmy the old father said to hold him, he was a crook, and so when the cop put the phone down he told Jimmy he would have to detain him. Jimmy at once told me to go back across the border into Canada and wait for him there, but I refused and I stayed there with him until the old father showed up and there was all hell breaking loose, but once the old father got his money back from Jimmy, plus the car keys and the papers, the American cops, who were sensible men, said the father had no charge against Jimmy and let Jimmy and me go back across the border. And there we were. We stood on the Canadian side and as we stood there, waiting for a bus, the Chrysler Imperial drove past with old Tom sitting up front beside his daddy and, as Tom went by, he turned around in his Homburg hat and his overcoat with the astrakhan collar and, so help me, he put his thumb to his nose and spread his fingers and gave us the raspberry.

We stood there in the snow, Jimmy and I, each of us with a suitcase, with that big murdering limousine splashing snowy slush on us as it went past, the old father sitting straight up behind the wheel and old Tom, thumb to his nose, his fat lips farting out a raspberry, and at that moment I had the first real laugh of our married life. We just collapsed and embraced, and I remember thinking that maybe it had started so badly it could only improve and we'd make a go of it after all. We had forty-six dollars, enough to get us as far as Montreal if we ate only chocolate bars and chips, which we did, and then for a day and a night we didn't eat at all while we sat around in Montreal waiting for answers to telegrams Jimmy had sent. (One to his older brother in New York, one to friend O'Keefe in Halifax.) At first we waited in the Greyhound bus terminal on Dorchester Street, but after a Traveler's Aid lady had asked me twice if I needed any help we got nervous and moved to the waiting room in the Canadian Pacific Railway station on Windsor Street, where we snoozed away the night on benches, and next morning went back to the Greyhound bus terminal to see if there were any replies to the telegrams. At noon a telegram arrived from O'Keefe. He had wired sixty dollars, which he said was his next week's pay. "Good old O'Keefe," Jimmy yelled, hugging me, but I kept worrying how we would pay good old O'Keefe back.

And so we bought bus tickets and went on to Toronto, where we spent our first night apart, me at the YWCA, Jimmy at the men's Y. The next morning we met before breakfast and read the want ads in the paper, then separated and went off to look for temporary jobs. And, miracle, miracle, we were both hired in the first jobs we applied for. Jimmy got taken on as a packer, stuffing shoppers' grocery bags at a checkout counter in a Loblaws' supermarket, while I was engaged that same morning as a Christmas help trainee by the T. Eaton Company. At lunchtime that same day I slipped out of the big T. Eaton store on Yonge Street, where they were giving us the training course, and ran down the street to the Canadian National Telegraphs office and wired my mother, saying I'd come to Toronto, had a job at the T. Eaton Company, and would write soonest, best love, don't worry. Nothing about being married to Jimmy Phelan. That would have been much too risky. I was under age, she could bring me back to Butchersville, and I guessed she would if she ever found out that Jimmy and I, both Catholics, had been married in a Unitarian minister's office, which doesn't count in the Catholic religion, I mean if both parties are Catholics.

Anyway, after getting that wire away and easing my guilt a little, I went back to the T. Eaton Company and was shown how to make out a sales slip and told how T. Eaton had founded a great business and helped build up Canada because he was the first merchant in Canada to open a dry-goods store with a strictly cash policy, but all through this I kept worrying about Mama, remembering how I had lied to her, and feeling depressed because

Toronto wasn't at all as I'd imagined it would be, not a bit like New York, which I had been in for a long weekend when I was fifteen, and not even as interesting as the part of Montreal we'd seen while we hung around the bus and railroad terminals there. And I worried about me and Jimmy and sex, and so by the end of the lecture on making out a sales slip I was ready to weep and went into the T. Eaton washroom, all prepared for a good self-pitying cry. But I never did cry. For there was another woman crying in the washroom, another of the Christmas help trainees, although she was old enough to be my mother, and when I asked what was wrong she said it was so long since she'd been to school she didn't understand the same as you, dear (meaning me), and she didn't get the part of the lecture about crediting a charge and so would be fired and she and her husband were in debt, Household Finance had closed in, she and her family had had to change their addresses twice and now daren't answer the door in case it was some-one from a collection agency, her husband had developed an ulcer with the worry, and if she didn't get this job today and make some money to help out— And by this time she was becoming incoherent and I, frightened by this tale of people getting in debt and living close to the line (we'd already spent nearly all the money O'Keefe had lent us), told her to hold on, wait a minute, then went out and borrowed a sales book, sat down with her, and went over and over the charge-crediting procedure until I was sure she had it right. After which she kissed me and said God would re-ward me and if ever she could help me with anything I was just to ask her. Then we went to another lecture and I learned that T. Eaton worked hard all his life, harder than any of his employees, and was sometimes too tired to eat his supper at night and always put the customer first, which we must do too. Then we went to the cafeteria for a cup of tea and the woman I had helped sat next to me and when

I asked her what part of the city would be cheap to live in, she got a *Toronto Star* and went over the Room to Let ads with me. The one she circled was Blodgetts' and that was how we ended up, Jimmy and I, living with Harry and Mother.

"God's own country, kids," Harry bawls. "God's own bloody country." We giggle. "Git up them stairs," Harry orders, smacking his wife's bottom. She turns to us, woebegone. "He always wants *that*," she says. Again we giggle. Harry gives us one of his large "double-intender" winks, then lumbers upstairs after her, old and heavy in his darned brown cardigan and floppy mud-colored slacks. Later, under the covers in our back bed-sitting-room, Jimmy and I clutch each other, repeating these catch phrases, retriggering our giggles. Our minds are full of Blodgett lore: we can close our eyes and see Harry in his favorite nook, scrunched down in his old cretonne-covered armchair, the chair planted foursquare in the bay window of his front parlor, his back to Gerrard Street, a case of Labatt's India Pale Ale on the floor within reach of his right hand, the wreckage of the *Toronto Star* and the *Toronto Telegram* strewn about his slippered feet. He has not moved out all weekend. Across the room the television flitters fitfully. Mother rises to adjust the rabbit ears. Harry talks. He talks. From time to time, like a blind man, he gropes for and finds a new bottle of ale, reaches it up to the wall bottle-opener without taking his eyes off the TV set, strikes the cap off, brings the foaming bottle top neatly to his lips. No drop is spilled.

"Trouble with you kids, trouble with you, you're like

bloody belted earls, you are, born with a silver frigging spoon in your mouths because you was born here. Yes, here. In Canada. This bloody country, I tell you, this *is* democracy, God's own bloody country, I say, and don't tell me the States, don't tell me the frigging Yanks are as good as we are, the frigging Yanks, I tell you I've been in Buffalo, I like people better, ha-ha, get it? That's one of my double-intenders. I been in Buffalo, now Mother, don't give me them nasty looks, it's just my way and a bit of fun never killed nobody.

"Mary-Jimmy, did I ever tell you kids how I come here? I come to Canada with a football team. No, straight up. We was rank bloody amateurs too, but good enough to play the best they had over here, which was not bloody much. Factory teams, mostly. Let's see, that's—what is it, Mother?—must be thirty, no, that's right, thirty-two years ago. Never mind, we got off the boat in Halifax, played there, then come on to Montreal, played a couple of matches there, then come on here. Toronto the Good. Second match we had here was with the Soap-O factory team, and yours very truly kicked the only two goals and afterwards Mr. Henry, he was general manager of Soap-O, a nice guy, he came up and offered me a job—just wanted me on his team, he said. So our team—Sunderland Wanderers, we was—frigs off back to blighty, God help them, poor sods, while I started at Soap-O sweeping floors, and I can hear you say, not much of a job, that, but, kids, I've not had one day's regret. Right, Mother?"

"Not one day's regret," Mother says.

"Seven months later I sent for Mother, yes, *her* sitting over there, my bloody fiancey, and I sent full fare too, oh, yes, and we was married right here, Bloor Street Baptist, eh, Mother? And let me tell you, not one day's regret about that neither. The Old Country, you hear some of these Old Country types here in Toronto going on about sodding England, don't make me wet my drawers, I'm as English as any man and so is Mother and let me tell you kids the sun can bloody set on the whole sodding country, I said set, from Land's End to John O'Groats, and sink into the bloody emerald sea—how's that, what's it? (a jewel set in a something sea). Yes, and what's the old country ever done for me, I ask you and I'll give you my answer straight up, fuck all—sorry, Mary, sorry, Mother—but Canada, that's another story, that's my country now, I'd bloody die for old Canada, I would. It's God's bloody country, yes, God's bloody country, and don't none of us forget it."

Christmas was over. At Christmastime Jimmy and I deceived our respective families by announcing our "engagement," then, courting the family seals of approval, went through a second marriage ceremony, this time in a Toronto Catholic church. My mother had to send written permission to the parish priest, which she did, but only after she'd written a letter warning me that in marrying the likes of Jimmy Phelan I was throwing my life away. Jimmy's mother felt much the same way; her letter to Jimmy pointed out that he could now see where uncontrolled "passions" led people: to a job packing shoppers' bags in a supermarket. Jimmy still had his Loblaws' job, but I had been fired by the T. Eaton Company right after the Christmas rush. Now I had a job compiling a list of Toronto dentists for a firm that specialized in making up directories.

Yes, Christmas was over in God's own country. Jimmy's mother said I had ruined his life and my mother said he had ruined mine, and we lay in bed giggling as we reread the letters, camping up these doom-sayings, but in the dark, afterward, I would sometimes wonder how true these predictions were. We were married now, officially, by the One Holy Roman Catholic and Apostolic Church, living in Toronto in God's own country, and the best we could do was make a combined salary of eighty-nine dollars a week and live on Gerrard Street with Harry and Mother Blodgett: Harry, who believed the millennium, was here because he was now supervisor of the night cleaning staff at Soap-O's Etiobicoke factory, and Mother, who gave thanks to her Redeemer for His eternal goodness in making her a chicken-plucker at Kemelman's Poultry in the Saint Lawrence Market. Yes, it was God's own country for the Blodgetts, with three square meals a day and lots of lovely beer and the mortgage half paid on their lovely home, and we giggled as we heard all this and remembered it in bed, clinging to each other, trying to make believe that we were in love, a part of us sensing the rim of hysteria around the edge of our giggles, for Harry and Mother were not just comedy relief. There was another side to them, a side we saw sometimes on Sunday mornings: Harry, stupefied with beer, asleep in his armchair, snoring in concert with Mother, who lay dead drunk at his feet, her mouth open, her teeth slipping, great dead pigs, the pair of them, in the cold winter winter sunlight of a Toronto Sunday morning, surrounded by empty beer bottles, the air rancid with stale cigarette smoke, while facing them, across the room, the television test pattern, blue and constant, hummed ignored. And even Harry's shout of "Git up them stairs" had a sinister ring to me sometimes as I sat in my cubbyhole office, compiling lists of registered dental surgeons, and imagined Harry rearing up like some old hippo over Mother and, sweet Jesus our Saviour, if huge Harry and mountainous Mother could make it in bed, then what was wrong with Jimmy and me? Either Jimmy came before he was inside me or just after, and often I would feel so frantic I'd have to go into the bathroom later when he fell asleep, sit on the throne, and finish it off. Afterward, sometimes, I would cry. Was it me or was it him? He was so proud of the size of his penis, it had to be my fault, but what good was the size of his prick to me when I never got time to come? Was I frigid, was that it? He implied I was colder than he was and once suggested that perhaps our difficulty was that while he found me beautiful and couldn't control himself with me, I didn't find him attractive and so remained cold with him. But I knew that wasn't true, his looks had nothing to do with it, I was cold to him all right, but cold because in some secret part of me I knew it had been a mistake to marry him. I had done a selfish rotten thing just because I wanted to get away to Toronto. But I was not prepared to pay the price for that mistake. I was not prepared to serve out a life sentence as Mrs. James Phelan. The truth was, I was twenty; I didn't want to live with anyone for a while, I wanted to be alone in my own room, to cook only when and if I felt like it, not to have to wash dishes or men's socks, and the thought of having Jimmy's baby, that was what brought on the real panic of those days; I saw myself becoming one of those drear, wan women who wander the supermarkets, aimlessly pushing wire shopping carts up and down the aisles of merchandise at three in the afternoon, their minds muzzy with Muzak, while up front on the shopping cart some infant slobbers and pees in its snowsuit and farther up the aisle its boily brother, aged three, noisily upsets a soap-flakes display. O diaphragm between me and all harm, I didn't have you in those days; we knew I should go to a doctor, but I was shy about it and so Jimmy went on using the french letters which were part of our trouble, for he hated them and my worry was that he'd forgotten to put it on and so, in the dark, when he would start to take my pajamas off, I'd interrupt him to ask, "Did you?" which made him cross and spoiled things.

But I feared his sperm. A mistake would send me on that long supermarket wander while the Muzak played

"Some Enchanted Evening," and so there were no enchanted evenings or afternoons between Jimmy and me, no, not ever. And I dreamed of abortions. I didn't believe I'd be able to go through with one. I suppose the last vestige of being a Catholic was the little part of me which saw it as murder, and when I was not dreaming about abortions sometimes I sat in gloom, thinking of what would happen if I *did* have a baby. I was sure it would mean postnatal depression. I had read an article about postnatal depression in *Canada's Own Magazine* and I couldn't get that article out of my mind. I read how some women get in such a state that they have to be locked up. In the article a Canadian psychiatrist was quoted as saying it happened to women who secretly didn't want babies, which was my case exactly. My abortion dreams changed to nightmares in which I killed the baby and flushed it down the toilet, nightmares so frightening and in which I did such horrible things that I've blanked them out forever.

Anyway, all this made me more afraid than ever of a mistake with Jimmy, and so I was always making excuses, saying I was sleepy or sick or telling lies about my period, which made him think I was frigid, and that, of course, made him resentful and it became more difficult for us to spend evenings together without passing snappish remarks, and so, I suppose to avoid talking, we began spending a lot of evenings at the movies.

Strange that I decided a while back that we went to the movies because Jimmy was a mad movie fan. When now, examining that life of ours—wasn't it I who drove us out all those nights?

And postnatal depression. Funny how long it is since I've thought of that. Or of Mackie.

Mackie, Mackie McIver. I can see her face more clearly than my mother's. Her hair is reddish, her skin freckled; there is just a hint of red rims around the lids of her light blue eyes. I wonder does she still wear those shirtwaist dresses, dresses with pleats which always made me think of the tennis dresses our mothers wore in the thirties? There she sits in her well of loneliness in the library at *Canada's Own Magazine,* at her jumbled but ordered desk, the phone cradled against her shoulder as, in that light, clear girlish voice, she tells some reader the size and population of Patagonia. Patient, tenacious, going back again and again to the files to hunt up some point. She did not give up. If ever she needs an epitaph, that sentence should be chiseled on the stone over her grave. *She did not give up.* Oh God, she did not give up.

Tall, I remember her as very tall. I wonder has any woman remained, will any woman remain as vividly on the retina of my memory? And yet the first time I saw her I did not notice her at all until she made her amazing offer.

I had been having the nightmares about flushing babies down toilets and was trying to think of a way to exorcise them, or at least exorcise that article on postnatal depression. But I didn't have a copy of it any more and I decided to reread it in hopes it hadn't been as gloomy as I thought. So I phoned *Canada's Own Magazine* and asked for a copy, but they said it was too far back, impossible to let me have that issue, but if I came into their library I could copy it out.

Next day I went up to *Canada's Own* on my lunch hour. I was directed to the library on the editorial floor, where I asked for the article. The librarian was a woman, and she sat me down at a desk with a nice reading light, and it was very warm and quiet there. When she brought the article I felt foolish, as though I were there under false pretenses, for I'd said something vague about wanting it for research. So I took out a piece of paper and made a couple of squiggly notes as I reread the piece. A voice said, "Excuse me," and I looked up and it was the librarian. "I was just wondering, are you researching this piece for someone, or is it just a personal interest?"

Which made me blush, I remember, and also made me furious at her, but I saw that she was blushing too; then she said she didn't mean to be nosy, it was just that she was short-staffed and was looking for a girl to help her in here. "And," she said, "you *look* like a researcher, you see."

"Well," I told her, "I am in a way. I work for a company which compiles directories and things. But I was just interested in this article for a friend of mine."

"Directories," she said. "Do you work for Lowrys?"

I said I did. She smiled, triumphant. "Oh, dear," she said. "They don't pay at all well, do they?"

And then, sensing the murder rising in me, she added very quickly, "I mean I used to work there myself once. I mean, I only said that because if you were at all interested in coming to work here, I'm sure we could pay more than they do. And you'd have more freedom. We'd pay—oh, let's see, say sixty-five dollars a week. Would you be at all interested?"

Well, of course I was interested; it meant a twenty-dollar raise and besides it seemed more prestigious to work for a magazine. So I said, "Yes, I suppose I am."

"Oh, great." (One of the things I remember best about her after all these years is the funny high whinny she gave when something really pleased her.) She gave it now and said, "Of course I'll have to speak to the editor. I'm not sure if he's back from lunch."

I said, "But there's no hurry. I could come in tomorrow, or any day that suits you."

"No, no," she said. She smiled. "You might change your mind. Now, you just wait here, will you please?"

She ran to her desk, grabbed up some sort of accounts book, and ran out. While I sat there at the reading desk, bemused, not really believing this was happening to me.

Until, after what seemed an awfully long time, back she came, very jumpy, very eager. She asked me to come with her.

And so I walked into my first meeting with the Warm Brown Turd, R. J. MacKinnon, editor of *Canada's Own Magazine*. That same R. J. MacKinnon who now, improbably, has been chosen to write the foreword to Hat's one and only book. I remember I felt dazed, as a prisoner might when led into the glare and confusion of a courtroom, for there were very bright overhead lights in MacKinnon's office and, off by one wall, two teletype machines mysteriously typed out stuff on their own, which was something I had never seen before and found distracting. There were two phones on his desk and he kept being interrupted by one or the other of them ringing and the librarian lady (I mean Mackie, which was the name I gave her, perhaps to pay her back for the name she insisted on giving me) anyway, Mackie, Miss Ruth McIver, the librarian lady, as I said, kept talking at MacKinnon, talking very fast in her high schoolgirlish voice, while he half listened and looked at my legs, and then, after a perfunctory question about my schooling, he quickly ascertained that I was married, that I had no library training and had been only a few weeks in my current job, and just as I was deciding that I had failed his examination and that as soon as he finished a conversation on the phone which had interrupted him he would tell me he didn't think I was quite what they had in mind, he said to the person on the phone, "Okay, go to hell," slammed the phone down, stared up at me, and sighed in an I-give-up manner. "Okay," he said. "Ruth here seems to think she can use you. I suppose it's up to her. I can give you fifty-five dollars a week, okay?"

"Sixty-five," she said sharply. MacKinnon looked at her, and there was, I remember, a warlike sort of pause. "Sixty," he said. "Take it or leave it." He looked at her, not at me. "She has no experience," he said.

Mackie (Miss McIver, the librarian lady) looked at me, alarmed. I said, thank you, sixty would be all right. Then I said I supposed I'd have to give a week's notice in my other job and I remember MacKinnon nodded and suddenly came up to me and shook my hand, saying, "Well, you'd better arrange the starting date with Ruth here. Good luck." And that she thanked him very gushily, then took my arm and walked me down a long corridor of editorial offices, going back to the library, and squeezed my arm and said, "Oh, boy. Wasn't that something? I mean, really *something*. I'm delighted, delighted. Aren't you?"

I must have looked confused, for she at once put on her stricken face again and said, "Look, is it the five dollars, for if it is, remember, I promised it to you and you're entitled to it and I'll give it to you myself, all right? It's worth it to me to have you, honestly, it is."

"But that's not necessary," I told her. "Sixty is fine, it's more than I'm getting now."

She stared at me there in the corridor, her eyes widening, then mysteriously filling with tears. She bent forward and her lips touched my cheek. "You *are* a dear," she said, blushing, blushing. "Can I ask you a very big favor?"

I said, "Yes, what?" and then she said, "I'd like to call you Maria. Is that all right?"

I said, "Yes, it's all right. But why?"

"Because you *are* a Maria and not a Mary. I hope you won't be offended, but Mary is stodgy and you're not stodgy, you're—well, you're just Maria, that's all. Do you mind?"

I thought at the time it was sweet of her. I thought her an extraordinary woman, hiring me on the spur of the moment, and if she wanted to call me Maria, why not? But now, thinking back to that time, I realize no man ever tried to change me as much as Mackie did, no man tried so ruthlessly to suppress the Mary Dunne I was in order to transform me into a creature of his imaginings. It took a woman to do that, it took Ruth McIver, whom I called Mackie and who was Miss Mouse to most of the people on the editorial floor, Miss Mouse, perennial spinster, the sort of woman who wasn't kissed even at the annual office party. But behind the façade of Miss Mouse was a Caesar of determination. Once she had decided I was Maria, she never called me anything else.

So I became Maria, Miss McIver's assistant in the library at *Canada's Own Magazine*. It was as though she had decided to destroy my old identity by inventing a new one for me. Oh, I know, that sounds Machiavellian, when the truth is my relationship with Mackie was probably a simple little Mammon fable, a story of my greed. Certainly it was the one time in my life when I was corrupted by someone's money. Poor Mackie, I'm being hard on her, she meant well. Yet when I think back to those times, to Jimmy and Mackie and me sitting down to dinner in her big house on Prince Arthur, I feel no auld lang syne.

Days, I was Mackie's Maria. Each night I went back to the Blodgetts' and our bed-sitting-room, where I was Mrs. James Phelan who badgered Jimmy into writing to his parents and to Dalhousie University so that something could be arranged and he could finish school at the University of Toronto instead of spending the rest of his life as a packer at Loblaws'. And something *was* arranged. His parents sent what money they could afford, but the fees were higher in Toronto and everything they sent him went for books, tuition, and transportation. Jimmy quit Loblaws', went to classes, and we lived on my salary. Dinners of Campbell's soup and a tin of Heinz spaghetti. No cigarettes, no movies, no new clothes. Nothing. When I look back on those few weeks, they seem to have been a softening-up process designed to make us ripe for corruption. And yet I, not Jimmy, was the one who wanted to resist it. I remember saying to him at the very beginning, "If there's one thing I don't want it's for Miss McIver to know how poor we are." "Why not?" he said. "It's nothing to be ashamed of." "Please, Jimmy," I said, "I have to work with her, she's one of those Lady Bountiful people, I don't want any favors from her, do you understand?" We were going to dinner at her house on Prince Arthur when I said it. I remember it was the first time we'd been invited there; it was our first evening out in ages. In those days I spent most evenings sitting in the Blodgetts' parlor, staring at television with Harry and Mother so that Jimmy would have the bed-sitting-room to himself for studying. The gay life.

I remember how impressed we were, that first night at Mackie's house. There was the house itself. Then she let slip that her father had owned a biscuit factory. Her mother died when she was twelve, leaving her an only child, Daddy's girl, living in that big house with her father until his death the summer before she met us. When dinner was served, it was brought in by a uniformed maid, and the meal was standing rib roast with a bottle of wine, trifle for dessert, and brandy with the coffee, and you can imagine that after our months on Heinz and Campbell's we fell on that food like the starving Asian masses, and Jimmy got high on the wine and two glasses of brandy and started answering all her questions, telling her about his life at the university, how he had gone back to school, how he felt like a struggling married adult among a bunch of feck-less kids, and before I could stop him he had blabbed our situation, how we lived on my salary, our lack of money, everything. Mackie refilled his glass, sucked in every word, and, before we left, insisted on showing us over the house, leading us into unused bedrooms, pointing out that her fa-ther's study was going to waste, saying how she had been afraid of living alone ever since her father had passed away and how she had nightmares, how she wished she had someone else to stay with her besides the maid, who was deaf and no use in an emergency. She let that idea lie with us, then invited us back to dinner again ten days later, and this time she showed Jimmy a car which had belonged to her father, which she never drove, saying maybe he would like to use it to get to the university, and then (bringing it out as if she'd just thought of it) saying how wonderful it would be if we moved in with her; we could use the rooms and the car, and Jimmy could drop us women off each morning at *Canada's Own*, then use the car himself for the rest of the day at university, then per-haps pick us up and drive us home in the evenings? Or would that be too much trouble for him?

Well, I looked at him and saw his mouth opening to say no trouble, he'd be delighted, so I cut in and said that it was very kind of her but we'd made an arrangement with the Blodgetts, we were more or less committed to it, et cetera. Anyway, I backed us out of it and, I remember, going home on the bus afterward Jimmy and I had a ter-rible fight in which I accused him of leeching off people, which was the worst possible thing I could say as he was touchy then about living off my salary. Which produced one of his deep sulks, so by the time we got home we weren't speaking.

But next day at work Mackie went back to the attack, starting in on me all over again. And when I said no she waited two days, then phoned the Blodgett house at a time when she guessed I'd be out, and, under pretense of asking for me, repeated her offer to Jimmy, saying she wished he could make me change my mind, she really needed someone to stay there with her, her nightmares were getting worse, we really would be doing her a favor, et cetera. So Jimmy promised to talk to me again and did, and he and I had a second row, an awful one in which the unhappiness of our life in and out of bed settled down on us and I cried, and after we'd made up I said all right, we'd go to Mackie's, if that was what he wanted.

I see that I make it sound as though I didn't want to go, but of course it's not so simple as that. I had never been really poor before, and living on top of each other in a place like the Blodgetts', was, I thought, part of the reason we fought so much. On the other hand I had never been as rich as Mackie, and the part of me that likes luxury saw myself living in that house on Prince Arthur with maids cooking dinner and making our beds, and after Butchersville (after any small town) city life seemed very grand. So it's not fair for me now, as it wasn't fair then, to put all the blame on Jimmy. This is a story of how I lost part of my innocence, lost part of that Mary Dunne who left Butchersville and never can go back. It is a story of what money did to *me*. If I am to learn anything from past mistakes, then there's no sense blaming it all on Jimmy.

At the end of that week Jimmy broke the news to the Blodgetts and I told Mackie we would come. I remember that Jimmy went over to Prince Arthur and warmed up Mackie's father's big Buick and he and Mackie drove back to Gerrard Street to pick me up and install me in our new home. It was Saturday afternoon. The bags were all stacked up in the front hall, and when the car arrived Harry and Mother came out of their parlor, looking very solemn, and invited us all in, Jimmy and me and the lady who was stealing their lodgers away. Then, in a gesture as grand as declaring a national day of mourning, Harry turned off the television set. He produced a specially purchased bottle of gin (for he thought I'd said I liked gin), poured great glassfuls for me, Mackie, Mother, Jimmy, and himself, and made a little speech, saying that Mother and he would be thinking of us, they wished us all the very best of luck and every happiness, a family of our own (Jimmy and I avoiding each other's eye at this), long life, and cheers, down the hatch, God bless. Then Mother and Harry both came to peck my cheek and shake hands with Jimmy and with the lady we were going to live with, presenting us with the rest of the gin as a going-away present, making us promise that we'd come and see them very soon.

But we did not go to see them, not soon, not ever. The following Christmas we got a card from them, a jolly Santa and his reindeer: "Wishing you all the very best, thinking of you, hoping to see you, Harry & Mother." We meant to send them a card but we forgot.

The next year there was another Christmas card, Jesus the Shepherd surrounded by Dear Little Lambs: "Wishing you all the very best, Violet Blodgett. P.S. Harry passed away last Aug. 31." I never knew her name was Violet. We had not written or phoned or called or even sent a lousy card. We were young; we had our troubles. If there is a hell it should be for selfishness.

But we had our troubles; we were full of them. I kept telling Jimmy the one thing we mustn't do with Mackie is take things we can't afford to pay back, so for goodness' sake don't drink her liquor, you had two drinks last night and two the night before, you can't make a regular thing of it and who's paying for the gas in that car, not you, you fill up the tank at Bolst's and charge it to her account, don't you? Don't you?

He said, "Have you ever listened to yourself, Mary?

You're not even twenty-one yet and you nag like my mother, nag, nag, nag, now shut up, will you?"

I said, "Look, I don't want to be beholden to her, that's all." "Well, we are beholden," he said, "so relax. She has pots of money, she doesn't know what to do with it, if it pleases her to act the fairy godmother to the pair of us, well then, good for her, I say. Let's sit back and enjoy it."

I looked at him and wondered how I could have married him. I'd thought he was like me, but he wasn't, I didn't know him at all; when you came right down to it he had no morals, none at all. I'd made a mess of my life, an awful damn mess. Oh, Jimmy, please, I thought, please have some independence, don't always *take* things, please, Jimmy, please, I want to love you, I do, I do.

But I did not love him. And he went right on taking things from Mackie, defiant, like a child making a noise after it's been ordered to stop. And yet while I was righteously blaming Jimmy, wasn't I just as bad, wasn't I also eating Mackie's food which our miserable rent couldn't even begin to pay for, wasn't I living in her house, riding in her car, and, worse, didn't I know very well I was the one she wanted to please, everything she did for Jimmy she really did for me? And what did that make me but a person with absolutely no morals at all? Because I knew what it was all about, I sensed it almost from the start, I just wouldn't face up to it. I mean, after that thing about my birthday. It was obvious.

Let's see. I went to work on *Canada's Own Magazine* I think it was the last week of January. My birthday is the seventeenth of March, Saint Patrick's Day. And that year it was my twenty-first birthday. But I did not want a celebration at Prince Arthur Avenue. So I said nothing to Jimmy; he wasn't one for dates, I knew he wouldn't think of it. A few days before the seventeenth, a present came from my mother and one from Dick and Meg. And, I remember, a present from my Aunt Martha. Anyway, I put them aside and said nothing about them, planning to open them myself, quietly, on the day.

On the morning of the seventeenth I got up early and opened my presents in the bathroom. My mother had sent me a wristwatch. I forget what the other presents were. I remember I wanted to wear the wristwatch at once, but it would be noticed, so I put it in my handbag and decided to keep it there until the end of the week, when the birthday would be safely over. Then I went down to breakfast, and sure enough, no word from Jimmy about what day it was. He didn't even say it was Saint Patrick's Day.

After work that evening Jimmy came around with the Buick as per usual and drove Mackie and me home. Still no word about the birthday. I remember I went upstairs, took a bath, and changed, and when I went down to the living room there was nobody there. The lights were out. Which was peculiar. I thought a fuse had blown, or maybe a bulb, and so went into the room by the light of the fire and was going toward the big tri-light lamp to check when suddenly the piano started playing in the next room and Gert, the maid, opened the sliding doors into the dining room, and there was Mackie, sitting up very straight at the upright piano, playing "Happy Birthday to You," and Jimmy standing by the piano singing it and the maid singing it, and on the dining-room table was a bottle of that fizzy wine that Mackie was mad for, Asti Spumante, and what were, obviously, presents.

"How did you know it was my birthday?" I blurted, looking at both Jimmy and Mackie as I said it.

"You can thank her," Jimmy said. "You know me and dates." While Mackie smiled and came forward. "I'm the librarian, remember?" she said. "I keep records." She kissed me, first on the left cheek, then on the right, like a French general, saying, "Many happy returns, my dear."

And Gert, the maid, said, "Happy birthday, Miss Maria." And Jimmy came up and grabbed me and kissed me (sticking his tongue between my lips as usual). I heard the fizzy wine pop and at that moment I was glad they'd remembered. I wanted a celebration. I was twenty-one at last.

Then, the presents. There was a box of Laura Secord candies from Jimmy, which was just right: it was what we could afford and they were chocolate-covered almonds, my favorites. Gert had made me two things: a gingerbread man with red icing buttons and a pair of red wool mitts to wear with my winter coat. The third present, the one from Mackie, wasn't as embarrassing as I was afraid it might be. It was a little gold bracelet, very thin, not *too* expensive, I hoped. Anyway, something I felt I could accept. So I put it on and tried the mitts on and opened the candies and held my glass of wine, tears, happy tears in my eyes as Jimmy, Gert, and Mackie drank a toast to my majority.

And then Mackie gave me the envelope. "And this," she said, "is something extra." I remember I felt afraid and didn't want to take it, I tried to hand it back to her, saying no, really, we were embarrassed, Jimmy and I, she'd been far too good to us already, isn't that so, Jimmy? and Jimmy agreeing, but with no determination (the rat), and of course nothing would satisfy Mackie but that I open the envelope. There was a letter inside. It went something like this:

Mr Gil Cameron,
Canada's Own Magazine,
Toronto
Dear Gil:

       This is to acknowledge receipt of Miss McIver's cheque for $200.00 tuition fees for Maria Phelan.

       As you know, I have a high regard for your opinions on acting potential, but I am sure you will also understand that I cannot accept Miss Phelan as a member of my evening class without first going through my usual interview procedures. If you will have Miss Phelan call me, I will set up such an interview as quickly as possible.

With warmest personal regards,

Catherine Mosca

Catherine Mosca's acting class was the reason I had wanted to come to Toronto in the first place. She was one of the founders of the New Theatre Group in New York, and her class is the only good professional one in Canada. Back in Butchersville I had daydreamed that if I ever got to Toronto, I would work at any job and save every penny and as soon as I had part of the tuition fee saved up, I would apply for one of her "interviews." Of course when we *did* get to Toronto there was the guilt about Jimmy's career, so when he went back to school I'd put my plans off for a year until, I hoped, he'd graduate and be able to support me. And now here I was, staring at a letter in which the fees were paid and the interview arranged, and it should have been like winning the Irish Sweepstakes. Instead, I thought of what had happened a few weeks back.

We were in the *Canada's Own* cafeteria when Mackie introduced me to Gil Cameron, the magazine's drama critic. I was twenty, I was stagestruck, I was excited to meet someone who knew the real stage, and I remember I blurted out some question about did he know Catherine Mosca, and he was nice to me, very gentle and said yes, why? And so I told him all about my ambition to come here, save my money, and get into one of Catherine Mosca's classes, and how I'd won first prize at the Dominion Drama Festival in Halifax, and on and on, I blush, I blush, why didn't I shut up?

Afterward I felt silly and said so to Mackie. I remember

she asked if Miss Mosca gave evening classes and I said I had no idea, I didn't imagine so. And that was all, I forgot it. Until this letter. Looking back now, I see that if I'd had the drive, the self-love, the hardness it takes for success, I would have gone over and kissed Mackie and thanked her for giving me this start. But instead I was filled with shame and hate, I saw her plotting it all behind my back, getting poor Gil Cameron to lie about my "acting potential," phoning Miss Mosca to inquire about evening classes, writing out her check, then getting Gil Cameron to send it on with a "personal" letter.

"No," I said. "I can't take it."

I put the letter down on the table, picked up my glass, and tried to drink the fizzy wine. "Now, Maria, that's nonsense," Mackie said. "We won't let you do it, will we, Jimmy? It's not even a present, it's a—well, call it a loan from me to you until you get on your acting feet. You can pay it back someday. Oh, Maria, don't you see? We know you have it in you, we all do. Just take it and enjoy it, for our sakes."

"I can't."

"But why, dear, why?"

How could I tell her, how could I tell her I felt betrayed? I had blurted out my secrets in public, and, as a result, strangers had been going around involving themselves in my private dreams. Didn't she realize that now I could never go to Catherine Mosca and apply in an honest, ordinary way? I felt like crying; I felt, It's my twenty-first birthday and I'm supposed to be an adult today but I don't feel grown up, I feel ten years old. They've spoiled everything. I put the glass down, said "Excuse me," and turned to run upstairs to my room, and as I did I saw the most unforgivable thing: Mackie putting up her hand to make Jimmy and the maid stay where they were, smug old Mackie "taking over." Not this time you don't, I thought. Not this time, damn you. I ran upstairs like a mad thing and locked the bedroom door.

Her voice. I can hear it still.

"Maria? . . .

"Maria, won't you come and have some supper? Gert's made you a birthday cake. . . .

"Look, Maria, those classes aren't a gift, you can pay me back. I promise. . . .

"Maria, I was only trying to help. We're all very glum downstairs. We need you. . . .

"Maria, I apologize. I know now it was nosy of me and I shouldn't have done it. But I didn't realize that it was going to offend you. I *am* very fond of you."

Then *he* came up.

"Mary, for God's sake. . . .

"Mary? Oh, come off it."

He began to sing:

> "Happy birthday to you,
> Happy birthday to you,
> Happy birthday, dear Sulky,
> Happy birthday to you."

That didn't work either. He went down and, I guess, ate his dinner. But she came right up again.

"Maria, I've been thinking. I'll get Gil to write tomorrow and say there's been a mistake, you're not ready to apply yet. Okay?"

"Okay," I said.

"Good. Now come on down and have some supper."

"No."

I know. It was childish of me, but *dammit.* Later, it seemed much later, he knocked and asked if he could come in. Mackie had gone to bed, he said, and he was tired and wanted to go to bed too.

I called out, "Look, just this once would you mind sleeping on the couch in the study?"

"Okay," he said.

He went away. It was the first time we'd slept apart since that third night of our marriage when I slept at the YW and he at the YM. Maybe that, our sleeping apart, was the worst thing I did that evening. For I set a precedent.

But no, sending him off to sleep alone wasn't the worst part of it, the worst part was that hours later, in the middle of the night, I got up, went down to the living room, and there, sure enough, was the letter from Catherine Mosca, sitting in the letters tray on the sideboard. I read the letter. I read it twice. And the worst part, the very worst, the most despicable part of all was that next morning I apologized. Mackie and I made up, and, so much for my independence; a week later her check had been cashed, I had passed my interview and was enrolled in Catherine Mosca's evening class.

Yet if I had not worked hard in acting class, I might still believe I was born to be an actress. "A so-called actress," as Ernie said tonight, his voice thick with that hatred of actors you find in so many people. Of course, Ernie doesn't just hate actors, he hates me in particular. Funny, I haven't thought of him since he left. Despite all that happened tonight, I did manage to excise him from my mind. Perhaps the truth about Ernie is that he does not stay in anyone's mind. He did not even stay in my mind before tonight, yet how could I have forgotten some of those things that happened?

I wish I had remembered him. I wish I'd had some warning feeling when I first saw *L. O. MacDuff* scribbled on the doorman's pad. But of course, as with everything else about Ernie, the L. O. MacDuff thing is not something one would remember. Only Ernie would remember it.

It was about half an hour after I tried to reach Mama in Butchersville that the phone rang again. Terence always answers the phone when he's home. But after a moment I heard him call out from his study.

"For you, Mary."

When I picked up the receiver in the living room, I could hear Beau's and Sam's voices in the background. Then Terence, hearing me on the extension, hung up, and all at once there was a strange heavy silence on the other end of the line.

"Hello?" I said.

"Maria?" A man's voice.

"Who is it?"

"It's me."

"I'm sorry. Who?"

"L. O. MacDuff. Didn't you get my message?"

"Oh, yes," I said vaguely. "But I'm afraid I—well, I have an awful memory for names."

"Oh, come off it, Maria," he said. "It's Ernie Truelove. Don't you remember the nickname you gave me?"

"God," I said. "Hello, Ernie."

"You *did* remember," he said. "You were just teasing, weren't you?"

"Are you here on a vacation?" I asked him, wanting to get off this name thing.

"Just a few days. I'm supposed to go back to Montreal tomorrow morning. That's why I phoned you. I—ah—I wondered if—ah—if you and your husband would care to join me for a drink tonight. My last night and all that. I'd like to kind of celebrate with someone I know. And—well, you're the only person I know here. Apart from the fact that you're the person I'd most want to see, even if I *did* know other people."

"Oh," I said. "Well, yes, but I'll have to check with Terence, all right?"

"Look," he said, "if you're busy, I mean if you have another engagement, I understand, of course. I know you must be mixed up with all sorts of interesting people, I mean, being married to Terence Lavery and all. Look"—his voice grew loud, hurting my ear—"I mean, don't be shy, tell me, forget it, just thought I'd call, that's all."

Now it was my turn to get loud and flustered. "No, listen," I said, "I just wanted to check with Terence—"

"No, be frank," he interrupted. "Look, we're old friends."

"I was going to suggest," I said, "that perhaps you'd like to come and have supper with us. Just potluck."

"Oh, but I couldn't put you to that trouble. I mean I didn't phone for that. I wanted to invite *you*."

"It's no trouble," I said. "We'd love to see you."

"Great." He did sound delighted. "I'm a fan of your husband's, you know. Look—can I bring a bottle of something?"

"No, just yourself," I said. "Is seven all right?"

"Any time," he said. "Seven will be fine. By the way"—a long pause, then he went on—"you—ah—you know that Hat was living at my place when he died?"

"No, I didn't," I said and just then I sensed he was going to say something I didn't want to hear.

"Well, he was. He used to talk a lot about you, Maria. I mean—well, you know he was in love with you right up to the end."

"Oh?" I said. What could I say?

"Yes, well, I just thought I'd tell you, I mean, no matter what he may have told you or written you, he did love you. I just mentioned it because there mightn't be a chance tonight, I mean with your new husband there and all."

"Thank you. I'll see you at seven, then, Ernie."

"Seven," he said. "Gosh, I'm looking forward to it, Maria."

"So am I. See you then."

"I'll be there," he said. "Lay on, Macduff."

He hung up. I remember thinking, That's it, "Lay on, Macduff," was his slogan, he used it all the time. I remember thinking, I hope he doesn't bore the pants off Tee, and then the thing he'd said, the thing I didn't want to think about, came into my mind and angered me all over again against Hat. I could just see Hat sitting in Ernie Truelove's place in Montreal, a Scotch in his fist, his wild black eyes fixed on his audience, as he dramatized how he felt about me, how he loved me, how, goddammit, he would always love me because, do you see, Ernie, Mary was the woman I really loved, she was the love of my life. And then, obliquely (or perhaps not so obliquely), the old hint of suicide, the last emotional stop pulled out to ensure that Ernie would not leave him alone. For, total actor that Hat was, the suicide threat meant the audience would rally round. Oh, how could I have wept for him so many times since I heard of his death?

I hung up the phone and thought, Why have I invited Ernie Truelove to supper? Why have I left myself open for another evening of reminiscence about Hat?

I was shaking. Adrenalin or fear, I don't know, but at that moment I willed Terence to appear and, as though by magic, he did appear, coming by the living room, showing Beau and Sam to the front door.

"Bye there, Martha," Sam told me.

"Bye, honey," said Beau.

They were putting on their coats in the hall. Both, I noticed, wore gray desert boots. Sam had a green bulky-knit sweater and Beau a maroon Swiss-velour shirt. Both had purchased flat British cloth caps. Beau's face is very fat, and the cap, when he put it on, looked like a lid on a kitchen pot. And Sam—well, Sam was simply too old for fancy dress.

"Be talking to you," Beau assured Terence.

"Yeah, we'll be in touch," Sam decided.

"*Ciao*," said Terence, closing the door on them, waving them a farewell, then turned, coming to me, smiling, his arms out to hold me, and I into his arms and held him tight, for in his embrace my fears went. I held and was held and was safe. I put my face against the lapel of his tweed jacket and rubbed like a cat.

"Well, now, Martha," Tee said. We laughed. "Yes, indeed," Tee said, "they don't know your name."

"Who does?" I said. "Sometimes I forget myself."

"Who's L. O. MacDuff?" Tee asked, suddenly holding me off and looking at me. "Some old love?"

"No, no. But he's coming to supper. I'm sorry, I couldn't get out of it, I'll tell you about it. Want some tea?"

"Okay. And let's go into my room and goof and gossip a minute."

Tee turned me toward his study and asked, "Good day?" and, without thinking, I said, "No, no, I've had an awful day, it started badly, it was just one thing—" and then stopped myself, remembering that nowadays I always seem to be complaining. I seem neurotic, self-centered, always talking trivia, I don't know how he can still like me. "I mean," I said, changing tack, "I had a strange sort of day. I had lunch with Janice Sloane, and that was very odd, I can tell you."

"Odd?" he said.

"It would take ages even to give you the gist of it. But one thing came out. Remember we used to wonder who it was told Hat about you and me? Well, it was Janice."

But Tee wasn't interested in that, that's the past, and he never thinks of the past. He kissed the nape of my neck.

"L. O. MacDuff," he said, "our mysterious dinner guest, he's the one *I* want to hear about. I bet he's an old boy friend."

"Nonsense," I said, but as I said it I remembered that Ernie had taken me to dinner a few times, and a memory of one night, vague, for I was high, when Ernie wept. That was all I remembered then, it was just a pinprick, I put it out of my mind. "Wait till you hear," I said to Tee. "Know what his real name is? It's Ernest Truelove."

"No wonder he changed it to MacDuff. Martha, you have to be joking."

"Stop calling me Martha," I said. "I'll begin to think it's my real name." We were in the kitchen now. I put water in the kettle and decided to tell Tee about that strange thing of forgetting who I was in the beauty parlor this morning, but "Teabags or tea?" he asked and I said teabags would do, and he went into the pantry, out of ear-shot, to get the teabags. When he came back I had begun to feel trembly again, and when I spoke my voice was shaky. "I mean," I said, "about names. It's strange, it's been such a funny day about names, it started this morning when the woman in the hairdresser's asked my name and I forgot, I couldn't remember, I just blanked out for a moment. It was like that time long ago I think I told you about, in Juarez, a real panic—"

But Tee came to me and held me, pressing me to him. "Now, now, take it easy," he said. "Don't get upset."

"And then when I did remember, I remembered my name as Phelan," I said. "Which was really depressing."

When I said *depressing*, Terence's eyes went neutral. Sometimes I think he thinks there's something wrong with me, something mental. "Oh come on," he said. "It's just your time of month."

But as he said it he looked at me with a sort of questioning look, and I thought to myself, He thinks I'm mad, he

152

does. My hand shook as I poured hot water into the tea-pot. I tried to sound light and casual.

"It was funny, that thing about my name," I said. "I mean, really. Who am I any more? All these names—who am I?"

"You are May-ree, May-ree," he sang, "and it's a grand o-o-ld n-a-a-me."

"Wrong. Ask Sam. My first name is now Martha."

He laughed, and if I had left it at that it would have been fine, it would all have passed off as a joke. But when I am nervous I am incapable of leaving things alone, I go on about them, and so I did go on and said, "But seriously, Dunne, Phelan, Bell, Lavery—just think if it were you, would you remember? I mean is it any wonder I can't remember my name now, when somebody asks me?"

He picked up the tray. "At least you're not L. O. Mac-Duff, yclept Ernest Trueblood. Let's take the tea into my room."

"True-love," I told him.

"That's even better," he said. "And was he a true love?"

"What's that supposed to mean?"

"I mean he sounded like some old boy friend of yours. Is he?"

"Of course he's not. You think every man I meet is one of my old boy friends."

"Sorry," Tee said. "You take the teapot, okay?"

"All right," I said, starting off down the hall. "I suppose he was a 'boy friend,' as you call it. I mean I went out with him a few times."

"In Montreal?"

"Yes. After Jimmy and I broke up. Hat was in Europe and it looked as though his wife wouldn't give him a divorce. Ernie worked in our office. He asked me out to dinner a few times, and I was lonely and went."

Terence pushed open the door to his room and put the

tea-tray on his long worktable. "Well, it's funny. When I told him I'd get you to call him back he said he'd wait in his room for the call. I said there was no need for him to do that. Then he got all upset. He said, 'No, no, you don't understand, it's important to me to see her, very important.' So I said, 'All right, but I'm sorry I didn't get your name,' and he sort of hesitated and then he said, 'Well, if you tell her L. O. MacDuff, she'll know who you mean.' Which I thought was an odd thing for him to say."

"It was a nickname I gave him. He was always saying, 'Lead on, Macduff.'"

"I thought it was 'lay on,'" Tee said. "'Lay on, Macduff.' Isn't that what Macbeth says?"

On the wall of his study Terence has hung prints and photographs of the great men he admires. I looked at the wall, staring at those famous faces, thinking, Maybe Terence does not believe me, maybe he thinks I was promiscuous before I met him. I have Hat to thank for that lie about being promiscuous, it's the sort of thing, once a man says it, other men believe him.

From the wall, Dostoevski, bearded like a Bible elder, stared down at me in contempt. Above him, in an early photograph, Proust saw through me with calm ellipsoidal orbs. Yeats, in Augustus John's portrait, ignored me to contemplate some pure beauty I would never be. All were men, all men judged me, all men were unfair, as Hat was unfair, and in my mindless tension it seemed to me that Terence was accusing me of having had an affair with silly Ernie Truelove and, worse, somewhere in the back of the panic of my mind was the memory of Ernie weeping, I could not remember why or when, but there, staring at and stared at by those great and famous men, I was again guilty of something, I knew not what, but guilty, yes, guilty. Self-condemned.

Ernie weeping—why could I not remember why or when

it was? What had happened to my memory? I stared at the wall as Terence poured cups of tea. Dostoevski, Proust, Tolstoi, Yeats. They knew who they were and, because they did, we, posterity, will always know. They wrote, therefore they are, whereas I, sitting glum on that sofa, was nameless, lost, filled with a shameful panic. I looked at Proust, the *flâneur*, who renounced his world for his work. I thought of his death, the great book finished after fifteen years, the last pages of corrections lying on the invalid's sickbed. And as I stared at Proust's strange eyes, some self-defense within me rose up to shift the intolerable burden of blame, and I thought to myself, Why did Terence put these great men on his wall, Terence who is so quick to judge me promiscuous? Isn't Terence afraid of being judged himself? My God, when I think of it, the arrogance of a man who could do the trivial work *he* does under the scrutiny of the likes of Tolstoi and Yeats. Proust gave up a world for his work. Terence wouldn't even give up a party.

And then, as though he guessed at my sudden anger toward him, Tee got up and put a Chopin record on the record-player. No one has known my moods as he does, and he was right, music was the best thing then. In my emotional state, music could bring tears, but tears lull me, whereas, as he knew, further talking would lead to my finding some pretense to pick a fight with him.

I stared again at the bearded elders, heard Brailowsky begin a mazurka, tried to think of the clear water sound of the music, but I was on the cliff edge and I knew it, on the edge of that state of mind where I will blame myself for anything, a state of mind where the world is not at fault, but I am at fault, and I said to myself, Be calm, be calm, listen to this mazurka, let the music fill your head, driving all thoughts away.

The music swelled, lulling me, and I turned to look at

Tee, who had stretched out on the daybed and was reading the *New Statesman*. He put his heel to his toe and shucked off one brown loafer. It fell to the floor. Heel to other toe as he shucked off the second loafer. It did not fall but lay on its side on the daybed while I stared at the loafer, thinking, I will not think about anything but that, the loafer, I will contemplate the loafer and listen to the music and I will not think. I-will-not-think.

Terence was watching me. He was just pretending to read his paper. I knew he had guessed the mean thoughts I'd been having about him, and now he was silently asking me what had I done with my life to give me the right to criticize what he had done with his?

And I said to myself, I'm not going to get into an argument with him about that or anything else. But it was no good. I did get into an unspoken argument. I said to myself, look here, now

There doesn't have to be any purpose.

There doesn't

have

to be

any PURPOSE.

Ordinary people live ordinary unmeaningful lives (I said to myself).

There doesn't have to be

any

PURPOSE.

Take women. Most women don't even live lives of quiet desperation. (Quiet desperation is far too dramatic.) Most women live lives like doing the dishes, finishing one day's dishes and facing the next, until one day the rectal polyp is found or the heart stops and it's over. And all that's left of them is a name on a gravestone.

But it was no good, he was judging me, I knew what he was thinking, and so I damn well judged him. I looked up at Dostoevski on the wall and, Look here Fyodor, I said to myself, would you have put aside your novel for a sure thing, for a little musical, the way Terence did? Damn right you wouldn't, Fyodor. But that little revue in London, that really is what Terence is best known for. I remember the afternoon after it opened, we drove up to the theater on Shaftesbury Avenue to see the notices on the marquee and the theater manager came out and took our photo with a flash camera beneath the critics' kind words. "Happiest romp in years—*Times*." "Laughed till I cried —*Sketch*." "Charming, with-it, up-to-the-minute!—*Mirror*." I stood there, arm-linked with Tee, smiling for the camera, stood there in a drizzle of rain, and was sad behind my smile, sad for the play Terence had abandoned because "they" had said audiences wouldn't like it, because "they" had pushed him to write this, and now "they" were vindicated by the inanities written over the marquee beneath which we posed. How dare you judge me, Terence, I said to myself, staring at him as he pretended to read his paper, how dare you? Let me tell you something, Tee. If you are with-it and up-to-the-minute, then you will never be ahead of it or outside it or apart from it, as genius is, as Proust was apart, as Dostoevski was not with it. I stared at him and I was Mad Twin and, Yes, yes, yes, I thought, you shouldn't worry about success. Do you hear me, Tee?

There are more things in
life than
instant
suck-cess.

And I remember as I sat there staring at him, angry tears in my eyes, the Chopin unheard, Tee, poor Tee, turned and looked at me and I saw that Mad Twin had been wrong again, Tee had not judged me, he never judges me, and who was I to sit meanly in judgment on him, I who would run to the window and jump if anything hap-

157

pened to him, for what I said to Hat long ago is still true, Terence is my savior, he restoreth my soul, he has made me happy and I should be ashamed of myself for wanting him to be old Fyodor (my God, I thought, imagine going to bed with that bearded madman with his gambling and his sick lusts after small girls), what normal woman would want a genius as a mate, what does it matter what posterity says about Tee, will I be around to hear the silence of those future years, of course I won't.

I had turned my head away so that Tee would not see my tears and now I wiped my eyes and looked back at him, but suddenly—I know, it doesn't sound sensible, but anyway, I caught him looking at me in a very cold, curious way, and I thought, Yes, he thinks I'm going mad, he's trying to find out how shaky I am. And as I stared at him he smiled, falsely, and I smiled back because I was afraid of him, yes, afraid, *even though I knew that only a mad person would be afraid of Tee.* So therefore I *was* mad, and I smiled and smiled and hoped I could deceive him, for unless I kept my mad side under control even Tee, good sweet Terence, would pick up the telephone and call in doctors who would sign papers (for your own good, Mary) and have me taken away and locked up in an asylum.

And if they do lock me up, then I really will lose my mind because I am the sort of person who is very susceptible to environment and if I were to be locked up with a bunch of mad people I would start mimicking them (that sounds mad: "mimicking them"), I mean if I am put in among people like that it could upset me so much that I really would become ill, I mean temporarily deranged, and that could become permanent, permanently deranged, and then they would throw away the key, and as all this rushed around in my head while I sat there cravenly smiling at Terence, my enemy, I began in my mind to say an act of contrition Oh my God I am heartily sorry for having sinned against Thee, because Thou art so good I will never more offend Thee and I will amend my life.

And now, sweet Mother of God, it was really bad, I was slipping over the cliff edge, smiling at Tee, who had got up from the daybed and was coming toward me, and I smiled to him, hello there, hello, I am all right, I was only joking about forgetting my name today, it was just a joke, Terence my love, I am fine, see, I am smiling at you, and now you stretch out your hand to take mine, but if I let you hold my hand you will discover that I am trembling, and of course that's why you want to take my hand, to see if it is trembling, yes, you don't want to hold my hand in a loving way, you want it as a doctor does, to feel my pulse, but I am on to that, my love, and so I embrace you hard and press myself against you, press so hard I control my shaking hands and I kiss you and pull you down on top of me on the daybed, pretending I am hot and excited, and then break away from you and go to pull down the blind while behind me I hear a noise which means you are undressing.

I remember standing there at the window in a sudden lucid moment, divorced from my fear, and I remember thinking, I am getting ready to make love to Terence, just as though I were a prostitute, for I am not doing it for love, or even for tenderness, but simply to prevent him from knowing the state I'm in.

I turned around and was going to say something, I think I was even going to confide in you, Tee, but there you were, waiting, and again I was afraid and so I began to pose for you as you sat there on the daybed, I began to take off my clothes, first my skirt, then my suit jacket, then my bra, stood there in panties, garter belt, and stockings, looking down at you with an actress smile, turned away from you, showing you my bum as I peeled off my panties, and you had your pants off too, you sat there in your shirt with your prick sticking up inquiringly from under the shirt-

159

tail and as you took off your shirt I bent to take off my garter belt and stockings and my face was close to your naked belly as you pulled your shirt off, and I remembered my doom dream, when naked is panic, when naked is the dooms, the glooms, the nightmare in which I see myself in unknown hotel rooms with nameless men; the men differ, but I am always the same. I come from the bathroom, naked, my hair down to my hips, my make-up on straight; I go toward the bed and the man stands up. He is naked and his prick is stiff. Naked means no sleep; stiff prick means fuck: it means finishing myself off in the bathroom later, or lie awake, unfinished, the man asleep beside me and I awake, a sad, female animal.

And now Terence came to me naked and I shook, but you held me, Terence, you pressed me to you and felt my shaking but you held me. I was drowning but I felt your body against mine, your body that fits mine as no other body ever did, your prick against my belly, and I knew I would not drown, for with you, naked is make it new, there is no past, you are my resurrection and my life and out of the depths I cry to you, and now Terence maketh me to lie down in green pastures, he restoreth me by his fingers inside me as he kisses my breasts and neck, and I take his prick in my hand and come up with him to joy, all my shaking stilled, to that joining, that Mass of the senses, that slow titillation of our parts, until I no longer have a mind, I am one with the moment as we roll and turn, and now we change rhythm, we move into that hot frantic driving, to that fuck that encompasseth me, we try to prolong it, hold it back, wait, wait, and now, feeling you drive inside me, excited, excited, I cry with joy, it is not as it used to be with others, there is no fear, there is no "Will I and when can I and if I can't then can I pretend it?" I feel you and know you're close and I am close, too close, and oh, make it last, think of something else to make it last, but we drive toward it and I feel you come and I come, we come, we come together and I shake and shudder, I shake and shudder and shake and shake. And lie still.

He lies beside me. There is sweat on my brow and my heart beats loud. But I am at peace.

We slept. I woke. I looked at the clock on his worktable. "Terence, it's six-thirty."

He yawned, "Eeeeeeaaahhh." He cat-rubbed his eyes with his knuckles, sat up, and switched on the light. I saw the tiger stripe of black hair which runs from his navel to his pubic bush. "How long did we sleep?" he asked.

"Two hours," I said, and then I thought, *Ernie.* I was going to cook the leg of lamb, but now it was too late. Terence reached over and kissed me. "Listen," I said, "could you nip down to the supermarket and get us some lamb chops? I was going to cook a leg of lamb but it's too late and the butcher's closed—"

He smiled and cut short my explanation by fondling my breasts. " 'Ow much are these? 'Ow about a couple of nice breasts? Tasty."

Sometimes he puts me off with those burlesque pleasantries, but this afternoon I was feeling so guilty about having to ask him to run down for the chops that I forgave him. I feel guilty with Terence. He has so much to do, yet I'm always asking him to help me with the few things I have to do. He's organized and I'm not. I remember thinking that people like Ernie Truelove are always on time. I jumped up, grabbed my clothes, and ran for my bathroom as Tee sprinted past me like some young naked satyr, making for the other bathroom down the hall.

In the bathroom, I looked in the mirror. My face smiled back at me, mirroring that quotation about "the lineaments of gratified desire," which described my lineaments very nicely at that moment, thank you and thank *you*, Mr. Lavery, sir. I thought of Hat saying, "All you want is to be fucked, fucked, fucked until the come is running out of you," and yes sir, Hat, I recommend it, it does wonders for premenstrual tension, and there in the bathroom as I began to clean my face, I thought of Terence going to get the lamb chops: he never minds doing an errand, because he loves me. Mackie never minded doing errands for me; there was no chore she would not do so long as she had me to herself. In one of the rows I had with him, Jimmy said, "Look, you go to work with her, you have lunch with her, you spend your evenings with her. I know, it's not your fault. I have to study. But dammit, Mary, except for the time we're asleep in this bed, when are you and I together? I mean, we used to talk about my job at Loblaws', about the T. Eaton Company and the Blodgetts and Nova Scotia and school and all those things we used to laugh about. But I tell you, kid"—he liked to say, I tell you, kid—"I sit here night after night at dinner listening to you and Mackie going on about *Canada's Own* and this one and that one, giggling away, the pair of you, and for Christ's sake I've nothing to say to you now, *she's* your buddy, you're more married to her than you are to me."

"Well, you're the one who's studying."

"And what about you? When you're not sitting in there with Mackie, you're out with a bunch of actors."

"I'm in acting class. The one you and Mackie so kindly arranged for me. What's wrong, do you want me to quit acting? Do you?"

"I'm not talking about acting, stop trying to change the subject."

"Who's trying to change the subject?"

"You were."

"I was not."

"You *were*. Anyway, I was talking about you and her. Do you realize that you and I can never sit alone in that living room? Do you realize I never can start a conversation with you without keeping an eye out for her ladyship to walk in, plunk herself down, and listen in on every word we're saying."

"Well, it's her house."

"Exactly. *Exactly*."

"You *were* the one who wanted to move in here, Jimmy, not me."

"Oh, Christ," he would shout and run out of the bedroom.

Yet even in fights we were three. After each row, when the thick silence of dissent perched over our meals, there was Mackie, passing sauce or more meat, eyes nun-glancing from Jimmy to me, maintaining a "tactful" silence which in effect condemned Jimmy, for in all the time she and I used to spend together she managed to ignore the fact of my marriage, never saying anything that would connect the Maria I was for her with that guilty young married woman who, each evening at some point of going to bed—undressing, combing my hair, brushing my teeth—had the same small unhappy thought: I hope he doesn't want to tonight.

Yet years later Hat screamed at me that all I had ever wanted was to be fucked, fucked, fucked. And I believed him. Just as I believed Jimmy when he said, "You know what you are, you're a virgin, that's what you are, you're as cold as a bloody plaster saint." Jimmy's right, I thought, I *am* cold, it's my fault, there's something wrong with me.

It's funny how I believed Jimmy, just as I believed Hat. In those days I thought men more intelligent than women. Yet I also believed I was very intelligent. It makes me smile now to remember my lost innocence, but when men said flattering things to me and wanted to hire me, when train conductors went out of their way to explain things for me, when other girls' fathers acted fatherly to me, it never occurred to me that it was because of my looks. I thought myself to be too tall; I thought my nose was too big; I wanted a bobbed nose and one of those meaningless doll faces people in small towns think pretty. Even with Mackie, I thought it was my brains that attracted her. I thought she'd taken that first shine to me and hired me because she too had once worked in the same awful directory place, and that she saw me as a younger version of herself. And it wasn't until she made that strange confession four months after I first met her that I realized my brains had nothing to do with it. She came out with it one evening when, typically, Jimmy was upstairs studying. And Mackie said, "I've been reading a book about romantic love, I mean the romantic love poets write about, a pure love that is romantic because it never can be fulfilled. Chivalric love, do you remember?"

I said yes, although I still hadn't caught on.

"Chivalric love," she said. "Chivalric, because it is doomed. Like my love."

And so, surprised, stupidly, I said, "Your love? I didn't know you were in love."

She smiled at me. "Oh, Maria," she said. "Do you remember the first day you walked into my office in the library? Do you know what happened? I looked up at you and felt dizzy. I felt I was going to faint. I remember the first thing I thought, when the dizziness cleared, was that your coat was cheap and your shoes were worn."

"*My* coat?" I said. "I don't understand, what had that to do with your feeling dizzy?"

"I mean," she said, "I didn't know you at all, I'd never seen you before, but I wanted to buy you a beautiful coat and beautiful shoes—which you should have. I remember thinking I would like to see your face framed in furs."

"Mackie!" (I was embarrassed. I remember I laughed, but she didn't.)

"No," she said, "it's true. I remember I brought you the magazine article you'd asked for and then I went back and sat down at my own desk and I said to myself, This girl will read the article she came to read and then she'll go away and I'll never see her again unless I do something about it, something extraordinary. Do you realize what happened that day, do you *realize* what it took for me to go back and talk to you and then, when you told me where you worked, I had this mad idea and I ran in to see Mac-Kinnon and asked for you as my assistant. Do you remember, Maria? Oh, what a day that was. Chivalric love, I said, Lord, I was a knight in armor that day, I had no fear, I really bullied old MacKinnon into taking you, remember?"

I sat staring at her as she told me this story. I remember thinking, Why, she's not even aware of the true meaning of what she's saying. I remember feeling embarrassed for her, yet protective of her too, thinking, She loves me and I don't love her, doesn't she realize I'm a married woman, poor thing, that's why she wants Jimmy and me to live with her, she's a Lesbian without knowing it. (I had only recently read about Lesbians, I didn't know much about them, but after she told me her story I remember thinking, There's something morally wrong about us going on living here, using this poor woman. We should move out. And I should get some other job.)

But I didn't tell Jimmy what she'd said. And we didn't move out. I chose to forget she'd ever said it. I thought her love was doomed, as she said it was. Nothing would ever come of it. Besides, I thought, how could I break it to her, how could I hurt her by telling her what I think is wrong with her?

She said her love was chivalric. She meant it was a pure love, a love in which she loved me more than she loved herself. But, of course, she was wrong. Her love was not chivalric, it was selfish. She was pleased with herself for having captured me and carried me off into her bookstacks and into her home. As, later, she was so jealous of my love for Hat that she must tell Jimmy about it, hoping to destroy it. I remember in the cab this morning I thought of Jimmy, who said he loved me but who in reality wanted a face and a body which happened to be mine. Sad as it sounds, Mackie was the same. For she loved a girl she invented, a girl she called Maria. There was no Maria. There was only me.

"Lamb chops," Terence said. "Want anything else?"

He was at the bathroom door, dressed, his hair combed. I said no, I had everything. I heard the front door close and I thought, Damn, damn, why did I invite Ernie Truelove to dinner? How much nicer it would have been to spend tonight alone with Tee. I thought, I won't bother doing my hair, I haven't time, I'll wear my fall, and I thought of the fall, sitting on its oval-faced styrofoam dummy head on my bedroom windowsill. I remember I thought, I'll finish up my face here in the bathroom, then put on my op-art dress, the one I got at Ohrbach's with the short skirt, it's swingy, and I was just lining in my mouth with my lipstick brush when I heard the doorbell. Terence forgot his wallet, I thought, he always forgets it when he changes clothes.

"Door's open," I shouted. I knew I hadn't locked the catch earlier.

I heard him come in.

"Did you forget your wallet?" I called, but there was no answer. I'd finished my mouth so I got up and went out into the hall, going to the bedroom for my dress. There, facing me in the hall, was Ernie Truelove.

And me with my terrycloth robe open, exposing to him my bare breasts, my panties. I clutched the robe shut. I could have killed him.

"Oh, gee, I'm sorry," he said, but his face was hanging open, his eyes were still glazed over by his staring at my breasts. I moved past him into my bedroom. I was shaking. I called, "I'll be with you in a minute. Go in the living room and—ah—get yourself a drink."

I heard his footsteps retreat. I started to get into my dress, and as I did his voice boomed out. "Gosh, Maria, I'm sorry, I didn't know I was early, I mean I didn't mean to inconvenience you like this. Gosh. Listen, just pretend I'm not here, okay?"

"Don't worry, it's all right, I won't be a minute. There's drinks on the living-room table and ice in the kitchen fridge."

"No hurry," his voice boomed. And then: "Hey, Maria, gosh, it's good to see you again."

Well, you've certainly seen plenty of me, haven't you? I thought as I slipped on my op art dress.

"Your husband home?"

"No, he went out, he'll be back in a moment."

"Gee, what a place you have here."

I was trying to fix my hair and put the fall on. Why couldn't he shut up and read a magazine or something? I rushed, and as soon as I'd finished I put on my red shoes, looked at my skirt in the mirror, then stepped out into the hall. I saw Ernie in the living room, but he hadn't yet seen me. I looked at him for a moment as he stood by the window, a large lumpish man, very Canadian square, in his navy blazer, white shirt, maroon tie, flannels, and sensible black brogues. As I went toward the living room he heard me coming and turned to peer at me in a way which made me think he ordinarily wears glasses. His eyes, I noticed, were a sea-gray color with strange amber flecks in the irises.

"Now," I said, very hostessy, "what will you have to drink?"

"Oh, whatever you've got."

"Well, we've lots of things. Rye, Scotch, bourbon, gin, vodka, sherry—I think we have just about everything."

"I would say you have," he said, looking around the room pointedly to show me he is aware of "everything." Hands clasped behind his back, policemanlike, he rocked gently on his heels. "Yes, I would say you have it made, Maria."

And of course the way he said it made me feel guilty, the guilty feeling you get when you meet old friends who have not been materially successful. "What about a Scotch and soda?" I asked.

"Well, let's see." He bent over the drinks tray, hands still clasped behind his back. "Ah, me. Choice is the foetus of unhappiness. Let's see-eee."

Silence for a moment, as he read labels on bottles.

"Hmm," he said. "There's always rye and ginger ale, the old Canadian standby."

"Rye and ginger," I said, moving toward the drinks.

"But, maybe that would seem corny to you?"

"Why should it?" I asked.

"Well, now that you're one of the 'smarts.' "

"Smarts?"

"You know," he said. "The sort of people who get written up in *Time* magazine."

"That's a new one. Smarts?"

"You're married to one, Maria, my dear. Your present husband was written up by *Time*, wasn't he?"

That "present husband," angered me, so I said, "Oh, come off it, Ernie. Since when did you become a professional hick?"

He laughed without amusement, throwing his head back to simulate mirth. "Professional hick, eh? That's rare. That is *rare*."

At that moment, I remember, Terence came into the living room. At once, Ernie stopped laughing. "This is Terence," I began, but Ernie cut me off at once with a great explosion. "Oh, you don't have to tell me, Maria, why I'd know your husband anywhere. It's an honor, a great honor to meet you, Terence."

"Well, how do you do," Terence said, smiling, embarrassed, holding out his hand, which Ernie took and held, saying, "Yes indeed, and what's more I've read your books and seen your revue and admired your drawings and let's not forget your play which I'm looking forward to seeing when it comes out with—who is it is playing the lead, is it David Niven?"

"Well, not actually."

"Anyway, I feel I know all about you. In short, Terence, I am a fan of yours, a real honest-to-God fan."

"Well, in that case I'd better get you a drink," Terence said hurriedly, going toward the drinks tray.

I had been putting ice into glasses and now I handed one of them to Tee, saying, "Ernie would like a rye and ginger."

"Rye and ginger?" Ernie said. "You're kidding, Maria."

"I thought that's what you said a moment ago."

Ernie laughed, and I remember thinking he looked like a cow in a Disney cartoon. "Now you have to be kidding," he said. "Where's that good old Canadian sense of humor?" He turned to Terence. "You see, Terence, she'd just called me a professional hick. So I thought I'd better act the part properly. Rye and ginger, ha-ha."

I remembered that he'd ordered rye and ginger *before* I'd called him a professional hick. I looked at him, thinking, Why are the awful ones, the horrors, why are they all *my* so-called friends? And, as if confirming it, Ernie turned to Terence, put his hand on Terence's sleeve, and said, "I called you Terence and I should know better. I know you British don't first-name every stranger you meet. And a good thing too. I'm sorry. Forgive me."

"No, no, that's all right," Terence said, embarrassed. "I mean call me Terence or whatever you like."

"Well, thank you," Ernie said. "Of course, in my own case, I like to be called by my first name. I hate my last name. Truelove. Wouldn't you?"

"Umm." Tee nodded his head affirmatively, like a boy who has just mastered a difficult point in class. "Now, what will you drink?"

"Teacher's," Ernie said. "Teacher's Highland Cream and a spot of water would do me nicely."

"And what about you, darling?"

"A martini," I said. I felt I was going to need it. I asked Tee if he'd got the chops and when he said yes I excused myself and went to the kitchen, thinking again, Oh God, why did I invite him?—and then, just as it did with old Mr. Dieter Peters this morning, my mulish, unbiddable memory yielded up a sudden isolated moment: Beaver Lake in Montreal, and I walking along the edge of the pond in the moonlight with Ernie Truelove, and I remembered that as we walked I was confiding in him and that later I knew it was a mistake. But I could not remember what it was I confided to Ernie. I thought, He took me out to dinner once or twice, the time I was living in Montreal and Hat was off in Europe and I was waiting for my divorce from Jimmy. But that was all I had time to remember, for at that point Tee came into the kitchen, carrying a martini for me, his look saying hurry back. I took the martini, said I'd be in in a minute, and began to rush, setting the table in the dining room, getting out a little jar of caviar and some melba toast, finally becoming so jittery about leaving Tee with Ernie that I stopped everything, took the caviar and toast, and went back into the living room.

"Caviar?" Ernie brayed.

"Oh," Tee said, beginning to spoon some out for him, "do you like it?"

"Well, let me say this." Ernie paused, put his hands on his kneecaps, and leaned forward like a judge announcing his decision. "Let me say it's not something which I've had enough of to allow me to become tired of it." Smiling; waiting for Tee and me to collapse in a fit of laughter. We did not oblige him, so he added, "Yes indeed. Caviar. The height of sophistication."

I remember at that point I asked him if he was still with *Canada's Own*. He said yes, he was still on the desk, and Terence asked if that meant copy-editing.

"Yes indeedy," Ernie said. "We also serve who only punctuate." He picked up his Scotch, drank as if it were Coke, then munched a piece of toast with caviar. "Deelicious," he informed us. "What a nice spread these fish eggs be,"—nodding wisely, licking his lips, leaning toward Terence. "You know," he said, "Maria here was quite the little Cassandra, in my case. She told my fortune once. She said if I didn't get off the desk then—that was years ago—that I'd stay on it all my life. Looks as though she was right."

"Your fortune?" I said. "I told your fortune?"

"Yes, don't you remember? It was just after I met you, I mean in Montreal. You were living in a flat on Ridgewood and you gave a party for old Mackie McIver one weekend when she came up from Toronto. Remember? I was there and the Sloanes and Eddie Downes. And after dinner you told fortunes."

"Not me," I said. "Mackie was the one who told fortunes." And as I said it I remembered her sitting on the floor in her good "dinner dress" (it was black velvet), looking like an old child as she read our palms. And reading mine, staring into my eyes as she told me things, things I knew then were disguised professions of love. "No," I said to Ernie. "Maybe my memory isn't great, but I do remember that. Mackie was the one who told your fortune."

"Wrong, Maria. Wrong. She did tell my fortune, but afterwards I asked *you* to tell my fortune and you laughed and pretended to read my palm and then you said that about my staying on the desk for life unless I left it within three months."

He was so vehement, I thought, Well, what does it matter? I said perhaps he was right, but I certainly didn't remember ever telling him that.

"Ah." He shook his head sadly. "There are so many things you don't remember."

"Like what?"

"Like, for instance, how you promised to phone me when you came back to Montreal. You've been back quite a few times since, but I'm still waiting for that phone call."

Yes, I suppose I did promise to phone him, I thought, but dammit, when I go to Montreal it's only for a few days, I can't phone everybody.

"Am I right, Maria?" he asked.

"Yes. I'm sorry."

Abruptly, he turned to Tee and thrust out his glass. "Can I trouble you for a refill?"

Tee got up and poured Ernie another Scotch. I went back to the kitchen. I thought, The sooner we eat, the sooner we'll be rid of him. I remember looking into the

living room and seeing the back of his head, his brillian-
tined brown hair carefully combed over a vulnerable little
bald spot at the crown. And as I stared at his head, he
leaned forward and placed the drink Terence had just
given him on a coaster on the coffee table. The neatly
combed-over bald spot, the precise gesture of placing his
drink, reminded me of his neatness in other things. How,
before he began his day's work as a copy-editor, he would
sharpen six pencils and arrange them in a row near his
right hand. How, the first night I was in his apartment, I
opened his kitchen cupboard to get a glass and there were
his dishes and glasses, stacked under neat typewritten labels: PLATES, SOUP; GLASSES, SHERRY; SAUCERS, SMALL; and
so on.

Always neat. And then (probably because I was in my
own kitchen at the time), remembering his neatly labeled
kitchen shelves, I remembered the first time I saw his
apartment. It was the night I came back from Ottawa after
the Senate divorce hearing: my divorce from Jimmy.
Jimmy had not been present in Ottawa. The grounds
against him had been adultery and desertion, both false.
The divorce was collusive because by then Jimmy also
wanted a divorce. At least I kept telling myself he did.
But I wasn't really sure. Perhaps he was saying it just to
save his pride? Anyway, when I arrived back in Windsor
Station in Montreal that night, I remembered how Jimmy
and I had waited in that same railroad station at the beginning of our marriage, waited for O'Keefe to send us
enough money to go on to Toronto after old Tom, the
idiot, had gone home to Halifax with his father. And, remembering, I felt down. I wasn't expecting to see anyone
there in the station. I had planned to go home and go to
bed. But Ernie Truelove and his girl were standing at the
ticket gate. Sally something, yes, Sally Harper, her name
was. Taller than Ernie, a redhead. They had come, they

said, to invite me to have supper with them at Ernie's place, and while I didn't want to go, I didn't know how to say no in those days, and so they put me into Ernie's little Renault and drove me up Mount Royal to Ernie's apartment, which was very close to Beaver Lake.

It was summer, very hot, and when I walked into the apartment I was met by a blast of talk, and people coming forward to kiss me or shake hands. Ernie had assembled nearly all the people I knew at that time in Montreal: Janice and Charles Sloane, Blair and Peggy O'Connell, the Leducs, Eddie Downes. It was a typical Montreal party, everybody talking at once, both men and women getting drunk. I remember that someone had cooked lasagna and Blair had brought flasks of Chianti and that when I went into the kitchen to help with the supper I opened the cupboard and saw Ernie's glasses and dishes all stacked and labeled in that odd way.

And it was then, staring at Ernie's cupboard, that I thought back to the events of the day: I remembered a near-senile senator asking me if there was any hope of "patching things up" between me and Jimmy and my saying, "No, sir, no hope," as my lawyer had instructed me to. But was there no hope? Wasn't the whole thing my fault? And what had I let myself in for? Hat was divorcing his wife and I was divorcing Jimmy and I was going to marry Hat. Hat wanted to marry me, but did I want to marry Hat? And suddenly I knew that marrying Hat would be the same thing all over again; the sex thing wasn't right with him, as it had not been right with Jimmy. I thought, There is something wrong with me sexually. If it's not right with me and Hat, it's my fault. And then, trying to cheer up, I decided that at least with Hat it was better than it had been with Jimmy. Besides, the divorces were all in court. We'd gone this far: too late to back out. And

I thought, I like Hat and I can learn to overcome this sex thing.

And as I thought those gloomy thoughts, roars of laughter were coming from Ernie's living room. It was like a wake; it was a bunch of people celebrating the death of my marriage to Jimmy. I felt sick, and so, when the other women in the kitchen weren't looking in my direction, I let myself out of the back door and stood there in the moonlight in Ernie's little back garden, and I was physically sick. Where, a few minutes later, Ernie found me, sitting on his solitary garden chair, my head between my knees. I said no, I wasn't drunk, I'd had very little to drink, but I remember he ignored that and suggested a walk along the lake to clear my head. And so we climbed up a slope behind his garden and there was Beaver Lake, it's a park pond, not a lake, bright and unreal in the summer moonlight.

So Ernie and I walked along the edge of Beaver Lake, the guest of honor with the host, the noise of the party behind us. I don't think I was even aware of Ernie, I was so full of my own miseries. And then suddenly he walked a few quick paces ahead of me, wheeled back, and stood there blocking my path.

"Why were you crying, Maria?"

I stared at him in the moonlight. There was something frightening about him. "Aren't you happy?" he asked.

And I, like a fool, began to cry again and said, "No, I'm not."

He caught at my arm and gave it a little shake, he was so eager to get my whole attention. "I love you," he said. "I've never loved anyone before."

I stared at him. I thought he was drunk. I said to him, "But what about Sally?"

"That's not the same. I like Sally, but look, *you* should

know. A person can't choose who they fall in love with, can they? I'm in love with *you*, Maria. You're the worst possible person, you don't care about me, you probably never think of me, but I can't help that. I love you. I will always love you."

I will always love you. That is what he said, and tonight, in the kitchen, just before serving dinner, it came back to me. And something else came back too, something Janice Sloane said to me earlier, at lunch, something about Ernie Truelove having broken up "with that girl, Sally something," and I thought, My God, it's true, he's broken up with Sally because he thinks he's in love with me, the lunatic, he still thinks he's in love with me.

And that frightened me. For it is frightening to be loved by someone you don't love, someone you don't even .care about. And I remember thinking, What if Ernie starts going on to Terence about this love of his, what if he manages to make Terence believe that there was something between himself and me? Which sent me hurrying back into the living room, the dinner not ready, afraid to stay away, afraid to miss what mad Ernie might tell Tee.

When I walked back into the living room, Ernie did a strange thing. He sat up in his chair, put his legs together, sticking them straight out in front of him, then raised them up as though he were doing some gymnastic exercise. And there, his feet together balancing in the air, staring at his large black brogues, he pronounced: "Well, let me say this. I think New York is—well, decadent is the only word for it."

Tee was pouring another drink. "Umm," said Tee.

"Let me explain what I mean by that, Terence," Ernie said. "As I see it, there are three types of people in New York. First of all, there are the people who were born here. Ordinary people who live in the Bronx, or wherever. You follow?"

Tee nodded. I thought how bored he must be.

"That's one category. Then there is a second category. People like you, Terence, whose specialized skills bring them to New York. Well and good.

"That's the second category. The third category is different. And it's a big one, believe you me. And let me say this. The third category is the reason that, for me, at least, New York stinks."

He turned to me, showing his large horseteeth, hissing out the word "stinks."

"The third category," he said. "The third category is made up of no-talent jerks, people who come here from other towns and, because they live in New York, somehow they think they're better than the rest of us. Do you follow me, Terence?"

"Umm," said Terence.

Ernie put his glass to his mouth. He had finished his drink and now he crunched the ice cube with his large teeth.

"Another drink?" Terence asked, and Ernie thrust his glass rudely in Terence's direction, then turned mad eyes on me. "I saw a play last night, Maria."

"Any good?"

"Well, the main feature of this thee-atrical performance was that an actor got up on stage and gave the audience a look at his bare bum."

"The *Marat-Sade*," Terence said, handing Ernie far too big a Scotch.

"His bare bum," Ernie said. "Now if that isn't decadence, what is?" He took a gulp of the Scotch. "Well, I guess it's all we deserve, this fag theater. I suppose it's a natural reaction."

"Against what?" Terence asked politely.

"Against this female domination of the North American continent," Ernie said. "That's what."

Headshaking again, a Savonarola warning against the evils of the times. "Yes, I suppose we have to have something for the fags too. I mean, show them a few male bums to excite them. I mean, is that any different from these so-called actresses? I mean, how do you like that? There isn't one so-called actress in the business today who isn't ready to get up in front of an audience of total strangers and walk around showing her naked boobs, just like a whore. Now, isn't that something?"

Looking at me as he said it: his mad eyes. I thought of earlier, my robe open, those eyes of his glazed over as he stared at my breasts.

"Styles change," Tee said. "A few years ago topless men in blue jeans were all the rage at the box office."

But Ernie was not to be deflected. "*You* were an actress," he accused me. "Would you take off your bra if a director asked you to?"

I looked at him, and Mad Twin rose up inside me. "You don't know what you're talking about," I said to him. "There are plenty of actresses who won't do those things."

"Then they won't get any parts." Horseteeth showing. Horrid laugh. "No, nowadays it's strip or get off the pot."

I got up and said I had to put the chops on. As I went into the kitchen his voice pursued me, booming, fading, coming up again: ". . . like or not like . . . I don't know about that . . . take me, I was one of those children other children just don't like. And you know, Terence, that has carried over into my adult life. I am not someone that other people like."

Correct, I thought, but, oh, why did Tee give him so much to drink? I swear he's getting drunk, Canadians get drunk, they seem to glory in it. Tee never understands that, he doesn't know them as I do.

"You mean in Montreal?" I heard Ernie say.

"Yes," Tee said. "I believe the city is very much changed."

"Yes indeed, you wouldn't know the place nowadays. Exciting things are happening in Montreal. You should come up for a visit. You could stay with me, both of you."

Some mumble from Terence and then the boom of Ernie's reply. "No, no, I'd love to have you as my guests, both of you. It would be an honor having the famous Terence Lavery stay with me."

"I'm-not-famous-don't-be-silly," Terence said in an embarrassed rush.

"You're not stuck up, I'll say that," Ernie assured him. "I'll tell you a secret. I have a photo of you pinned up on my wall. One that appeared in the paper, of you and Maria, the time you were married. I had a print made up of it, and if anyone asks me, I say I know you. Not true, strictly speaking. I know Maria. But now it will be true. Because I've met you at last."

Mumble from Tee.

"I mean it's sort of like a pin-up, this photo," Ernie said. "You know. Pretending about girls."

"But you weren't pretending," Tee said. "You do know Mary and you said she's in the picture."

"Looking lovely. Just beautiful."

There was a silence and then Terence mumbled something and a moment later was beside me in the kitchen, raising his eyebrows, jerking his head toward the living room. I looked and saw Ernie out there, his back to me. He seemed to be blowing his nose.

Terence whispered, "We were talking about you. He said you were lovely. Then he began to weep. What's going on?"

I said, "Please. Go back in. I'll serve dinner in a moment."

It was a stupid thing to say, that thing about dinner. But I was flustered. I gave Tee an imploring look and he nodded and went back in. I began to rush the dinner, all the time trying to see and hear what was going on in there. Tee went back and sat on the sofa, his long legs crossed, his arms spread-eagled along the sofa's back. Ernie, facing him, sat forward in his chair, eager as a job applicant. And as I carried plates and dishes into the dining room I heard Ernie say, "Yes, my own writings. Yes, that was and is my ambition. Like Hat, Mary's husband. We both hoped to write something worth while."

I thought, I must keep him off Hat. I'll announce dinner. I went in, and as I did Ernie stopped talking and rose up with exaggerated politeness, gesturing for me to sit down. He staggered slightly.

"Ernie's been telling me about his writing," Tee said.

"My unpublished novel," Ernie said. "You're in it, Maria. Yes, yes, you're in it, all right. I have this marvelous scene between you and Mackie McIver. She still asks after you, you know."

"Oh," I said, very cold. "How is she?"

"Oh, same as ever. Any time I go to Toronto, I always drop in to see her at the library. And we talk about you. Funny. She's very fond of you, in a strange sort of way."

"Mmm," I said. I turned to Terence. "Tee, will you help me with the plates? Dinner's ready."

"Tee?" Ernie said. "A pet name, is it? I know Maria's a great one for pet names. Remember, Maria, you were the one who christened Mackie 'Mackie.' For Mack the Knife."

It had nothing to do with Mack the Knife, I thought. Where did he get that idea? And then, as we settled in at the table, Ernie still holding on to his Scotch, he took a drink and said drunkenly, "Yes-sss, it suited her too. She put the knife in you, didn't she? You know, telling Jimmy about you and Hat."

Quickly I snatched up the red-currant jelly and offered it to him. "Try some of this with your lamb."

He stared at the dish. "What is it?"

"Red-currant jelly."

"With lamb? I never heard of that."

"Perhaps it's a British taste?" Tee suggested.

"Mint sauce is British too," Ernie informed us. "*That* I do know. I must say, however, to be perfectly frank, I prefer mint jelly. That's the Canadian thing to have with lamb."

Tee stared at his plate. I thought, Why is it always my friends who are the really giant bores? Ah yes, Ernest True-love, what a brilliant conversationalist you are. Will you please shut up?

But oh, no. He was off again.

"Yes, I've noticed that about the British," he said. "They like those made-up sauces. HP sauce and A1 sauce and Worcestershire sauce and another one—let me think, yes, I remember, Lea and Perrin's sauce. No, I guess that's the Worcestershire one. Yes. Funny, isn't it, that they're so fond of all those sauces?"

"The cooking's so bad at home," Terence said, rising and pouring wine.

"Is that a fact?" Ernie said. "I've never been there, you know. Of course the poor eat very badly, right?"

Terence looked startled. "Yes, they do. As they do in most countries, I suppose."

"Ah, but in England you have this class thing. I hope I'm not offending you."

"Should I be offended?" Terence said, smiling.

"Well, you're upper-class, aren't you?"

Terence laughed. "My old mum would be very pleased to hear you say that. She's an awful snob."

"Yes," I said. "And she's a char at the Ministry of Transport offices in London."

"Char?" Ernie's head went up. "What's that?"

"Charwoman. Cleaning woman," Terence said.

"Ah, come on. You're having me on." Ernie laughed his horselaugh and gulped at his wine, but I saw that he was angry. "I may be a professional hick," he said, "but I do know an upper-class British accent when I hear it. You can't tell *me* you're working-class. Because I *am* working-class. My dad's a plumber in Brockville, Ontario."

"Well," said Terence, switching accents, "I do talk ever so nice, but you mustn't pay no heed to that. I'm a bloody great fraud, mate."

But Ernie was not amused. His face was red with drink and discomfiture.

"Honestly, Ernie, it's true," I found myself saying. "Terence won a scholarship to Oxford."

"Exactly," Ernie said. "Oxford University. It's a long way from Sir George Williams College, where I went. In Montreal. A YMCA school." He turned on Terence. "So let me say this. I don't know whether you're joking about your mother being a cleaning woman. But I am *not* joking. I am not middle-class. No one could ever take me for middle-class."

He turned to me. "You, Maria," he said, "you're middle-class. Your father was a stockbroker, wasn't he?"

"No," I said, "he was not a stockbroker, how could he have been? You don't have stockbrokers in a place like Butchersville. My father was a small-town businessman with a lumber business that went bust, and if it hadn't been for the war, God knows what would have happened to him."

Terence had begun to laugh, seesawing over his plate of food. "My old man, yes, my old man's a bigger bust than your old man—talk about snobs."

I looked at Ernie, sure that this would be the final insult, but there he was, beginning to break up himself, old

Ernie, turning, pointing to me. "Isn't that funny, her boasting about her old man—failed, lumber—yes, I agree, that *is* rare. *Rare*."

I sat and stared at them and felt as I did long ago when boys laughed at me because I was a girl, and I said to myself, Terence is not disloyal to me, he's just trying to smooth things over, but it *seemed* disloyal and I found myself with tears coming into my eyes, and then, worse, their laughing stopped and they looked at me, concerned.

"It was just a joke," Ernie said. "Just a joke, Maria." And I saw Tee look worried and I thought, He believes I'm mad, yes he does, and anything to stop him thinking *that*, so I began babbling, sounding rambling and disconnected, I suppose. I don't remember, but I remember lying and saying my tears had nothing to do with their laughing at me, they had to do with something unpleasant that happened to me earlier, something I'd just remembered.

Of course they both asked what it was, this unpleasant thing, and, I don't know why, I found myself starting to tell them about the man who insulted me in the street this morning. And when I said this man, a well-dressed, normal-seeming man, had said something filthy to me, Ernie's face went suddenly eager. "Said what?" he asked. "I mean what exactly did he say?"

"Oh, just something obscene."

"But *what?*" he persisted, and, angry with him, I thought, All right, Ernie Truelove, you asked for it. I leaned in Ernie's direction, stared into his blind amber-flecked eyes, and said, "Well, this man said to me, 'I'd like to fuck you, baby.'"

Ernie's face tightened. I mean I actually saw the skin tighten, saw his ears go flat. He put down his fork very deliberately and sat, his blind stare fixed on his plate. A perfect blush spread from his jaw up his cheeks as he contemplated again what the stranger had said. "Gosh," said

Ernie. "Gosh, and yet"—he turned to Terence—"do you know, Terence, I sometimes say to myself, Well, there but for the grace of the five hundred miles that separate me from a woman like Maria, well, there go I."

I don't think Terence understood. "What?" said Terence, pouring wine into Ernie's glass.

"I mean, I could be that man," Ernie said. He looked at Terence, then at me, as though daring us to contradict him. He picked up his knife and fork and cut a piece off his chop.

"I'm mentioning this," he said, "because it might interest Terence. Creative persons are often interested in hearing about abnormal states of mind." He laughed and raised the piece of meat to his mouth. "Such as love," he said. He put the meat into his mouth and began to chew and talk all at once. "Yes," he said, "love. Let me tell you, Terence, what happened to me nine years ago. I'd come down to Toronto for the day for a meeting at our main office at *Canada's Own*. After my conference with MacKinnon, our chief, I went into the library to look up something. And there she was."

Still chewing, he turned to me, his mouth half open, showing the food particles. "Yes," he said. "Maria. I can even remember what she was wearing, it was what they call a shirtwaist dress with red and black—no, it was pink and black candy stripes. I remember the pink matched the pink of her lips. And I remember I asked her for some files and she brought them to me, but, you know, I didn't do a stitch of work. I just sat there until plane time. And let me say this. I was in love. Yes indeedy."

"Of course," Terence said, trying to make a joke of it, "that famous Dunne mesmerism."

"Yes, yes," Ernie said. "And do you know, although I didn't see her again for four months—four whole months —I don't think there was a single day I didn't think about her. And you'd better believe this. I didn't even know she was married. I never even noticed her wedding ring. Isn't that something?"

"Umm," said Tee.

"I guess I'm talking too much?"

"My ears are burning," I said. "Come on, let's change the subject."

"Change the subject?" Ernie fixed me in his stare. "Why, you changed this subject, all right, all right. Me. You changed my whole life."

"Come on," I said. "What an exaggeration."

He shook his head, staring at me. "Oh, no," he said. "Oh, no, it's not."

He stared at me. I stared at him, at this forgotten admirer who said I changed his life. In the carnival hall of mirrors which is our memory we distort what we see. In Ernie's mirror image of me, I am magnified, elongated into a girl who led him on, the object of his great, unhappy, unfulfilled love. While he, in the equal if opposite distortion of my mind's mirror, is reduced to a squat manikin from my past, a dull stranger, remembered only for his minor quirks.

I stared at him as, guiltily, he gulped his wine. "I know," he said. "I'll bet I'm boring Maria. In the past she often brought it to my attention that I bored her. And it's true, I'm not very interesting. I know. But perhaps Terence would be interested?"

In the living room the phone began to ring.

"I'll get it," I said to Tee.

"No, I'll get it, it's for me, most likely."

There was no escape, Tee was up and out of the dining room. The phone stopped ringing and Ernie and I sat there, embarrassed. Tee's voice from the living room: "Hello? . . . Yes, how'd it go? . . . Mnn . . . mnn."

While Ernie slewed around in his chair. "Alone at last."

"What did you say?" I said, making my voice as cold as I knew.

"Philadelphia?" Terence said on the phone. "Why not New Haven?"

"Why did you never phone me when you went back to Montreal?" Ernie asked.

"I forgot."

"Are you mad at me, Maria?"

"Well," I said, "wouldn't you be, if you were me? Going on about my not phoning you. I've only been back in Montreal twice, both times on very short visits. I can't phone everybody. I'm sorry."

"Am I everybody?"

"How many weeks?" Terence said on the phone. "Five?"

"Ernie, don't be silly. I told you. I forgot."

"All right, then you forgot. I suppose, gosh, I suppose that's the ultimate, yes, the ultimate insult. You forgot. That takes care of me, doesn't it?"

"Please," I said. "I'm not feeling well tonight. Let's not start some big thing."

"Put Jack on," Terence said on the phone.

"I still love you," Ernie said to me, glancing back surreptitiously into the living room as he said it.

"Oh, that's nonsense."

"I do."

"Oh, shut up. How could you?"

"How *could* I? Because I can, because I do, because I can't help myself. I told you all that. Don't tell me you don't remember?"

"But I don't."

"Oh, come on, Maria." He stared at me reproachfully.

"Look," I said, and now I too was glancing back furtively at the living room, where Tee was. "All I remember is you took me out to dinner a few times while I was waiting

186

for Hat to come back from Europe. You knew I was going to marry Hat. I told you."

"You did not," he said, nearly shouting. He peered drunkenly over his shoulder at the living room, then faced me again. "You did not," he said more quietly.

"Well, I thought I did, but never mind. There was nothing between you and me. What business was it of yours what was going on with my private life?"

"I was in love with you," he said. "That's what business it was."

"No, no, put Jack on again," Tee said to the phone.

"All right," I said to Ernie (thinking, This is stupid, it's degrading, how did I ever get into it?). "But I never said I was in love with *you*."

He hung his head. "You let me think you were."

"When?"

"Those times I took you out."

"I don't remember anything of the kind."

"But you do remember I took you out?"

"So have a lot of other men."

"Oh, Maria," he said. "Don't, please. That night you stayed over at my place, we discussed it all night long. I'll never forget that night, Maria. Never. I've never been the same since."

I did not answer. I looked into his drink-stunned eyes and thought, *I don't remember*. What does he mean, I stayed over at his place? I did not remember.

In the next room, Tee's voice said, "No, that was the first option, I believe. Check it and you'll see."

I thought, Nothing ever happened between me and Ernie, that's nonsense. And then, in panic, I thought, What if there *is* something wrong with my memory, some Jekyll-and-Hyde thing? What if I've done things I simply don't remember?

I sat staring at him. I heard myself say, "Ernie, that was—well, it was a long time ago."

"For you, maybe," he said. "For me, it—gosh, it's—gosh, it's as clear as the night it happened."

"When *what* happened?" I was shaking and he saw that I was shaking and that seemed to excite him.

"You may say you don't remember," he said in a loud, indignant voice. "You say you don't remember it, gosh, you say you don't remember what was the most important and most—gosh, the most emotional evening in my whole life."

His eyes glaring; it's catching, hysteria, I could feel it starting up in me as we faced each other, hysterically aroused, the food forgotten, even Terence forgotten. It was as though Ernie and I were alone in the apartment. And then, very deliberately, in the loud, overemphasized voice of a drunk person, Ernie began to speak again. "Oh, yes, Maria, I suppose you'd like to forget that. You have a talent for forgetting what really happened, haven't you? You use people, then you let them drop. Yes, my Lord, when I think of it, the roll-call of the fallen, yes, the ones who've fallen out of your favor, like Jimmy Phelan, I only met him once or twice, but he was a very nice guy. A *very* nice guy. And poor Mackie McIver, all right so she said some things about you and Hat, and why not, she was fond of Jimmy too but anyway, dammit, that woman was like a mother to you, she put you through acting school, you lived in her house, and I happen to know you never write or phone her, oh, yes, you let her drop, just like you let me drop, just like you let Hat drop. Poor Hat, waiting for you all those months. God, when I think of it. Goddammit, Hat was my best friend."

And while I heard all the rest of it, it was that that I fastened on, Ernie as Hat's best friend, it struck me as ludicrous, it made everything else he said suspect. "Hat's best friend?" I said. "Oh, come on, Ernie. It's not so."

"It is so!" he shouted. "I was with Hat the night he died. I was the last person to talk to him, the last person he saw."

Once before, I was told the details of a death. Ralph Davis read the report of the inquest and told my brother, who told me how the hotel maid in the Park Plaza in New York knocked on the room door at eleven in the morning, got no answer, went in, using her passkey, saw the man on the bed, began to back out, thinking him still asleep, then saw his opened eyes, staring at the ceiling. How she went out, locking the door again as she had been instructed to do in such cases, and ran down the corridor to use the house phone. And when Ernie said he was the last person to talk to Hat, I thought of the last person who must have talked to my father, the woman (whoever she was) who checked into the hotel with him the previous afternoon. They must have undressed and got into bed right away, for the coroner put the time of death as late afternoon or early evening. I see my father begin to make love, then slump over and die. I see the woman's fear as she tries to revive him. I see her stare at his open eyes, wondering whether to close them and cover him up, but she cannot do that, for then the authorities would know someone was with him at the time of his death. So she gets out of bed, puts on her clothes, and leaves the room, closing the door on him. It grows dark; he lies through the night, dead eyes staring at the ceiling, the glare of the New York sky casting its red pall over his naked body. First light, then morning sunlight and, at eleven, a passkey in the door, his vigil ended.

I sat and remembered it all, saw that which I never really saw. When my father died, I was two thousand miles away in school. If Ralph Davis had not told Dick and Dick had not repeated the story to me, I would never have known it. I would be a different woman today. I did not want Ernie to tell me how Hat had died. He died in Montreal, and he died suddenly, was all that man said that night at Molly Lupowitz's party.

But there was Ernie, mad Ernie, glaring, and, God, I'd have done I don't know what to get off the subject of death, so I said, "The evening—I mean the evening you were talking about, the night you say I stayed over at your place, when was that, Ernie? Please, I'm not pretending, it's just that there's something funny with my memory today, I can't remember things. I mean I can't remember *anything*."

Which seemed to mollify him a bit, for he picked up the wine bottle, poured the dregs of it into his glass, drank it in a swallow, nodded, leaned forward, nodded again, and said, "All right. Very good, let's assume, yes, let's assume you're not kidding me. Yes, we assume that. You don't recall that evening which, as I said, was the most important, the most emotional evening of my whole life. Well, where does that leave me, Maria? Hmm? I'll tell you where. It leaves me looking like what I am, no doubt, a goddam stupid fool to be in love with a woman like you. A *fool*."

"Ernie," I said, "I wasn't trying to hurt you, honestly, I wasn't. I just—I mean, I'm terribly confused today."

"Yes, Maria," he said, "I would say you are confused. Perhaps you forget these things because you simply cannot face remembering them. But now, let me say this. I don't think you should be allowed to forget them. You know the maxim: those who cannot remember history are condemned to repeat it? Do you really want to repeat your life? *Do* you?"

"No," I said. "I suppose not."

"All righty. Then I will tell you what happened that evening. Let's see." And he began to talk. After a minute Terence re-entered the dining room and sat down again at the table. But Ernie paid no attention. He had begun his tale. He was the Ancient Mariner; he fixed us with drunken eye: we were captive.

"Do you remember the beginning of that night, Maria? Do you remember I was sitting in the downstairs bar of the Tour Eiffel with Hat? It was about eight in the evening and we'd been there about two hours and old Hat was getting stoned. I'd been helping him on a story, doing the legwork on it, yes, and anyway, there we were, Hat and I, shooting the breeze at the bar, when who walked in but the one person in the world who can make my heart stop. You just stood there in the doorway, looking at us, not saying anything, and Hat looked over and saw you. I remember he said, very offhand, 'Hello, there. Join us, won't you?' But you ignored that and walked past us and sat down at a table in the corner of the room. And Hat turned to me and went on talking in that high voice of his, but I couldn't keep up my end of the conversation, Maria, not with you there. I mean, any time I'm in the same room with you—even now—I feel so excited, I have—well, I feel sort of breathless, you know?"

"Oh, Ernie, for goodness' sake."

"No, really, I mean it."

"All right, you mean it," I said. "But please, can't we talk about something else?"

"Have some more wine," Terence said, rising, going to the sideboard for another bottle, but as he went past me he gave me an odd sidelong look which made my heart begin to race again. What must he be thinking? Did he think there was something between me and this damn Ernie? Angry and afraid, wishing that my heart would quiet down, I turned to Ernie, and, oh God, Ernie was crying. Tears were in his eyes, childish tears, a childish grief, unconcealed, unashamed.

Behind me at the sideboard I heard a popping sound, as Terence pulled the cork from a bottle of wine. And in the silence of the moment that followed we both heard Ernie sob. It was awful.

"What's wrong, Ernie?" I asked foolishly. "Aren't you feeling well?"

"I-I-I—" he began, but could not go on, relapsing into his harsh sobbing.

"Look," I said, trying to sound cheerful, "let's you and I talk about this some other time. After all," I said with a false laugh, "poor Terence has had enough of my former life told him by me—enough to last him a lifetime."

Ernie, still sobbing, swiveled around in his chair, caught his breath audibly, stared up at Terence with naked tear-wet face—Terence, who, stiff with embarrassment, came forward from the sideboard and hastily poured great dollops of wine into our three glasses. "But Terence seems," Ernie began, "I mean he seems a nice guy. And if he wouldn't mind too much, I'd like to recall that night for Maria, I mean to get it off my chest, as they say. I feel it would be a great help—if Terence doesn't mind too much?"

"I don't mind," Terence said in a rush of embarrassment.

"Well, thank you." Ernie took a wad of yellow Kleenex from his pants pocket, blew his nose, seeming to get hold of himself. Uneasily Tee sat down, putting the bottle of wine on the table next to Ernie, then turned to me with a look which tried to make a joke of all this. Of course it wasn't a joke and he knew it, but his look calmed me a bit. At least he was on my side.

"So," Ernie said, "to go back to that evening." He nodded, leaned forward, then nodded again, as though he had just found his place in a book he had been reading. "Anyway, I think, he, I mean Hat, had a date with you and he'd forgotten. And you guessed where you might find him. Right?"

I nodded. It wasn't hard to know where to find Hat in those days.

"Anyway, there you were, Maria, sitting in a corner of the Tour Eiffel bar, and there was Hat, talking to me. A waiter went over to get your order and then came back to us at the bar. And said to me, 'Excuse me, sir, but that lady wishes to speak to you.' And of course I thought the waiter had made a mistake, so I turned to Hat and said, 'She means you.' But the waiter said, 'No, sir. You,' and pointed to me, and I looked back at you, Maria, and you nodded, yes, so I went over to you and, remember, you asked me to buy you a drink? And, by golly, I did, I sat right down beside you and ordered and there we were, chatting away, just the two of us, my gosh, me and my dream girl."

"A-hem," said Terence, grinning at me. "Let's have some coffee, shall we?"

"I'll get it," I said, jumping up, but Ernie looked at me. "Please?" he said. Terence gestured to me to sit and, defeated, I sat while Ernie went on with his tale. "So, anyway," he said, "the waiter brought our drinks, and there we were, Maria, sitting together at the table in the corner, and just as you raised your glass and said, 'Cheers,' old Hat got down off his bar stool and weaved across the room. I can still see him standing over us, staring down at us. He looked at me, then at you, and he said to you, 'Haven't you made a mistake? I thought *I* was your dinner date.' And you said, 'No, I'm going to ask Ernie if he'll buy me dinner. He's taken me out lots of times.' 'When?' said Hat. 'When you were running around Europe this summer.' And when you said that, Maria, Hat glared at us, remember?"

"I've told you, Ernie, I don't remember."

"But you *must* remember that. Those mad black eyes Hat had. Glaring at us. I'll never forget it."

I looked over at Tee, who sat, head down, staring at the place mat.

"Yes," Ernie said. "I used to be afraid of Hat, you know. Anyway, he looked at us and then he said, 'Who'd believe it? May-ree-and-her-True-love, Mary's little True-love'— you know, sort of singing it, sneering, you know. And you just got up—oh, you were terrific, Maria—you got up and you picked up your gin and tonic and you up-ended it over his head, oho, you should have seen that, Terence, the gin and tonic running through Hat's hair and down his face, and Maria here said to him, 'Sober up,' and went right past him and walked out, and I went after her, and then the waiter ran up the stairs after us, so I paid the bill and as I paid the tab I could see old Hat still standing there by the table and he was toweling his wet hair off with a waiter's napkin; I suppose it was funny, I suppose you could call it comic, but you know, Maria, it wasn't funny to me, because all my life people have made fun of me, and if you're called Ernest Truelove, what else can you expect?

"But that night you, Maria, you made up for all of that. Yes, and we went to dinner, I remember we ate in the La Salle Hotel, the old downstairs room with checked tablecloths, it isn't even there any more, and we had wine with dinner and talked a lot and I remember realizing that you were very emotional about what had just happened, the row with Hat, and because of that the drinks sort of hit you; anyway, what I'm trying to say is that you got high, I guess, while I stayed sober, and we went from the La Salle, back to my place, remember, on the mountain, near Beaver Lake, and I broke out a bottle of Napoleon brandy that Sally had brought me back from the duty-free shop on her trip to Europe, and we settled down to some serious drinking then. Gosh, I guess you don't remember that, but all of a sudden, Maria, you stopped talking for a while and sat there, and then you said it was a mistake, this idea of your marrying Hat Bell, that you couldn't be happy with anybody and you knew it, that you were unlucky to yourself and unlucky for other people as well, and that your father had come to a bad end or something, and that you would too.

"You see how well I remember it, Maria, yes, I can see you sitting there on my rug, sitting at that picture window I have that looks out on a view of Montreal, all the lights lit below us, and you talking and me sitting opposite you, listening to you, and the lights began to go out as the dawn came into the room. Terence, maybe you'll understand it better than Maria here, because Maria doesn't even remember it, she says she doesn't, but anyway, it was dawn and she'd just finished telling me she wasn't at all sure she should marry Hat Bell, that she could never make anybody happy—anyway, suddenly I got all my courage up and I said to her, 'Maria,' I said, 'if you married me, I wouldn't care if you made me happy. Just being near you would be more happiness than I could ever hope for. Because I love you, Maria, I really do love you, I love you the way no one else loves you. I mean unselfishly—*unselfishly*. Why, listen,' I said, 'if you don't want to marry Hat Bell and you want to get away—to Europe, say—I'll give you two-thirds of my salary, no strings attached, no questions asked, and you just go away for a year, or for as long as you like.'

"And, golly, you'd better believe it, Maria, when I said that in the dawn, years ago, I meant it, I meant every word of it, I still mean it, come to think of it, for if you love someone, really love them, it doesn't matter what they've done or will do, it doesn't matter about their goodness or badness, or what sort of person they are, for if you say you would kill for them or be killed for them, then what does good or evil mean?"

"That's nonsense, Ernie," I began, but he held up his large hand as though to silence me, then turned to Terence and said, "No, I'll bet Terence knows what I mean. Anyway, as I was saying, it was dawn that morning and I'd made this declaration to you and we were sitting facing each other on my rug and suddenly you leaned toward me, Maria, your eyes shut, your face tilted up as though waiting for a kiss, and I remember how I felt, it's far too intimate to describe in front of a third person, but anyway, we kissed each other, and I'll never forget that moment when I kissed you, Maria, I'll remember it all my life. I'm sorry, I know I'm out of line, but I just want to tell you one thing. Just one thing. And that is: I would live my life over again just for that one moment, yes, I'd put up with my childhood and my name and people making fun of me, nobody really liking me—yes, and the worst of it is that I don't blame people for not liking me, because even *I* despise people like me and I know in my heart that I'm not like Terence, although I want to be; I know in my heart that everything I've ever done or ever will do will somehow be third-rate, yes, even my novel I'm writing, the book I have such dreams for, yes."

His blind eyes, bloodshot from tears, from drinking, sought me as though he waited for me to say something. I sat stiff and I controlled my trembling; but my heart frightened me. I said, "Have you finished?"

"Yes, I have finished, at least I guess I have. I guess that's it, that's all, that's my big story. Boring, isn't it? I know. What I don't know is why I inflicted it on you, on both of you, for really, I guess, its importance is all in my mind; you don't even remember it, Maria. You were kind of high at the time and it was just a kiss, nothing happened, except that you said you were fond of me—"

"Look," Terence said, "you've finished this story, haven't you?"

There, in the dining room, amid the wreck of dinner, glasses, dishes, wine bottles, there settled on all three of us an instant of total immobility, as though the film of our lives had jammed. We sat, frozen in stop frame, until suddenly Ernie's head jerked forward and he turned to me, his face screwed up in a painful parody of a boy's embarrassed grin. "Yes," he said, "I guess I have finished. Eh, Maria? Golly, I've gone and done it again. Made a fool of myself, imposed on people's kindness, irritated the people I most want to be friends with. You and Terence. Golly."

Having castigated himself, he, like all those people who are quick to apologize, considered himself at once forgiven. He grinned again and said, "What a horse's ass I am. I'll bet that's what you're thinking?"

Terence, embarrassed and angry, shook his head and stood up. "Let's go inside and have a brandy."

I said I would get coffee and I remember that in the kitchen, pouring water into the Melitta filter, hearing Terence open the sideboard to get brandy glasses, I felt my heart again, so loud and hard inside me that I wondered, My God, what if it's *not* nerves, what if there is something wrong with me, what if it's a rheumatic heart or something like that I don't even know about, what if I topple over here in the kitchen and die, it would serve Ernie right, coming in here and starting up all this fuss and nonsense, I suppose I did use him that night long ago, because I wanted to get back at Hat, but it shows you, if you use people you pay for it, as tonight I am paying, years later, for that one silly kiss I gave Ernie. And as I stood there in the kitchen getting the coffee, I heard Ernie's loud voice say, "No, I thought maybe at the funeral. I was expecting *her,* I guess, not you. I thought she'd probably come up on her own."

"She didn't know anything about it," Tee's voice said.

"But what about my telegram? I sent her a telegram."

"Oh?"

"Yes, advising her. You know, I was sharing my apartment with Hat at the time he died."

"I didn't know that," Tee's voice said.

"Yes, we were very close in the last year or two. I was his best friend, poor guy. I made all the funeral arrangements, notified his family, notified everybody. And Maria. I definitely remember sending her the wire."

Tee muttered something I didn't catch. My hands shook so I had to put the kettle down and sit down. I put the kettle on the kitchen table. I sat at the kitchen table and laid my cheek against the table's wooden surface, and when I did my eyes were reflected in the aluminum of the kettle beside me, my eyes were like my father's dead eyes, Hat's dead eyes, and in nightmare I saw Mama dead too, lying now on the kitchen floor in Butchersville, the wind from under the doorjamb blowing her gray hair into her dead, staring eyes—

"Mary, what's the matter? Are you sick?"

Tee was at the kitchen door. He came to me, sat on the chair with me, put his arm around me, and felt me tremble, felt me shake, saw the state I was in, but I wasn't afraid of him any more, he was alive, he was life, not death. I held him and I thought, He is my savior, he restoreth my soul. I heard him ask again what was wrong and all the unreasoning, unreasonable emotions of my state spilled out beyond my control and I held him, kissed him, weeping, saying, "Tee, Tee, I love you, please love me?"

"Of course. Of course. I do."

"And that damn Ernie," I said. "I'm sorry I asked him, but please, I don't want to talk about deaths or funerals, about Hat, you know, I just don't feel up to it."

Tee got up, shut the kitchen door, then said, "Look, I'll say you're sick, you have a sick headache or something. You don't have to put up with that bloody man. He's bonkers. Now, don't worry, you're fine, you'll be fine. Come on, we'll go in there and you'll say good night to him and then I'll have a coffee with him and get rid of him."

"But I can't do that, I can't leave you."

"You can and you will," Tee said. "Come on, now."

He took my arm and opened the kitchen door and we went in to meet Ernie, who turned from the window, brandy sniffer in hand, and I had been right, he did wear glasses, for as he turned to face us he whipped off a pair with that curious vain, guilty look of a person who is trying to conceal the fact that he wears glasses. He shut the hinges with a *clack,* stuffed the glasses in the side pocket of his navy blazer, advancing on us, showing his teeth in a false smile. "We-ell, arm in arm, the perfect picture of young love. I will say you two make a handsome couple. Yes, I'd say that."

"I'm afraid Mary's not feeling well," Tee said. "She has a sort of sick headache and I've convinced her we wouldn't mind if she simply says good night and climbs into bed with a couple of aspirins. Don't you agree?"

"A sick headache," Ernie said. "Well, that's—ah, yes, that's bad. I'm sorry."

"*I*'m sorry," I said. "But I'm afraid I'm not much company for anyone when I'm feeling like this."

"It's all right, don't worry, I'm sure Ernie understands," Tee said hastily.

"Of course, of course," Ernie boomed. "Now you go on to bed. Gee, it was great seeing you again, Maria, just great, good of you to invite me, it just about made my whole trip to New York, and say, listen, I'm sorry if I went on too much about the past, et cetera, but I guess you know now that you're on my mind most of the time; anyway, I mustn't keep you standing there with that splitting headache, I'll just say good night and push on now."

"No need to rush off," Terence said to him. "Stay and have a nightcap with me. I believe Mary made coffee."

"Yes," I said, "it's all made."

"No, no, I really must go, I've imposed quite enough."

"Well . . ." Tee said, giving in.

"Yes, I must," Ernie said again.

"Well, in that case," Tee said. "Yes, and it was—ah, yes —nice meeting you."

By that time Tee, in some mysterious way, had stage-managed Ernie out of the living room and into the hall and Ernie had picked his horrible brown cocoa-straw hat off the captain's chest by the front door. My heart stopped being so loud. My tremor diminished. "Yes, and nice meeting you," Ernie was saying to Tee. "As you know, I told you, I'm one of your greatest fans. Yes, indeed."

"Good-by, Ernie," I said. "And take care."

"Good-by, Maria. And don't forget you promised to give me a ring when you come to Montreal."

"Yes," I said.

"Good-by, then."

"Good-by, Ernie," Tee said, opening the apartment door.

"Oh. One thing." Ernie paused by the captain's chest, hat in hand, turning back to me. "Just for curiosity's sake, I mean, I was talking to Terence just now and it came up, I mean about a telegram I sent you telling you about Hat's death. Apparently you never received it?"

I shook my head. Down Tilt.

"Then—I mean, did you get the letter, the one I sent on a few days later?"

"What letter?"

"A letter Hat wrote to you the afternoon of his death."

"A letter?" I said dumbly.

"Yes, he spent the afternoon writing it."

"But what letter? I never got any letter."

"Well," said Ernie, "I mailed it out to you. It was addressed to you, but there were no stamps on it. So when I sent you the telegram telling you Hat was dead, I held on to the letter, thinking I'd—ah—I'd give it to you when you came up to Montreal for the funeral. Then, when you didn't come, I mailed it on to you, here in New York."

"Where did you mail it to, what address?"

"To—ah, to Gramercy Park."

"You sent the telegram there too?" Terence asked.

"Yes."

"Well, that explains it," Terence said. "We weren't living at Gramercy Park then. We moved here over a year ago."

"But the letter," I said. "I mean, why wasn't it forwarded? What happened to it?"

"I don't know," Terence said.

"Gee." Ernie shook his head. "You never got it? Gee, I often wondered about that letter, I even thought of getting in touch with you about it. At the inquest, you know, they asked if Hat left any message and I said, 'No,' because, strictly speaking, that wasn't a message, was it?"

Through the opened front door of the apartment I could see one of our neighbors, an old lady with a wen on her forehead, passing down toward the elevator, listening in. I leaned over, took Ernie's sleeve, drew him back into the apartment hall, and shut the door. "Now," I said. "What message? What inquest?"

"Darling, take it easy," Terence said. "Relax, it's all right, calm down."

"*What* inquest?"

"Well, there was an inquest," Ernie said. "He was under psychiatric care during those last months."

"With Ranald MacMurtry? Dr. MacMurtry?"

"Yes, your friend, wasn't he?" Ernie said. "He testified

at the inquest, I remember he said Hat was a manic-depressive. There was the question of whether it was suicide or an accident."

"Suicide?" I must have been too loud or quavery, for Tee patted my arm as if to quiet me.

"Yes, the autopsy showed he died of a combination of barbiturates and alcohol. He started drinking again after you left, you know. And then, after a couple of bad bouts, he went back to this Dr. MacMurtry, and things went better for a while. He stopped drinking. But about a week before he died I noticed he'd begun nipping at the bottle again. And just about that time he began talking about you. That was always a bad sign. Anyway, that Saturday afternoon I was watching the Grey Cup game on television and he—ah—he didn't come in to watch, and that was funny, he was a football fan, as you know, but anyway, when I went out to the kitchen to get me a beer, there he was sitting at the kitchen table with his portable and a bottle of Scotch, and he'd written sheets and sheets of typescript pages and while I got the beer he addressed an envelope and folded all the sheets and stuffed them in and he said, 'I want to send this to New York airmail, how much do you think it will be?' Well, I have a little postage scale in my room so I took the letter and weighed it and we didn't have enough stamps in the apartment, so he said, 'Look, if I don't get to the office on Monday morning, will you promise me you'll mail this? It's important.' Well, of course, when I'd weighed it I'd glanced at the address and seen it was addressed to you, so I said something comical like 'I see you're writing my dream girl again,' but he just gave me a sour look, you know, and took up the Scotch bottle and went into the living room and asked how the game was going. And that was it; we watched the end of the game together. I was going out to a dinner party later, it was Saturday night, you know, Saturday night in Montreal, so I showered and dressed and when I was leaving, about seven or so, Hat was still sitting at the TV set, and I noticed he'd pretty well killed the bottle, so I said to him, 'Look,' I said, 'there's all kinds of food in the fridge, you'd better eat some of it if you want to stay in shape.' He looked up at me and he said, 'Good-by, Ernie. Enjoy yourself.' And that was it. I went out and came back late and went to bed and it wasn't until next morning, the Sunday, I woke up about noon and the door of his bedroom was still shut so when I made coffee I thought I'd bring him a cup to wake him up and when I went in there he was on the bed, lying on his stomach—"

"All right," Terence said, "let's skip the details."

"Oh. Yes, gee, sorry, Maria."

"And there was an inquest?" I asked.

"Yes, like I told you. Apparently he'd gone to bed sloshed and he took some sleeping pills, and then probably woke and took some more. You know, when he was drunk he'd forget what he'd taken. Anyway, it was an overdose. They found about fifteen pills in his stomach. That was what did it."

"Oh, Mary," Terence said, for I was trembling. I must have looked as though I was about to keel over. Terence led me back into the living room and sat me down on the sofa. Ernie came and stood at the door of the living room. I remember looking up at Ernie, at that smug, sneaky face, and I thought, Was the letter sealed or did he read it? I wouldn't be at all surprised if he did.

"Was the letter sealed, I mean the letter to me?"

"Sure, gosh, yes, of course. All I did was put stamps on it."

I looked at Terence, who sat beside me on the sofa, his arm around me. "Tee, what if the letter is still there, I mean at the Gramercy Park address?"

"No, no," Terence said. "The mail has all been forwarded to us. They still send it on, even the junk mail."

"Was there a return address on the letter?" I asked Ernie.

"I don't remember—ah—I don't think so."

"Then, maybe the letter's in the Dead Letter office?" I said.

"Hardly." Ernie shook his head. "No, I happen to know that after six months the post office destroys them."

"Are you sure?"

"Look, Mary," Terence said, "I don't want to make an issue of this, but the point is, Hat is dead and this letter didn't exist for you until Ernie brought it up. I very much doubt that you could ever find it now and, even if you did, what good would it do to read it?"

"Well, it might answer the question of suicide, for one thing," Ernie said.

"And what good will that do anybody? He's dead, isn't he?"

"It would set *my* mind at rest," Ernie said.

"And Mary's mind? What if the letter's a diatribe against her? You were telling us earlier that nobody loves Mary the way you do; well, if you love her so much, Mr. Truelove, I don't know why you're so anxious that she read a letter which might hurt her."

"*Touché*," Ernie said loudly. "Yes, *touché*. And I notice you're no different from anybody else, Terence, despite the fact that you're supposed to be a creative and sensitive person. You couldn't resist getting that dig in about my name, could you?"

"You wet idiot," Terence said. "Who cares about you or your name?"

"Please," I said. "Please, just don't fight."

"I'm sorry, darling," Terence said, but Ernie wasn't having any of that, he was all heavy breathing and drunk stare, his head lowering as though he were going to charge. "Oh, yes, let's not fight." He mimicked me. "Yes, let's shove everything under the rug and forget it. Yes, Maria, that's your style, all right."

Terence stood up suddenly. Ernie at once backed off, hunching his shoulders in a defensive boxer's stance. "Terence," I said. I was hysterical. "For God's sake," I said.

"All right," Terence said. "But he'd better leave."

"Yes, get rid of me," Ernie jeered. "It's painful to be reminded, isn't it?"

"Out," Terence said. He moved on Ernie, and at that moment the tension inside me, my hammering heart, my shaking, my wanting to scream, to weep, all of that, all of what I call Mad Twin, exploded in me, and I (or Mad Twin) got up, pushed myself between the two men, pushing Terence away, taking hold of Ernie Truelove by the front of his blazer and shaking him, yes, shaking him, while a voice I did not know as mine shouted out, "What do you mean, my style? What am I to be reminded of? *Did* you read Hat's letter or didn't you?"

And as I shouted this at Ernie, Terence had taken hold of me and was pulling me away, saying, "Mary, come on, darling, come on, get a hold of yourself, darling."

"No, no, I want to know, he's just accused me of causing somebody's death, he's just said it was suicide. Well, was it?"

"Nobody knows, it was probably an accident," Terence said.

But Mad Twin would not be calmed. "All right, but what about this letter, what did it say? I bet *he* knows, I'm sure he read it before he mailed it, he's the sort who would read it, you did read it, didn't you?"

Ernie: his head jerked up as though I had aimed a blow at him. His stare: drunken, dulled, yet frightened by my hysteria. "Golly, Maria. Honest. Cross my heart, I didn't."

"Are you sure? Listen, I'd rather you had, I mean, I want to know."

"Word of honor, Maria, I never read it."

"But it was a long letter, you know that much? Sheets and sheets, you said?"

"Yes, it was."

"Well, then, what do you think was in it? What did he say about me in those months, what did he say at the end?"

"Do you really think you should go on with this?" Terence asked.

"I have to, I have to know, I mean was it suicide, or wasn't it? Was it because of my leaving him, or what? I've got the rest of my life to worry about this."

"Well, if you really want to know—" Ernie said, and stopped.

"Yes, I do, go on."

"Well, he used to say—I mean, to complain that you never wrote to him."

"But why should I? We were divorced."

"I know, golly, it doesn't make sense, I used to tell him that myself. But he kept thinking he would hear from you."

"That's ridiculous."

"I know, Maria, but he—well, look, you'd better believe it, he was a bit odd there at the end. I mean —oh, about ten days before he died he got this crazy idea that you were in town. You weren't, were you?"

"In Montreal? Of course not."

"Well, Hat thought so. We phoned all the hotels, and then we decided you were perhaps staying with some friends."

"*We* decided? What do you mean?"

"Well, gee, you know, I love you too, I was interested too. And, besides, golly, well, I always did old Hat's research for him."

"Oh God," I said and laughed. I suppose I was hysterical.

"Anyway," Ernie said, "after I'd phoned and asked

around I was sure Hat was wrong and I told him so. But he insisted he'd seen you coming out of the Ritz Hotel a few days before. And then—it was on the Thursday, a few days before he died—I came home one evening after work, it was about six o'clock and I went up the stairs and got out my key to open the front door and as I did I heard Hat's voice saying from inside the apartment, 'Come in, Mary.' It was spooky. I opened the door with my key, and there was Hat sitting in a chair facing the door, staring at me."

"Drunk, I should imagine," Tee said.

"No. And you've never seen anybody look so disappointed. And he said to me, 'She was here today. Mary was here.' "

"But that's nonsense," I said. "He *must* have been drunk."

"No, wait. Here's what he said. That morning, Thursday morning, he said he was standing in the living room of the apartment, looking out the window. He used to do that a lot when he was depressed. He'd stand there in the living room, looking through the slats of the venetian blinds. He could see, but he couldn't be seen. The street is at window level, do you remember?"

"No," I said.

"Anyway, he was looking out the window that morning when suddenly he saw you coming up the street. He swore it was you, although I told him he must have made a mistake. But he said, 'No, it was Mary, she was only thirty feet away. I was staring right at her through the blind. She checked the number of the building, then turned and came in, and I heard her footsteps on the little flight of stairs out there. I heard her move right up to the apartment door, and then she stopped. It was very quiet. I knew she was hesitating, and so I said, just as I did now, "Come in, Mary." And suddenly I heard her footsteps running downstairs again. So I opened the apartment door, but she was already out of the building. I ran to the street entrance, but she had disappeared. She was nervous, I suppose. I'd be nervous too, if I was coming back to somebody.' "

"He thought I was coming back to him?"

"Yes. And he said, 'It's all right, I'm expecting her any moment. I've been waiting here ever since.' And there he was, he'd been sitting in that chair all day, waiting."

"Jesus," Tee said.

"And listen to this," Ernie said. "Hat sat all night in that chair, waiting for you. *And* all the next day, the Friday. *And* all Friday night. Oh, it was spooky, all right. I was worried, you know. And then, on the Saturday morning, when I got up, there he was still sitting in the chair, but now there was a change. He had a bottle of Scotch beside him and he'd had a couple of belts. And then, around noon that Saturday, he suddenly got up out of the chair and went into his room and came out with the bottle and his portable and sat down at the kitchen table. And said to me, 'Well, that's it, I guess. She decided against coming back to me. She's left town and I'll never see her again.' And he started to type. And then, later that afternoon, as I told you, I came into the kitchen again for a beer and there he was finishing all those sheets, and I asked was he working and he said no, he'd been writing you a letter. And honestly, Maria, this is what he said, what he really said. He said, 'You see, I think there are a few things that girl should know. I mean this is the end for me. I've given up. I'll never see her again. So I wrote her.' He held up all those sheets. 'As you can see,' he said, 'I had quite a few thoughts to get off my mind.' And then he sealed and addressed the envelope and I weighed it, as I told you, and promised to mail it for him on the Monday."

"Jesus," Terence said again.

"And that's the whole story, Maria. I mean, the letter had something to do with this idea he had that you'd been in

Montreal, come right to the flat, then decided not to see him. And that's it, that's all I know."

"As you say," Tee said, "that's it." I saw him give Ernie a meaningful look and then he said, "Could I see you a moment?" They both went out into the front hall and I heard them whisper male whispers about me. Then they came back, Ernie first, Ernie saying, "Well, gee, I really must be getting along now. Listen, and thanks for dinner and everything. And—ah—I'm sorry about the letter, golly, Maria, as I said, there's nothing I wouldn't do to prevent—I mean I'd never want to see you hurt or anything. As Terence here says, and he's right, all that is water under the bridge, no sense you worrying about it now."

"Yes," I said. "Yes. Well, good night, Ernie."

"Good night. Sorry if I got out of line."

"That's all right, you didn't."

Terence shook hands with Ernie and we all went back into the front hall. Ernie took my hand between his large damp palms and pressed it, staring at me with blind eyes. "Good night, dear," he said.

I withdrew my hand. Terence handed him his cocoa-straw hat, then held open the apartment door. Ernie put the hat on his head, shifted the angle to make sure it was secure, then, with a clumsy, half-humble bow to us both, turned and walked off toward the elevator. In my last sight of him, as Terence closed our door, he reached furtively in his side pocket for the glasses he had concealed, put them on, then moved forward more confidently, as though restored to sight.

"I think you need a drink," Terence said, turning to me, holding me. I pressed my face against his coat and heard my heart beat, loud. I felt he must hear it too, but I said, "No, not a drink. I'm all right." I said I had better do the dishes, and so Tee said he would help me, and I remember carrying dishes in from the dining room and putting detergent in the dishwasher while Terence said he thought Ernie wasn't normal, there was something mad about him, and I remember talking about Ernie for a bit, but in my mind was that picture of Hat in Montreal, half mad, standing in Ernie's living room, peering through the slats of the venetian blind at some girl he imagined was me come back to him at last. And when I thought of that I stopped talking to Tee and stood there in the kitchen, staring at the sink.

"Mary, are you all right?"

"Yes," I said.

"Would you like to lie down? I'll put these dishes through and make some coffee. Lie down for a few minutes and I'll bring you a cup."

I said yes I would and I went into the bedroom. In the bedroom I put on all the lights and sat on the bed and thought about that long letter Hat had written. He wrote the letter to rebuke me, then killed himself to give point to his rebuke. Yet the letter never reached me. Until today I did not even know he was a suicide. Nor will I ever know, for sure. Yet in his bungling didn't he achieve the most subtle revenge of all? The letter was probably a rehash of the reproaches he shouted at me in our last days together. But I cannot be sure: I do not know what it said. Not knowing is the worst, it is those other things I do not know, like the name and the face of the woman who was in bed with my father the afternoon he died, it is those things I will never know, they are what frighten me, and it is because of them that I can no longer find my way back to the Mary Dunne I was in my schooldays, to that Mary Phelan who giggled and wept in the Blodgetts' bed-sitter, or to that girl who laughed long ago in a winter street when Hat cried, *"Mange la merde,"* when such things were funny, when I was Mary Bell. I will not even be able to go back to today when I am Mary Lavery, for today was a warning, a beginning, I mean forgetting my name, it was like forgetting my name that day, long ago, in Juarez, I will forget again, I will forget more often, it will happen to me every day and perhaps every hour, and as I sat on my bed and thought of that, the dooms came down, the Juarez dooms.

Terence came in and saw me. "What is it?" he asked, but I could not tell him. "I don't know," I said. "I'm down, I feel down."

He came and lay beside me on the bed and held me, but it did not help. I felt the dooms, I felt as though I had been plugged in to some strange electric current and that current ran through me and made me tremble. It was the dooms, the Juarez dooms, and this time I knew it would never go away, I would tremble and shake for the rest of my days. And now that it had come upon me, Terence would leave me, the doctors would advise it, they would lock me up, and so I began to weep and Tee kissed me and said, "Listen, darling, listen, the best thing to do about all that is to forget it. You know the way Hat drank, he wouldn't know what he was doing, and besides, even if it were suicide, it had nothing to do with you. Whatever was wrong with him was wrong long before you met him."

"Ranald said that too," I said. I felt like someone making conversation.

"Ranald who?"

"MacMurtry, the psychiatrist."

"What did he say?"

"Oh, it was long ago, he told me whatever was wrong with Hat had something to do with his family—his parents."

"Well," said Tee, "you see. Now, try to forget it."

"It's not that. It's me," I said. "I'm afraid and I don't know why. I think something's happening to my mind."

"Nonsense," Tee said.

And the phone rang. We lay and listened. "Don't go," I told Tee. "It's him again, it's Ernie. Or Janice Sloane. Or somebody else I don't want to speak to."

"No, it's Bowen for me. I'll be back in a moment." I lay and did not weep but my heart frightened me, the electric current ran in my body: it made me tremble; it would not go away; it was here to stay.

"It's for you, love," Tee called from the living room. "Your mother."

My mother has cancer, a rectal lump, and when they do the operation they will simply open her up, look at what is there, sew her up again, and send her home to die. In the Juarez dooms, all things are black. In the Juarez dooms, fear comes like vomit in my throat and the electric current runs in my body, making my heart thump and my hands shake, and when I picked up the receiver and said, "Hello," my mother knew at once.

"Mary, it's me. How are you? Are you all right?"

"Sure. I'm fine," said some tape-recording within me.

"You don't sound fine. Are you ill?"

"I'm fine, Mama. I got your letter today."

Her voice, far away in Butchersville, ignoring what I'd said: "Listen, Mary, were you calling me?"

"Yes."

"Ah, I thought it was you. Mrs. Daly at the phone office said it was New York, so it's Mary, I said to myself, I hope she's all right, why would she call? So, anyway, I thought I'd better call you back. What is it, dear, is there anything I can do for you?"

"Is there anything I can do for *you?*" I asked. "I mean about the hospital?"

"The hospital?"

"Your letter," I said. "About that lump of yours. How do you feel? Are you worried about it?"

"So that's why you called. Of course, why didn't I think of that? Oh, Lord. I didn't mean to scare you." And she laughed.

"What are you laughing about?"

"I forgot what a worrier you are, dear. Now, don't you be upsetting yourself, sure it's only a minor thing, it's not much more than having a boil lanced."

"Still," I said, "there'll be an anesthetic. You might feel sick after it. Why don't you let me come up and take care of you for a few days?"

"Oh, Mary dear." And I heard my mother laugh again. "Ah, you're sweet," she said. "And I always love to see you. But why waste a lot of money just for a day or two? Why not come up and bring—ah, Terence? Come up and stay a while, when the weather's a bit better?"

"But I wasn't talking about a holiday," I said.

"I know, dear, I know. You're worrying about it being cancer, aren't you?"

"Are *you*?" I said.

"Well, I am, a wee bit."

"Then maybe you'd like me to be there?"

"And have you worrying for the two of us?" my mother said. "Is that it?"

"Oh, Mama, I'm not worried. It'll be all right."

"Well, of course it will"—her voice, the voice of my childhood, that voice which said a kiss would make the hurt all better. "Yes, of course, it'll be all right," my mother's voice said. "Why, Dr. McLarnon says this sort of lump is common as carrots in women of my age. Oh, of course I know it could be serious, I'm not daft. But I'll say my prayers and put myself in God's hands. That's all any of us can do."

God: I see Jesus, effeminate and sanctimonious; he wears a wispy brown beard and a white nightgown. He holds his hand up, palm outward, as though stopping traffic. He stops me. When his name comes up in our conversations, my

213

mother and I become strangers in a darkness, far away from contact with each other, strangers on a long-distance wire.

"Yes," I said. "I suppose so."

"Tell you what, Mary. I'll get Dick to phone you the minute he gets the results. All right?"

"All right." I did not tell her I'd already spoken to Dick.

"So, don't worry," my mother said. And then: "How are you, yourself? You sound a bit down in the dumps."

"I am, a bit," I said. "But it will pass. I hope."

"Of course it will. And Mary?"

"Three minutes," an operator said.

"All right, Operator," my mother said. "We're just finishing."

"Mama, what was it you were going to ask me?"

"It doesn't matter, it was nothing," my mother said in a rushed voice. All she could think of now was that the three minutes were up. "Good night, dear. We'll keep in touch."

"Mama?" I said. "Mama? I want to ask you something. Do you think I've changed much in these last years?"

Again she laughed. "You haven't changed at all, you're still talking over the time limit."

"No, seriously."

"Look," said my mother, "good night, now. You haven't changed for me. You're my daughter, you'll always be the same to me. Good night, darling."

And she hung up.

"Anything wrong at home?" Terence asked, coming in from the kitchen with two cups of coffee. I told him about the letter this morning and about my earlier phone call to Dick.

"Poor you," Tee said. "What a day you've had. No wonder you're feeling low."

I looked at him when he said that. Did he know? He sat facing me, smiling, sympathetic, sipping at his coffee. Did he know the Juarez dooms were on me, the electric-current dooms which cut me off from everyone else, for in these dooms it is not the world which is at fault, it is me who is at fault, my fault, my fault, my most grievous fault, yet I do not know my fault, the Juarez dooms are not about real things, I do not think about Hat's suicide, I do not know what it is I have done, and so, not knowing, I cannot forgive myself. I know only that I have done wrong, that I am being punished, that I will never be happy again. The greatest happiness would be to be as I was a few hours ago, before these dooms came upon me. But that will never be, I will get worse, I will end in a madhouse, a vegetable, smeared in my own excrement, unable even to clean myself, and once I think of that I know Terence is the one who will be forced to commit me to the asylum, and now I am afraid to be in the same room with him, for he will see how mad I have become and I must be cunning and escape, so I say to him, "Yes, you're right, I *have* had a hard day. In fact, I think I should take a hot bath and go to bed, if you wouldn't mind too much?"

"Sure," he said. "Go ahead. I'm going to bed myself in a moment." He smiled at me.

So I escaped him.

But not the dooms. Naked in the bathroom, I stood and stared at myself in the full-length mirror. I had run a bath, but just as I went to get into the tub I saw myself naked in this mirror. I looked at my face, a mask which looked back at me, at my body, which hid what happens inside it, for this is hell and I am in it, the strange current runs in me, it will never turn off, I will get worse, I will lose not only my memory but my mind, and at the end I will be that vegetable squatting on the floor of the asylum's disturbed ward, unable to say its name, any of its names, for it has forgotten, therefore it is not, it has no name, it cannot even clean itself. And death which frightened me all day, death which brought hints of these dooms, death did not frighten me now, death was quiet graves, Hat's grave, my father's grave, stone markers in the snow. I thought of snow as I put on my dressing gown and went out of the bathroom. I thought of the white, light, rubble-filled space, the one I see below from the kitchen window. I went into the kitchen, but I was quiet, I did not want to disturb Terence. I heard him moving around in the bedroom as I shut the kitchen door. I went to the kitchen window and opened it. I climbed out of the window onto the fire escape. The iron steps of the fire escape were warm against my bare feet. The building next door to ours was torn down some months ago; they are going to put up a new apartment building in the empty space. I looked down at the narrow dark areaway four stories below the fire-escape railing, but I was not drawn down to that darkness; I was drawn beyond it, to those strange palisades made of old wooden doors which wreckers erect around these waste lots. The street light shone on the whitish, dusty, brick-rubbled rectangle where that building used to be. I would have to climb up and balance on the fire-escape railing, then jump far out, jumping the ditch of the narrow areaway, to fall where I wanted to fall, inside the wooden palisades, into that white, light, brick-rubbled rectangle.

I put my hand on the railing. I looked down and at once felt giddy. I could not climb up onto the railing. I could not balance up there. I was afraid, very afraid to be out on the fire escape at all, so I ducked back through the kitchen window. I shut the window.

I went into the bedroom. Terence was in bed, half asleep, a book lax in his hand. I got into bed, lying well away from him. The electric current ran within me. I listened as he let the book drop on the floor. He leaned over, his body touching mine. He kissed my cheek.

"I love you," he said.

"I love you," I said.

He reached for the bedside switch. "Want the light on?"

"No."

He switched off the light. I lay very still, wondering why he did not hear my heartbeat. If I was afraid to jump off the fire escape, then I am more afraid of physical pain than I am of these dooms. If Hat killed himself, it was a stupid, selfish thing to do. Hat was always the actor, always making dramas out of his fairly ordinary problems. And, at the end, so caught up in his self-dramatization that he overplayed his role. But if I make that harsh judgment on Hat, then what was I doing, play-acting out there on the fire escape? And what are these dooms of mine but a frightening, unreal play going on inside my head, a play I must sit through and suffer, for if I do not fight them, the dooms will not leave me?

And so, here in the dark, I closed my eyes and went back seventeen years. They were waiting: Mother Marie-Thérèse and the class. She wrote it on the blackboard. *Cogito ergo sum*. My hand went up. *Memento ergo sum*. And see, when I put my mind to it, I did manage to remember most of the thoughts, words, and deeds of today, and now I will not panic, these dooms may just be premenstrual, I will not overdramatize my problems, I am not losing my memory, I know who I am, my mother said tonight that I am her daughter and while she lives I will be that, I will not change, I am the daughter of Daniel Malone Dunne and Eileen Martha Ring, I am Mary Patricia Dunne, I was christened that and there is nothing wrong with my heart or with my mind: in a few hours I will begin to bleed, and until then I will hold on, I will remember what Mama told me, I am her daughter, I have not changed, I remember who I am and I say it over and over and over, I am Mary Dunne, I am Mary Dunne, I am Mary Dunne.

THE NEW CANADIAN LIBRARY LIST